ANNALISA DAUGHETY

LOVE IS MONUMENTAL

A WALK IN THE PARK – BOOK 2

BARBOUR
PUBLISHING

Cover design: Faceout Studio, www.faceoutstudio.com
Cover photography: Steve Gardener, Pixelworks Studios

Published by Barbour Publishing, Inc., P.O. Box 719, Uhrichsville, OH 44683, www.barbourbooks.com

Our mission is to publish and distribute inspirational products offering exceptional value and biblical encouragement to the masses.

ecpa Member of the
Evangelical Christian
Publishers Association

Printed in the United States of America.

DEDICATION

This book is dedicated with love to Kristy Coleman, Vickie Fry, and Kelly Shifflett—the best friends a girl could have! I cherish all the memories we've made—college road trips, first apartments, traveling through Europe—and everything in between. Through every struggle of my adult life, you've been there to help me find humor in the situation. Thank you for all the prayer, laughter, and support.

SPECIAL THANKS

The author would like to thank Vicky Daughety, Sandy Gaskin, Rebecca Germany, Christine Lynxwiler, Victor Pillow, Jan Reynolds, and Megan Reynolds for their assistance with this project. Thanks to Bramblett Group of Henderson, Tennessee, for wonderful publicity and photos.

Cast all your anxiety on him because he cares for you.

1 PETER 5:7 NIV

CHAPTER 1

It was going to be a perfect night. The apartment was spotless, the aroma of pot roast filled the air, and both cats were behaving. Vickie Harris peeked into the oven and couldn't help but smile. The crust on the homemade apple pie was browning evenly. Just like Gram's. She glanced at her watch. Nearly time. She grabbed a pair of her good plates from the cabinet and set them out on the counter.

She scanned the dining room to make sure everything was in place. Her gaze landed on the lone candle in the center of her cherrywood dining table. It had never been lit. Somewhere in the back of her mind, Vickie could hear her mother's voice: *"My interior decorator says that having new candles in the house is tacky. Makes you look like a bad hostess. The wick should always be burned as soon as you set them out."* Although she hated to heed her mother's advice, she still struck a match and lit the candle. As a born-and-bred Southern belle, even the appearance of tacky was to be avoided like the plague.

The buzzing of the doorbell sent the cats scurrying to the bedroom. Even on a good day, they weren't the most hospitable of animals. Vickie pulled her vintage apron over her head and hung it on the hook next to the oven.

She peeked through the peephole and opened the door. "Come in."

Dawn Andrews stepped through the door. Her tousled dark blond waves with their buttery highlights made her look like she'd just stepped out of a salon. "Thank you so much for doing this," she exclaimed, her blue eyes wide. She flung her designer bag onto the couch and walked through the living room to the kitchen.

Vickie closed the door and followed after Dawn. "You know how much I like to cook. It isn't a problem at all." She smiled. "Isn't he going to think it's weird that you're having him come to someone else's apartment for dinner though?"

Dawn smiled, her small white teeth gleaming. "I guess that's a chance I'll have to take. I'm redoing my guest bedroom, and my winter clothes are everywhere." She paused as she lifted the lid to the slow cooker and inhaled. "Yum," she said, beaming. "Besides, if he were to experience my cooking skills on a first date, the relationship would end before it began."

Vickie giggled. "It can't be that bad."

Dawn rolled her eyes. "There's a reason the hostess at the Chinese place around the corner knows me by name." She paused. "And the pizza delivery guy is practically on my Christmas-card list." She grinned. Dawn had moved into the apartment building a week after Vickie, and despite their differences, they had become fast friends. Back when they were both newcomers to the city, a love of expensive clothes and old movies had cemented their friendship.

"So who's this new guy, anyway?" Vickie asked, leaning against the counter.

Dawn grimaced. "I hate to admit it, but this one is a setup."

Vickie's eyes widened. "You? A setup? Surely not." Dawn was one of the most vivacious people Vickie had ever met. She had men of all ages clamoring for her attention. During the five years they'd known each other, Vickie had lost count of the interesting dates she'd gotten to hear about. There was the doctor who'd flown Dawn in a private plane to see U2 somewhere out West. The lawyer who'd arranged for jewelry on loan for a red-carpet event at the Kennedy Center. The artist who'd painted her portrait and included it in his show at a local gallery. And Vickie had lived vicariously, relishing the stories.

"I know. Not really my style. But I've been so busy with work lately. One of my clients found out I was single and insisted she pass my e-mail address along to her nephew." She shrugged. "Normally I would've just said 'no thanks,' but this lady was a real spitfire. I helped her plan a charity gala, and she took charge like a general." Dawn laughed. "I figured it would be easier to agree to at least let the guy e-mail me than to fight her."

"So? What's his story?" Vickie asked.

Dawn dusted an invisible speck from her red silk sleeveless sweater. "He's a detective. And he's a little younger than me."

Vickie raised a perfectly plucked eyebrow. Dawn was one of those ageless women. They'd never discussed it, but Vickie's best guess was that her friend was in her late thirties. "The detective part sounds good. How young?"

A slow smile spread across Dawn's face. "Don't look like that. I'm not robbing the cradle or anything. He's thirty-three."

Vickie held her tongue. This would be the perfect opportunity to ask Dawn her actual age. In the past, Dawn had only referenced being "in her thirties" but hadn't specified. Yet wasn't directly asking someone their age a little tacky? "Thirty-three is a good age. Old enough to be a grown-up about things, but still young enough to be adventurous."

Dawn laughed. "I suppose. His e-mails have been quite funny. And we've been speaking on the phone a lot this past week. He seems very sure of himself. But not too sure. You know?"

Vickie nodded that she did, in fact, know. Although she wasn't totally sure she did. "Are you nervous?"

An incredulous expression flashed across Dawn's flawless face. She shook her head. "Not at all. Why?"

"If it were me, having a guy over for dinner and meeting for the first time. . ." Vickie trailed off. "I'd be a wreck."

"Normally I wouldn't have invited him for dinner. I would've just suggested coffee or something. But we've been having this conversation about hating those normal setup kind of dates. Coffee, drinks, dessert. You know. The normal stuff." Dawn glanced at her watch. "Then he mentioned a home-cooked meal, and it sounded so nice."

The sound of the kitchen timer filled the room. Vickie grabbed a pot holder and pulled the piping hot apple pie from the oven. She set it carefully on the stove. Gram would be proud.

"Wow. You went all out. You didn't have to do that," Dawn said. "And don't worry. I'm giving you full credit." She grinned. "I've finally learned not to date under false pretenses." She shrugged. "This is who I am. I like take-out and consider popcorn a food group. He'll either like me or not."

Vickie gave a small grin. "My guess is he will. They all do," she said thoughtfully.

Dawn regarded Vickie seriously. "Don't start that again. You are gorgeous. I wish you'd get out there and have a little fun. I think you should take that coworker of yours up on his offer to set you up with his cousin."

Vickie felt the blush creeping over her face. She concentrated on straightening the kitchen towels, racking her brain for a way out of the conversation.

Dawn leaned forward, peering at Vickie's red face. "Is there something you're not telling me?"

"I'm meeting him for coffee tonight." She refused to meet Dawn's gaze.

Dawn let out a squeal. "Yea! I'm so excited. So have you talked to him? E-mailed him? Do tell."

"I'm no good over the phone. So that was out of the question. I guess I could've done the e-mail back and forth thing, but it seemed to me like a very impersonal way to get to know someone."

"You and your rules. So what? You're meeting him blindly?"

Vickie shrugged. "You make it sound crazy. Yes. But Chris promises me his cousin is a great guy. He's thirty-one. Never been married." She sighed. "I'm sure he's nice."

"It's been awhile since you've gone out with anyone," Dawn said.

"I know. I hate this kind of thing. I wish I could just marry some guy I've known forever and skip the awkwardness of dating."

Dawn laughed. "You've been skipping the awkwardness of dating by refusing to do it. It's about time you got back out there. Don't be nervous though. It'll be fine."

Vickie wasn't so sure. But last week she'd looked at the calendar and had been sad to realize it had been six months since she'd so much as had coffee with a man. The fact that she had an upcoming birthday had prompted her into action. "I'm sure you're right." She motioned around the kitchen. "I think you're all set here. Have a good time."

"We won't stay long. It's a nice evening. I'm thinking maybe we'll go for a walk after dinner. I'll lock up when we leave."

"Thanks." Vickie smoothed the blue wrap dress she was wearing. "Does this look okay? It isn't too dressy, is it?"

"You look fantastic. Very Jackie O."

Vickie managed a smile. "Don't let Jake and Lloyd bother you. Shut them up in the bedroom if they decide to come out of hiding to terrorize you or anything." The cats could be a handful at times, but Vickie couldn't imagine life without them.

"Don't worry. We'll get along fine." Dawn walked her to the door. "Thanks again for cooking and for letting me use your place. I owe you big-time. And I'll swing by tomorrow for a report on your coffee date."

"It's really just a meeting. Not a date."

Dawn shook her head. "Call it whatever you have to call it, as long as you show up."

Vickie closed the door behind her, her heels clicking against the wooden floor. She hoped courage would kick in somewhere between the apartment and the coffee shop. Because she needed it.

CHAPTER 2

Thatcher Torrey leaned back in his weathered leather chair and sighed. His day had quickly gone from bad to worse when he'd walked into the faculty meeting a few minutes late only to be called out in front of the entire history department. He'd been aware of the decline in history majors in recent years, but he hadn't realized how upset the higher-ups at the university were. Since he was one of the professors who'd been around the longest and the one everyone assumed was a shoo-in for the department chair position that should be opening up soon, he supposed it was only logical that they might hold him partially responsible.

"Dr. Torrey, thanks for finally joining us," Roger White, the dean of academic services, had said as Thatcher slid into a chair. From the tone of his voice, Thatcher had known better than to share the story of the flat tire he'd had that morning on his way back to DC. Even a valid excuse wouldn't hold up in this particular courtroom. "You've been here for several years. Perhaps you'd care to offer a theory on the decline of our history majors. You know, we were once considered one of the premiere programs in the country. Any thoughts, Dr. Torrey?"

Thatcher couldn't remember a time when he'd felt more ambushed. Even worse, he'd spotted the smirk on Clark Langston's face from across the room. Thatcher and Clark's rivalry went back twenty-plus years to high school. So when Clark had joined the history department last year, he had become a daily thorn in Thatcher's side.

Thatcher had cleared his throat and plunged ahead with an answer. "I think we're still considered one of the premiere programs in the country, sir. I'm sure just as with enrollment numbers, the number of students who choose a particular major ebbs and flows as well. I feel sure our numbers will be back up soon." He'd quickly taken his seat before any other questions could be asked of him.

"Tough one, buddy," his friend and colleague John Reynolds had whispered from behind him.

"Would anyone else like to speculate on the dismal numbers?" Dean White looked around the room.

Thatcher hadn't been surprised to see Clark raise his hand. "I have a theory," he'd said, rising to his feet. Even though it was a casual meeting, Clark was wearing a jacket and tie. "I think one of the biggest problems facing the program might be the archaic teaching methods used by some of our faculty." He looked pointedly at Thatcher. "Students today are used to being constantly stimulated. They want to have access to their class work on their iPhones or laptops. You can't expect them to be excited about a standard old-school lecture. I think that is a big problem."

Thatcher shifted uncomfortably in his seat. It was no secret that he resisted the technological advances some professors embraced. He much preferred the old-school style of teaching. He'd shared his opinion on the subject many times with his colleagues. Creating a Facebook group for his classes was not on his agenda, and it never would be. He was convinced there was another way of reaching the students without jumping through hoops. A history class was no place for some kind of dog and pony show. As far as

Thatcher was concerned, any student who expected simply to be entertained should sign up for another professor. He'd earned a reputation as being a tough but fair teacher, and he didn't see any need to change his methods.

"Thank you, Dr. Langston. I can see you've put a good deal of thought into our problem." Dean White nodded in Clark's direction. "We're forming a committee to discuss implementing some new strategies in attracting students. I would like for you to join us if you're able."

Clark nodded solemnly and glanced at Thatcher out of the corner of his eye. "I'd be glad to. I want to do everything I can to make sure this program is the best it can be. Even if it means making some changes."

Thatcher had felt his blood boiling. The audacity of this man was unbelievable. Swooping in here and trying to take over. Thatcher had barely heard another word for the rest of the meeting. Now in the solitude of his office, he tried to pinpoint the moment where his career had taken a wrong turn. He was certain it was the day Clark was hired.

A tap on the door startled him. "Hey, man." John walked into the cramped office and took a seat in the wooden chair opposite Thatcher's desk. "That guy really has it in for you."

Although John was Thatcher's closest friend on campus, he didn't know the real story behind Thatcher and Clark's relationship. Thatcher didn't like to air his dirty laundry to anyone. It would be unprofessional.

"We've known each other for a long time. He's never been a fan of mine." That statement wasn't entirely true. Clark and Thatcher used to be friends. A long time ago. A fight that came to blows during their senior year of high school had effectively ended the friendship, and the fact that both had planned the same career path didn't help to mend things. Thatcher had kept up with Clark after college through alumni news, but their paths hadn't crossed—until Clark had interviewed for a position in Thatcher's department last fall and, much to Thatcher's chagrin, been offered the job. They'd spent the past year managing to be civil toward one another, but Thatcher had an idea those days were over.

"I hate to be the bearer of bad news, but word around here is that Clark's after the department chair position. I guess that doesn't surprise you." John didn't meet Thatcher's eyes.

Thatcher let out a grunt. "Not exactly. Especially considering his recent golf outings with Dean White. Such a kiss up."

"You should also know that he's been saying some pretty bad stuff about you to anyone who'll listen. Mainly quoting some of your former students who say they feel like they didn't learn as much as they could have because you didn't utilize all the technology available." John picked up the paperweight from Thatcher's desk and turned it over in his hand. "I doubt the students actually said those things unprompted. I have a feeling he's been coaching some of the female students to say what he wants them to. What a nineteen-year-old sees in him is beyond me."

Thatcher raked his hands through his hair. "I don't understand why this is happening."

"Look, we all know that no one works harder than you. No one is more devoted to this job and these students. You practically live up here during the school year." John motioned toward the faded blue couch in the corner that often served as Thatcher's bed.

"It looks like dedication isn't enough anymore. Maybe it's time for me to move on and let Clark take over. But somehow, I doubt he's going to be happy until he's completely ruined me."

"About that. . ." John trailed off. "Any chance you want to tell me the real story behind you two? Whatever happened was more than twenty years ago. Is it a grudge still worth holding on to?"

Thatcher met John's gaze. "The grudge is his, not mine. As far as I'm concerned, we could've moved past it. But he clearly isn't ready to let it go." That was Thatcher's way of saying he wasn't ready to share. Thankfully, his friend knew him well enough not to press the issue.

John nodded. "Guess not." He paused. "Thatch, there's one more thing."

Something in John's voice made Thatcher uneasy. "What's that?"

"You and I both know you should be the obvious choice for department chair once Dr. Gregory retires at the end of the year. But I think Clark is launching a full-out campaign. Not only is he becoming golf buddies with Dean White and calling you out every chance he gets, but now he's on some kind of mission to put himself on the national map."

Thatcher was confused. He knew of Clark's ambition at the university. But the national map? "What do you mean?"

John leaned forward. "There may not be any truth to this at all," he said, his voice lowered. "But I played racquetball this morning right after one of Clark's graduate assistants. As he and his partner were leaving, I overheard their conversation. He said Clark was hot on the trail of some great historic discovery. He mentioned Abraham Lincoln and some documents but then clammed up when he noticed me."

"Abraham Lincoln?" Thatcher let out a heavy sigh. "That figures. Remember when they found that inscription on Lincoln's pocket watch? That was huge news. Anything to do with Lincoln is newsworthy. Even after all these years, the public is still fascinated."

John nodded. "Do you think there are really Lincoln items still out there that haven't been discovered?"

Thatcher shrugged. "I guess it's possible. And if there are and Clark finds them. . ." His voice trailed off.

John set the paperweight back on the desk with a *thud*. "Then I'd dare say he'd be named the next department chair and our lives would be misery."

The men exchanged glances.

"It seems to me you only have one option." John rose from the chair. "I'll see if I can find out anything else about the documents."

"And it looks like I'm going on a treasure hunt." Despite the circumstances, Thatcher couldn't help feeling a twinge of excitement. A showdown with Clark had been twenty years in the making, and he wasn't going down without a fight.

CHAPTER 3

I'm telling you. His arms were too hairy." Vickie curled her feet underneath her and sank deeper into the plush navy sofa.

"Seriously? Hairy arms?" The incredulous tone was audible in Kristy O'Neal's voice despite the miles that separated them. "I think you've used that excuse before. Maybe you should come up with a new one."

Vickie sighed. "Other than that, I'm sure he is perfectly nice. Some kind of manager or something." She examined her french-manicured nails. "But all I could see was hair. Not only on his arms, but there were little tufts poking out of the neck of his polo shirt. Like Chewbacca from *Star Wars*." She shuddered. "Ugh."

Kristy let out a groan. "Vick, you never cease to amaze me. I think you could find something wrong with Prince Charming himself."

Vickie doubted she'd ever be so lucky as to find a Prince Charming. And as the days drew ever nearer to the date circled in thick red marker on her calendar, she'd settle for an earl or a duke. She wasn't picky—or at least she didn't mean to be. But it seemed her friends held a different opinion.

"I should've taken a picture on my phone when he wasn't looking. You'd believe me then." She paused. "I'm telling you, Chewbacca."

"Where'd you find this guy, anyway?"

Lloyd jumped into Vickie's lap, purring for attention. She absently stroked the gray cat's head as he rubbed against her. "Chris set us up. He's told me nearly every day for the past month about his single cousin. You know how much I hate setups. But he finally wore me down." She sighed. "Plus, I figured it was time I tried a new tactic. Clearly my whole 'waiting on the perfect man to find me' plan wasn't working very well."

"Does this mean that all the rangers at work knew about your date? If so, be glad you aren't at Shiloh because you'd never hear the end of it." Kristy worked as a park ranger at Shiloh National Military Park in Tennessee.

"That's the beauty of living in a city like DC. Plenty of people have lives way more interesting than mine to talk about." Vickie giggled. "Not like you, out there in the middle of nowhere where it's big news if you so much as catch a cold."

"Hey, now. Don't talk bad about my town." Kristy had grown up fifteen minutes from Shiloh's four thousand acres and had spent her childhood among the cannons and monuments. She was connected to the land there in a way most people couldn't understand. Last year, she'd given up her job as a ranger and planned to leave Shiloh for good in order to get married. But when her fiancé left her at the altar, she'd managed to get her old job back. Today, she was happily engaged to Ace Kennedy, a wonderful man, and they planned to make their home near the boundaries of the park. Vickie was thankful things had worked out so well for her friend.

"I'm kidding, and you know it." Vickie sighed. "Believe me. Sometimes I think about chucking it all and moving back to Tennessee myself." Vickie had been raised right outside of Nashville and had worked with Kristy as a seasonal ranger at Shiloh during college. Her parents still had a home in Tennessee, although they spent a lot of their time traveling these days.

Kristy was silent for a moment. "Not that I'd discourage you too much, because I'd love to have you live nearby. But I thought you loved it in Washington. Are things not going well in our nation's capital?"

"Oh, you know how it is. I get this way every year." Vickie switched the phone to her other ear and glanced over at the calendar. One week to go.

"Birthdays aren't supposed to be things you dread, remember? You should be celebrating another year of health and wisdom and all that."

"I'm thankful for my health. But at this point, I'm beginning to doubt my wisdom. If you'd told me ten years ago that on the cusp of thirty I'd still be waiting to fall in love for the first time, I'd never have believed it. But here I am. I've never even had a movie-worthy kiss," she said glumly.

"Now wait just a minute there. I seem to remember during our junior year that—what's his name? Brian Jones, I think it was. Anyway, didn't he kiss you after that formal banquet? You know the one. You wore that gold dress that Ainsley had worn in her sister's wedding."

Their friend Ainsley Davis was the other member of the "three musketeers posse" they'd jokingly established while they were in college. The three of them had gotten their start with the National Park Service as seasonal rangers at Shiloh. It seemed so long ago. Ainsley was currently on a temporary leave of absence from her job as a ranger at the Grand Canyon. At least Vickie hoped it was temporary.

Kristy continued. "I mean, he liked you so much he rented a tux even though all the other guys were in suits. *And* he brought you flowers. Wasn't that movie-worthy?"

Vickie blushed at the mere memory. "Not in my book. Besides, he barely kissed me." She paused. "Are you really going to make me relive that moment?"

Kristy laughed. "I guess not. Although it's still beyond me how someone can barely kiss you. Either he did or he didn't."

Vickie couldn't help but laugh. "Maybe that's only something that could happen to me."

"Must be." Kristy was quiet for a moment. "Seriously, though. How are you really doing? Hairy men aside."

"My parents are coming to town to take me out for my birthday. You can imagine how excited I am about that."

"At least try to have fun. You know they mean well," Kristy said. She knew all too well the difficulties in Vickie's family.

"My dad means well. My mom, not so much," Vickie said glumly. "How much do you want to bet that within the first ten minutes, she'll say ugly things about my haircut, my clothes, and my apartment decor?"

"She only wants the best for you."

"Yeah, well her idea of the best and my idea of the best are usually two different things."

"At least your parents love each other." Kristy's parents had gone through a nasty divorce several years ago, and even though she was an adult, she still had problems adjusting to their situation.

Vickie groaned. "You're right. I just wish Mom could be more tolerant of me. Or maybe if I had a few brothers and sisters for her to worry over, it wouldn't be so bad. Being the only child isn't all it's cracked up to be."

Kristy laughed. "Poor, pitiful Vickie."

Vickie grinned despite herself. "I know, right? I'm awful. I'm sure it will be fine. They've made reservations at Citronelle, so at least I know the food will be good. I partly think they're only coming because Mom's been hoping for an excuse to eat there." She watched as Lloyd jumped from her lap and curled up underneath the coffee table. "How about you? What's the latest from West Tennessee?"

"Well. . ." Kristy trailed off. "The wedding plans are moving slowly. We've finally picked out a few potential dates but still haven't settled on a location." She sighed. "To tell you the truth, I don't even care. I'm ready to marry him. It doesn't matter the day or the place or what we wear." She sighed. "I'm sure it has something to do with the fact that I've been through all this before."

Vickie was silent. She remembered the day more than a year ago when Kristy, clad in a beautiful wedding dress, had stood in front of her closest friends and family and explained to them that there wouldn't be a wedding. It was no wonder she wasn't the most excited wedding planner in the world. It must dredge up old wounds. "Have you thought about eloping?" she asked gently.

"Ace would do whatever I wanted. But I feel like that would somehow be cheating him, you know? Just because I nearly married the wrong man is no reason to deny Ace a 'real' wedding. And before you say it, I know that a nice wedding does not a marriage make. But still. I want to celebrate our love for each other in front of the people we care about."

"That makes sense."

"To tell you the truth, we're sort of considering a destination wedding. What would you think of that?"

"I think that sounds nice. Where are you thinking about?"

"Maybe somewhere along the Gulf Coast. I've always thought a wedding on the beach could be fun. And at least that way, it would just be the people who mean the most to us who attend." She paused. "Because those are the only people who'd bother traveling so far."

Vickie giggled. "Well count me in wherever you decide to do it. I could use a little vacation."

"As my maid of honor, I expect you to follow us to the corners of the earth." Kristy laughed. "And it certainly sounds like you could use a vacation. How about work? Is that at least going okay?"

"If it weren't, I'd go crazy. Things at work are going great. They've offered me a different shift, but I haven't decided yet. It would be four days a week but longer hours."

"But a three-day weekend? Sounds great to me," Kristy said.

"I guess. Although I mostly see it as three days alone with nothing to do. Those cooking classes I was taking are over. I guess I could see if there's anything else I'm interested in. Maybe painting."

Kristy was silent for a moment. "Or maybe you could take some action. Sign up for an online dating service. Pretty soon, you'd probably have someone to spend all your extra spare time with." Kristy and Ainsley had been trying to get Vickie signed up for online dating for the past few years, but she refused.

"I'm not going to meet someone online. My luck he'd be some kind of serial killer or stalker or something. No thank you. I'll just meet someone in a normal way."

"Whatever. But if you ask me, it's about time you do something drastic."

"Drastic isn't my style." They said their good-byes, and Vickie glanced again at the calendar. Which was worse? Being all alone or being out of her comfort zone? Maybe Prince Charming would show up on her doorstep next week to wish her a happy birthday. But if not, maybe it *was* time to get a little drastic.

CHAPTER 4

The cancer has spread. At this advanced stage, I think the best thing we can do is try and keep her comfortable." Dr. Matthews's face was devoid of emotion as he delivered the news. "I'm sorry, Miss Wyatt. We're out of options for your mother's treatment."

"What about another round of chemo?" Katherine Wyatt asked, trying to ignore the sharp pang in her stomach. She hoped she wasn't about to be sick right there in the doctor's office. She looked into his stony face. Although on second thought, maybe that would at least cause him to react. She still wasn't sure he was a real person. Katherine had often joked to her mom these past weeks that he must be some kind of vampire or something. Jane Wyatt had accused her only daughter of watching too many movies and had continually assured her that Dr. Matthews was the best in the business.

"She hasn't responded to any of the chemo we've tried." He shook his head. "I know how difficult this is for you."

Katherine leaped from the chair. "Do you? Do you really? Have you ever had to stand by and watch as your mother wasted away right in front of your eyes?" Tears began to trickle down her face, and she angrily brushed them away. "Have you sat in a hospital where the people treat you like you're crazy for hoping or for believing a miracle can happen?"

Dr. Matthews regarded her quietly, his expression never wavering.

"I didn't think so. She's all I have. I'm only twenty. I'm not ready to be all alone in the world." She knew how childish she must sound, but she didn't care. She grasped the edge of his large desk as if it were a lifeline. "There has to be something else you can do. What about a transplant? If she could get a new liver, she could be fine, right? I could give her part of mine. I read somewhere that they can regenerate."

The older man let out a deep sigh. "Miss Wyatt, again I am sorry for your situation. We don't think you're crazy for continuing to hope for recovery. It is wonderful to see a patient and family keep their faith through a tough diagnosis. But it is my job to make sure you know the facts. And the facts are that chemo didn't work and your mother isn't strong enough to withstand a transplant. So even if you were a perfect match, it isn't a viable option." He closed the chart in front of him as if to indicate the discussion was over.

Katherine sank back down into the chair. "There has to be something that can be done."

"I think perhaps you should speak to your mother. She and I have already discussed the situation. It was her idea for me to explain it to you." He rose from his desk and peered at her from beneath his round glasses. "I'd recommend that you try not to upset her with your desire to pursue other options. She's had a tough day. I've seen patients in her condition live for many months, possibly even a year, depending on how things go. She still has some good times ahead of her."

Katherine stood from the chair and let the doctor walk her to the door. "So that's it. You're just giving up."

"Miss Wyatt, we can continue to evaluate her to see if there are any changes. I assure you that if she's ever a candidate for any other treatment, I will let you know. But at this point, I would strongly suggest you let her digest this information before discussing with her how you think she should proceed."

Katherine nodded. "Okay." She felt weak. How could she face her mother now? They'd always shared everything. Her mom would know immediately how upset she was. And right now she was expecting Katherine to stop in and tell her all about registration for the upcoming year of college classes.

Katherine pasted on a happy face before stepping into her mom's room. She'd taken a few acting classes. This was California, after all. Surely growing up a stone's throw from the HOLLYWOOD sign was good for something. "Hi, Mom," she said brightly, stepping into the sterile hospital room.

Jane Wyatt looked up from a sudoku puzzle and smiled. "How was your day? Did you get all registered?"

Katherine's resolve to be upbeat faltered. She managed to keep the happy expression on her face, but she was sure her mom could see right through it. "Registration was a pain, as usual." She stood awkwardly at the foot of the bed. Her mom had always been one of the strongest people she'd ever known. Surely she could beat this, no matter what the doctors said.

Katherine's mother patted the bed. "Sit down, honey. I know Dr. Matthews spoke to you this afternoon. I wanted you to hear it from him first because I knew if I tried to tell you, you'd come up with a million reasons the diagnosis was wrong."

Katherine perched carefully on the bed and took her mother's hand. "I'm sure he has to say that, Mom. But we both know you're a fighter. Remember when you were in that car accident and the policeman said he'd never seen anyone walk away from something like that. This could be just like that."

Her mother reached up and stroked Katherine's face. "Oh,

honey. You know this isn't the same thing. And for us to pretend this might turn out differently wouldn't be right. I need to help you deal with this." Her voice broke. "I can't leave you until I'm sure you'll be okay."

Katherine felt the hot tears spill down her cheeks. "I'll never be okay without you here, Mom." She choked back a sob. "You've been beside me my whole life. I can't." She inhaled. "I can't do this alone."

Jane leaned her head against the pillow and shut her eyes. "Katherine, I think it's time for me to tell you the truth."

"What's wrong?" Something in her mother's voice made her nervous.

Her mom opened her brown eyes, the eyes that everyone said were almost a mirror image of Katherine's. "Honey, I've done an awful thing. I hope you can find it in your heart to forgive me."

The thought that this woman who had practically devoted her life to her daughter could even think that she might not be forgiven was crazy. "Oh, Mom. I can't imagine you doing anything that bad. Just tell me."

Her mother gripped Katherine's hand tightly. She drew in a ragged breath. "There's something I need you to do for me."

"Anything."

"Go home and look in my closet. Up in the very top there's a box. I want you to go through it tonight." She squeezed Katherine's hand. "Promise me you'll look through the contents with an open mind."

CHAPTER 5

Happy birthday, darling." Vickie's dad beamed at her as the waiter set two slices of cake on the table. The decadent chocolate cake with creamy chocolate icing looked delicious.

"Thanks." Vickie smiled at him then glanced at her mother. "Are you sure you don't want some? You're welcome to a bite of mine."

Vickie's mom shook her head, a disdainful expression on her face. "You know, dear, now that you're thirty, your metabolism isn't as fast as it used to be." She smoothed her perfectly coifed blond updo and eyed Vickie's heaping forkful of cake. "With your petite frame, you're going to have to be very careful with your figure from here on out."

Vickie sighed. "I know, Mom. You've been warning me of that for years."

"Marilyn, she's no bigger than a minute. Never has been. Let her enjoy her cake," Dad chided.

Mom shrugged her shoulders. "Walter, I simply want to make sure she realizes that it won't always come so easy. And since she's still single, she needs to make sure to keep her figure trim;

otherwise, finding a man will only get harder."

Vickie wished the floor could swallow her whole and put her out of her misery. "Mom. I'm fine." She met her mother's icy blue eyes. "I had a date last week, actually. So don't worry."

"Did he ask you out for a second date?"

She should've known better than to share that information. But she wanted her mother to at least know that she wasn't totally hopeless. "No. He has my number, though. I'm sure I'll hear from him soon." As if she'd accept a second date with the hairiest guy she'd ever seen. But there was no need to tell her mother that.

"Oh, Victory. Don't you know that if a man is interested, he's going to book the second date right then and there?"

"Please don't call me that. My name is Vickie." Mom was the only person in the universe who called her Victory, but then she had been the one who'd chosen the name. She'd been furious when Vickie hadn't had it put on her college diploma. Having it on her Social Security card and birth certificate was bad enough.

"Fine." Mom's face clouded over. "I'll indulge you. But you spent eighteen years going by your given name, and I still think you've made a mistake by letting people call you by a nickname instead."

"How about you open your gift?" Dad had spent a lifetime trying to keep the peace between his wife and daughter. He handed Vickie a tiny blue box.

"Thanks, Daddy." Vickie took the tiny blue box and untied the ribbon. She lifted the lid and pulled out a three-stone diamond necklace. "Oh, it's beautiful." And it was. The one thing she and her mother shared was taste in jewelry and clothes. Simple, tasteful, and elegant. Those were the key ingredients to their style.

"I thought you'd like it." Mom gave her first real smile of the night. "Your dad gave me diamonds for my thirtieth birthday. So I thought you should have some, too."

"Thank you both. And thanks for flying in to see me. It means a lot." And it did. Despite the differences she and her mother had, Vickie still loved her parents very much. Her thoughts went back to Kristy. It was nice to see her own parents together and still happy after so many years. Even though she didn't want to emulate their specific relationship, they still gave her hope that she could find her own happiness someday.

"Now," Marilyn said once coffee had been poured. "Tell us how work is going."

Vickie smiled. "Fantastic. I'm to the point where I can comfortably talk to visitors about any of the monuments along the National Mall, although the Washington Monument is still my favorite. But I'm trying to branch out some."

"That's wonderful. I'm sure you're very good at it." Dad had been Vickie's biggest supporter when she'd decided to pursue a full-time career with the National Park Service. Mom, not so much.

"So I guess I can give up the hope that you'll move back to Brentwood and get a respectable job?" she asked.

"Mom. We've had this discussion before. Being a park ranger is a perfectly respectable job." Some things never changed.

Mom heaved a great sigh. "You wear polyester pants every day. And a hat. Darling, that was okay when you were in your twenties. It was kind of like playing dress-up. But now you're a grown woman. It's time to get a real career."

Vickie felt the heat of anger rush over her face. "What, like the one you had? If I remember correctly, you were a part-time waitress at the Chili Bowl before you met Dad. So maybe you aren't exactly the right person to be giving out career advice." She knew it was a low blow. Her mother never spoke of the years she'd spent growing up in the mountains of east Tennessee. Instead, she had always said her life didn't start until the day Walter stopped into the restaurant. He had been on his way to Knoxville on business but had been so enchanted by her that he'd proposed to her on the spot. Mom hadn't even gone home to get her things. They'd driven to Gatlinburg, and by the time she called her parents to tell them where she was, she was a married woman. She'd spent her life accompanying Dad on business trips, decorating and redecorating their home, and entertaining friends. Only Vickie knew she'd always been self-conscious over not having a college degree. Mom had made that confession when Vickie was filling out college applications.

Ever the peacemaker, Dad put his hand on Vickie's arm. "Now, now. Let's not say things we'll regret."

"Fine." Vickie took a sip of water to calm herself down. "I'm sorry, Mom. But I happen to enjoy my career very much. And I don't plan on leaving it anytime soon."

"Suit yourself. I'm only trying to help. I'll have you know that several of your high school classmates live in the same neighborhood in Brentwood. Their husbands golf together, and their kids take swim lessons at the same club. And I know they all enjoy being Junior Leaguers." She sighed. "That was the life I'd always imagined for you."

Did her mother honestly not know her at all? "I know it is. But that isn't the life I want for me. I really love what I do. And I love living in DC. I wish you could just be happy for me."

The waiter chose that moment to bring the credit card receipt. Vickie and her mother eyed each other as her dad signed the paper. "I'll go get the car," Dad said, "and pick you two up out front."

"I am happy for you, Victory. But I don't want your life to pass you by while you're leading tours for vacationing families. I want you to be a part of a family. And now, turning thirty." She clucked her tongue. "*Tick tock*, dear. *Tick tock.* Let's hope your date from last week calls you again. I don't want to see you wind up all alone."

Vickie closed her eyes. Her mother had been ticking down her biological clock since she was twenty-three. That was how old Mom had been when Vickie was born. "Thanks, Mother, for that reminder."

"I'm just saying. You are in your prime baby years right now. Much older, and you'll be considered at an advanced age for pregnancy." Mom smoothed Vickie's hair. "You're a beautiful girl and so smart. I only want you to be happy." Her kind words took the sting out of her previous comments. Vickie knew that deep down, her mother did love her. Even if she had trouble showing it.

"Have you talked to Gram lately?" There was one topic guaranteed to make her mother uncomfortable. And after the night she'd just experienced, Vickie felt perfectly justified.

"No. I guess I should check in on her soon." Mom's eyes clouded over. "Have you? Talked to her, I mean." Since she left home all those years ago, Mom had barely given her family the time of day. She'd lavished impractical gifts on them during the holidays but had spent most of her adult life separating herself from her humble roots.

"I talk to her a few times a week." Vickie leveled her gaze with her mother's. "She's not well. Ever since Grandpa died, her health has gotten worse." Vickie sighed. "It wouldn't kill you to go for a visit. I know she'd like it."

"Maybe I will," Mom said. "Oh, there's your father with the car."

Vickie shook her head. Sometimes she felt like the adult, especially where her mother's relationship with Gram was concerned. Why was her mother so stubborn?

Twenty minutes later, Vickie trudged up the stairs to her apartment. Each time she saw her mother, it was like she'd gone through a battle. And she felt like she had the scars to prove it. Somehow, Mom always came out unscathed.

The phone was ringing as she unlocked the door. She rushed over and grabbed it, banging her shin on the coffee table in the process. "Hello."

"Happy birthday," Kristy said. "I tried to call earlier, but I guess you were out celebrating."

"Some celebration." Vickie quickly filled her in on the evening.

"Ugh. Sorry. I can't believe she pulled out the biological clock comment. That's brutal." Kristy's voice was filled with sympathy. "It sounds like you'd have had a better time on your couch, watching TV with Jake and Lloyd."

Vickie looked down at the cats sitting on either side of her. "You realize that it's their fault I'm single."

"Your cats? How is it their fault?"

Vickie laughed. "No. The fault lies with their namesakes. Jake Ryan and Lloyd Dobler. If I could find guys like that in real life, I'd probably be happily married by now."

"Fictional heroes from '80s movies?" Kristy laughed. "I've always wondered who it was you were waiting for."

"It's my birthday. Indulge me here. Remember how in *Sixteen Candles* Jake made her that birthday cake and was there to pick her up after her sister's wedding? Totally rescued her. And in *Say Anything*, I love, love, love the part where he holds up the boom box outside of her window. But I loved it even more when he guided her around that glass on the sidewalk. He just cared about her so much."

"Okay. I know turning thirty has been difficult for you. And I know dealing with your mother makes it worse. But can I point out that if you met a real-life Jake or Lloyd, you'd probably have some problem with them. Like Jake isn't smart enough or Lloyd doesn't have enough ambition. Something like that."

Vickie thought about it for a moment. "Maybe I'm turning over a new leaf now that I'm thirty."

"Oh yeah? How so?"

"I've been doing a lot of thinking lately. I've decided that everyone might be right. Maybe it's time for me to get out of my comfort zone a little bit. Go out with guys I'd normally turn down. That kind of thing."

"If I say I'll believe it when I see it, will you be mad?" Kristy teased.

"How can I convince you that I'm serious?"

Kristy was silent for a moment. "I've got it. You have to promise that you'll ask out the next available man you meet. No matter what."

"Um. I've never asked out a guy before. I didn't even participate in Sadie Hawkins in college because I hated the thought of asking someone out."

"Exactly. What better way to get you out of your comfort zone than to do something totally out of character?"

Vickie thought for a minute. She wasn't sure she had the nerve to ask out someone she didn't know. Although she wasn't sure she could ask out someone she knew, either. "Okay. . .maybe I could do it?"

"Not maybe. You can. This will be like your birthday present to yourself. You, taking charge of your dating life." The excitement was evident in Kristy's voice. "Promise?"

Vickie scratched Jake behind the ears. Maybe it was time for her to take charge. She was tired of just letting things happen to her. "Promise." They said their good-byes and hung up.

Vickie laid her head back on the couch. Thirty. It wasn't a bad age. Even if her mother could still relegate her to feeling as if she were fresh out of college, Vickie knew better. She'd been on her own for a long time. Made her own money. Her own decisions. She was proud of her independence. But it was time to admit she was also a little lonely. Despite her apprehension about taking charge of her dating life, it also made her feel a little bit empowered. And that was a good feeling.

CHAPTER 6

As soon as Katherine got home from the hospital, she went upstairs to find the box her mother had told her about. Sure enough, it was there. Then she marched downstairs and called Blake. She could only face so much alone.

When the doorbell rang twenty minutes later, she was waiting in the foyer. She opened the door and threw herself into his arms. "I'm so glad to see you."

He kissed her on the cheek. "You sounded pretty upset on the phone. What gives?"

Blake followed her into the house, and she led him into the living room. At twenty-eight, he was eight years older than she was. They'd met last summer, right after she and her mother had returned from her post-graduation cruise. Katherine had gotten a job with a temp agency for the summer to make some extra money for college and had gotten placed at the accounting firm where Blake worked. First, there'd just been harmless flirting around the coffeepot, but once her assignment ran out, he'd asked her to a movie. They'd been dating ever since.

Her relationship with Blake was the one thing she and her

mother didn't see eye to eye on. Her mother was horrified that Katherine had gone into her freshman year of college dating an older man. According to her mother, she was missing out on the social aspect of college that was so important. Her mother had always wanted her to join a sorority and be actively involved on-campus, things she herself had never gotten to do. But Katherine had chosen to work and spend time with Blake instead.

Now as they stood in the living room, she told him quickly about her mother's diagnosis and the doctor's stoic demeanor. "It was like he's already given up."

Blake pulled her close. "I'm sure it isn't like that, honey. He likely doesn't want to give you false hope." He leaned his head back and met her teary gaze. "It's probably better that you go ahead and accept the truth."

She pulled away from him. "So you're on his side. You think I should just go ahead and start planning her funeral."

He loosened his tie and shook his head. "That isn't what I said." He reached over and rubbed her shoulder. "But I do think you should prepare yourself for the worst."

Katherine started pacing the length of the living room. "I'm not stupid. I know the odds aren't in her favor." She stopped in front of him. "But I need to be able to believe that she could get better. That's the only way I can get through this for now."

Blake sighed. "How is she taking it?"

Katherine shook her head. "We haven't talked about it much. She primarily wanted to apologize to me instead of talk about her illness."

"Apologize? For what?"

"I don't know."

He frowned. "I don't understand."

She suddenly felt foolish. "She told me there was a box in the top of the closet that I needed to look through with an open mind."

"Is there?"

"Yes, there's a box there."

"So what's in it?"

She ran her hand over her face. "I know it's crazy, but I wanted you here before I opened it."

Five minutes later, with Blake settled on the sofa for the required moral support, Katherine walked in with the box. What would be in it? She couldn't imagine.

She sank onto the floor in front of Blake, set the box down, and lifted the lid. Lots of cards and letters. She immediately saw her name on the front of many of them.

She picked the top one up and peered at the postmark. A year ago. Her hand trembled as she opened it. A greeting card. "To my dearest daughter, on her high school graduation," she read aloud.

"From Mike?" Blake leaned forward to look at it closer.

Katherine sat very still, wishing she could believe that this card was from the only man she'd ever known as a father. Mike had adopted her when she was two, because her biological father had been—according to what her mom had told her when she was twelve and old enough to ask questions—unprepared for fatherhood and not interested in the responsibility. She opened the card slowly and a check fluttered to the ground. And it wasn't signed by Mike.

"Whoa." Blake whistled softly as he saw the hefty amount. "I take it that's from your biological dad. That's a lot of zeroes."

Katherine felt like the air in the room had suddenly grown thinner. "Why would she not have told me?"

Blake didn't answer.

She reached in again, digging to the bottom of the box. She came up with a small envelope addressed to her mom. She opened it and a photo fell out. She held it under the letter without looking at it while she read the scrawled words. "I spent time with him when I was younger," she whispered, more to herself than to Blake.

"Really?"

She looked up at him. "Yeah, listen to this—'She cries all the time, Jane. It tears my heart out. The only time she isn't crying is when she's playing with Easton. One thing I did right as a dad, I guess. Buying her that puppy to play with.' " She pulled out the photo, stared at it, and handed it to Blake. "Look. On the back, it says it's me, age two, and Easton, also age two." In the photo, Katherine's head was thrown back in laughter, and a chocolate lab was licking her face with a pink tongue. "Don't we look like buddies?"

Blake laughed. "You were a cute little thing."

She took the photo back. "This is so weird." She laid the photo and letter aside and dug in again. There were more letters to her mom telling about how much she cried while she was with him, all dated before her second birthday. Then there were a lot addressed to her. At first she read the cards and letters to Blake, but when she realized there was a card—and a check—for every birthday, and letters several times a year just to say hello and he loved her, she felt too sick to keep reading them aloud. She'd read one, lay it down, and grab another one. Over and over again.

One time, she was vaguely aware of Blake getting up and getting something to drink out of the fridge then coming back to sit on the floor beside her. Finally, she finished going through the whole box and looked up at him, her heart heavy. "I don't understand why Mom kept this from me."

"Are you angry?"

Katherine sighed. "How can I be angry with my mother, especially considering the news we just got?" She shook her head. "At this point, I'm just confused." She leaned against him. "I'm not sure what I'll say. I'm going to the hospital first thing tomorrow and am hoping to have it figured out by then."

Blake pushed to his feet and looked down at her. "I'm sure you'll know what to say. You and Jane have always been able to talk about everything." Katherine's close relationship with her mother had always bothered Blake. He didn't understand why she would share the details of her life, especially when they concerned her relationship with him. She'd told him a million times that her mom was both her mother and her friend, but he could never get past it.

"Yeah."

"Hey. . ." He tugged on her hand and pulled her to her feet. "Let's go out for dinner. I think it'll do you good to get out of the house tonight."

She looked down at the box. The last thing she felt like doing was eating, but she knew if she said that, he'd say that she had to eat to keep up her strength. She nodded. "Okay. I don't like being here without Mom anyway. I hope the doctor lets her come home tomorrow."

He nodded and grabbed her hand. "Let's go."

She let him lead her out the door and into his waiting convertible. He chattered all the way to the restaurant about an incident at work, but her mind was a million miles away. Part of her wanted to stop him and have him drop her off at the hospital. But her mom had clearly told her to go home, look through the box, and come back tomorrow. Maybe she was trying to figure out what to say, too. She leaned her head against the leather seat and let the warm July breeze wash over her. Tomorrow she would get some answers.

CHAPTER 7

The fluttering in Vickie's stomach began as soon as she opened her eyes. Memories of last night's birthday dinner with her parents and the silly promise she'd made to Kristy flooded her mind. What had she gotten herself into? She threw on a satiny pink robe over her nightgown and padded down the hallway. Coffee. No more thinking until she had a cup. At the sight of the freshly brewed liquid, she smiled. Whoever had invented the timer for coffeemakers deserved a Nobel Peace Prize.

Her favorite coffee mug was on the counter, right in front of the coffeemaker. The spoon to stir in creamer was already inside. Vickie knew if her friends could see the scene, they'd laugh. But it always made her feel better to have things prepared. For as long as she could remember, her nightly ritual had consisted of putting out her mug and spoon, grinding the coffee, and setting the timer. Sometimes she would go so far as to put out a skillet and plate if she planned to fix a scrambled egg, which was her breakfast of choice.

Jake lazily sauntered into the kitchen, stopping every now and then to stretch. Vickie bent down and scratched between his ears. "Good morning, sleepyhead." She grinned as he regarded her seriously for a moment. "Today's not going to be the day you start speaking, huh?" she asked as he went back the way he came, presumably to lounge on the fluffy bed he'd claimed soon after she'd rescued him.

Vickie poured coffee into the waiting cup and loaded it with sweetener and creamer. She plucked a peppermint coffee stirrer from the container and watched as the creamer swirled with the coffee. For a moment, she closed her eyes and enjoyed the scent. Okay. Her first day post-thirtieth birthday wasn't too bad. She could handle it.

An hour later, she was dressed and ready for work. As soon as she stepped out of her building, the humidity washed over her like a blanket. Why did she even bother putting on makeup? At least she'd thought to use waterproof mascara this morning. Just in case she had to follow through on the promise she'd made to Kristy last night.

It was only a five-minute walk to the Metro. That was one of the reasons she loved her location so much. Quick access to transportation was vital in DC, and being so close to Metro Center meant she was close to any of the lines. As usual, she silently applauded herself for choosing her apartment. When she'd first moved in, the area had been an up-and-coming neighborhood, but with so many renovated condos and apartments in the area, it had quickly transformed into a hip area for young professionals. Although Vickie had never classified herself as "hip," she was happy to at least be surrounded by hipness.

She exited at the Smithsonian stop and managed not to bump in to anyone. Late July was still prime tourist season, so this was quite a feat. Even though it had been five years since she'd moved to Washington, she never tired of walking to work. She could see the Washington Monument almost as soon as she stepped off the escalator from the Metro. If she stopped and looked in the opposite direction, the U.S. Capitol was in view. When she'd first started, the other rangers who were stationed along the National Mall assured her there'd come a time when she wouldn't notice the monuments, but so far that hadn't happened.

"Mornin', Vickie." Ranger Chris Michaels nodded at her as she walked into Survey Lodge, the main ranger station for the monuments. All the park rangers who worked along the National Mall had to check in at Survey Lodge before heading out to their appointed location.

"Good morning." She smiled. "It's already a hot one out there. And by the number of people getting off the Metro, I'd say we're in for a busy day."

He grimaced. "Is it bad that I'm already wishing for October? Cooler weather and smaller crowds sound nice about now."

She flipped on the computer. "I don't mind the crowds. But fall weather sounds nice."

Chris raked a hand through his brown hair and placed his hat on top of his head. "Guess I'd better go. I'm spending the day at the Jefferson Memorial. How about you?" he asked.

Vickie sighed. "Lincoln Memorial."

He laughed. "You say that with such excitement. I thought you liked the Lincoln."

She shrugged. "I do like it. As a visitor. But I prefer to work at the Washington Monument. I'll get through it, though. At least the weather guy this morning said the chance of rain had all but disappeared." Her mouth turned upward in a smile. "See, I'm trying to look on the bright side."

"Good luck." Still chuckling, Chris made his exit, leaving Vickie alone with her thoughts. She quickly checked her park service e-mail. Not much there. A reminder about ordering winter uniforms, but nothing that required immediate attention. She glanced at her watch. She still had five minutes before she needed to leave. That was one perk of getting to work a little early each morning. She hated to feel rushed.

She logged on to her personal e-mail and clicked on a new one from Kristy. A nervous quiver hit her stomach as she read the reminder. What had she gotten herself into? She logged off and grabbed her hat. Worrying would have to wait. She had a ranger talk to give.

CHAPTER 8

The moment he stepped off the Metro, Thatcher was reminded of his rule against setting foot on the National Mall during the summer after 8:00 a.m. The people were practically shoulder to shoulder. Why would anyone on vacation want to be out this early? Or in these crowds, for that matter? Thatcher's idea of a vacation was total seclusion. Except for his dog, Buster, and a fishing pole. He didn't even want to hear a radio.

He stopped short and looked around in disgust, already regretting his decision to visit the mall. But he was here. So he may as well go ahead with his plan. Ever since John had filled him in on Clark's plan to locate the rumored Lincoln documents, it was all he could think about. The very idea that Clark could become department chair—and his boss—was more than he could take. If those documents did exist, he would find them. And if that didn't secure his spot within the university, maybe it was time to move on.

A sharp jolt on the back of his heels startled him. "Ow." He turned quickly to face the culprit of his pain.

"I'm so sorry, sir." The young woman pushing the stroller

couldn't have been a day over eighteen. "I didn't notice that you'd stopped until it was too late." Her brow furrowed in worry. "Are you okay?"

Thatcher glanced from the woman to the gurgling baby strapped in the stroller. "I'm fine. Don't worry about it." He grinned, and the baby gave him a large smile that displayed two bottom teeth. "That's a sharp-looking fellow you've got there." He nodded toward the child.

The young woman beamed. "This is Luke. He's seven months old."

Thatcher managed a smile. "Fun age." He looked at the infant again. "I hope you enjoy your trip." He turned his back on the pair and quickened his steps. He jogged across Fifteenth Street right before the light changed, and passed by the line of people waiting to get passes to the Washington Monument. He should've known better than to come this way. What was wrong with him? Foggy Bottom Metro would've been a little closer to the Lincoln Memorial, and he could've bypassed most of these tourists.

He was so used to getting off the Metro at the Smithsonian station for his daily runs that he'd automatically disembarked there. He dodged another stroller near the World War II Memorial and finally made it to the path alongside the reflecting pool. The Lincoln Memorial loomed ahead, in all its majestic glory. Thatcher had always admired its resemblance to the Parthenon in Athens. Greece remained near the top of his list of places to visit, and he hoped someday he'd find the time.

He slowed his pace and stood at the bottom of the many stairs leading to the memorial. Throngs of people were already milling about, despite the early hour. He listened to their laughter and watched as they photographed one another, first with the Lincoln Memorial in the background and then facing the other direction with the reflecting pool and Washington Monument in the back of the shot. This was a prime spot for family photographs.

"Can you take our picture?" The young man held a digital camera in Thatcher's direction. "We're on our honeymoon," he explained, motioning toward the pretty girl who stood at his side, beaming.

"Sure." Thatcher took the camera as if it were a foreign object. "Tell me how to work this thing." His own camera still had the wind feature and required a roll of film, and he was pretty sure the same roll of film had been inside for the past five years, since Buster was a puppy.

"Oh yeah," the newlywed said. "Just press this button. You'll be able to see the shot on the screen."

Thatcher moved the camera around until the couple was in the center of the screen. "One, two, three," he said, pressing the button and capturing their smiling faces. He handed the camera back to the man.

"Thanks." The couple was already reviewing the photo on the screen, giggling about the face the girl was making.

He walked off, shaking his head. Young love was a sight to behold. He barely remembered being that age. He'd tried so hard to block those years out, and most of the time it worked.

Thatcher made it to the top step, and the statue of Abraham Lincoln came into full view. He had to admit, it was breathtaking. There was something almost magical about it. Larger than life, Lincoln sat gazing out over the crowd. You almost expected him to rise up from the chair and deliver a speech. Thatcher stood for a moment at the base of the statue. Were the rumors true? Was Clark really on the trail of an amazing discovery? These past several days, Thatcher and John had tried to find out more information, but so far nothing had turned up.

He noticed a sign next to the statue that advertised ranger talks for the day. The first one was scheduled to start in fifteen minutes. Since he didn't have any place to be, it couldn't hurt to stick around. He might learn something.

CHAPTER 9

Counting the years she'd spent as a seasonal, Vickie had been giving ranger talks for nine years. So you would think that by now she'd be over feeling nervous before a talk. But no. She always felt a flutter in her stomach just before that moment when she welcomed the visitors. Today was no exception. She took a deep breath.

"Good morning," she said to the small crowd of visitors waiting near the sign that advertised the times of today's ranger programs. "Welcome to the Lincoln Memorial and to our nation's capital." She smiled brightly as a few more people joined the circle around her, her eyes landing on a tall, well-built man leaning against a large column. He caught her eye and nodded. His thick dark hair was a little shaggy, the ends curling over the collar of his polo shirt.

Vickie launched into the first part of her talk, where she discussed the monument itself. "The memorial was commissioned in 1897, but construction didn't begin until 1914. It took eight years to complete." She motioned at the statue of Lincoln behind her. "This statue is nineteen feet tall and nineteen feet wide. It was made from twenty-eight marble blocks." She took a breath. "Quite a few myths are associated with the statue, just as quite a few myths are associated with President Lincoln himself." She smiled at the group. "Contrary to what you might've heard, his hands aren't spelling anything in sign language." She watched as everyone shifted their gazes to the large hands on the statue. "Instead, his left hand is in a fist, symbolic of his action during the Civil War. His right hand is open, symbolizing how he forgave the South and invited them back into the Union." She paused. "Another myth that's been perpetuated through the years is that the face of Robert E. Lee is on the back side of the statue, gazing across the Potomac River toward his home." She paused. "False. I assure you, his face isn't back there." She paused. "I know because I took the liberty of sneaking back for a peek right after I started working here." The crowd laughed. Vickie waited until they were quiet to explain the different types of marble and limestone used to build the monument.

"Moving on to the life of the president, we have to discuss what was going on while Lincoln was in the White House." She pointed to a Boy Scout in the front of the circle. "Can you tell me what major event was happening at that time?"

"The Civil War," the scout said, clearly proud of his knowledge.

"Very good." Vickie nodded in his direction. She motioned to the wall that was to her right. "One of Lincoln's most famous speeches can be found inscribed here. The Gettysburg Address. Did you know that the president wasn't even the keynote speaker that day?" Most of the crowd shook their heads. "Even so, he delivered one of the most famous speeches ever given, one that history students still learn from today." She noticed a few glazed-over expressions and decided to skip over the next part and go straight to the end. "As you probably know, Abraham Lincoln was assassinated six days after the Civil War ended. This memorial to our slain president is one of the most-visited locations in the world, and scholars continue to discuss and debate Lincoln and the impact he still has on our world today." She smiled. "I'll be around if anyone has questions; otherwise, enjoy the rest of your day."

The crowd began to thin out. She knew if any of the other rangers were around, she'd probably take flack for giving such a short talk. But it was early in the morning. And as usual, whenever she saw someone yawning or looking around, she always took it as an insult. Would thirty finally be the year she stopped taking things so personally?

"Excuse me," a deep voice said behind her.

She turned and came face-to-face with the man who'd been leaning against one of the columns. Now that he was closer, she could see a few strands of silvery gray in his dark hair. His chiseled, tanned face was smooth and unlined.

"Yes? Did you have a question?"

"I haven't been to the Lincoln Memorial in years. That was an interesting talk." He grinned, his brown eyes sparkling.

Uh-oh. The promise she'd made to Kristy last night came rushing back. She quickly glanced down to see if there was a ring on his finger. There wasn't. Had he seen her look? Of course, a man not wearing a ring didn't mean anything. Some men didn't like to wear rings. Or he could have a girlfriend or a fiancée. Men should really be required to wear engagement rings. *Say something, Vickie.* "Thanks." *Brilliant.* She smiled and looked around. "Um... are you here with your family?" So much for smooth. But at least if she found out now that he was here with his wife and kids, she wouldn't make a fool out of herself by asking him out.

A tiny bead of sweat trickled from her forehead, and Vickie resisted the urge to remove her hat and wipe it away. If only she'd have included a special clause in her promise to Kristy that she'd only ask out a man if she were in normal clothes. She was suddenly all too aware of her green pants and Smokey Bear hat.

He narrowed his eyes a little. "No. I'm alone." He cleared his throat. "Actually, I live here."

"Oh. Me, too." She fought the urge to groan. Of course she lived here; otherwise, what would she be doing delivering a ranger talk? She forced a smile and ignored the blush she felt creeping across her face.

The grin he shot in her direction displayed a dimple in his right cheek. "I see."

Her heart pounded against her chest. How should she do this? Should she ask him for dinner? *Would you like to grab a bite to eat later?* Or was that too much? Maybe just coffee. Or ice cream, since it was such a hot day. She'd try to ease into it. "We don't get too many locals here. Are you out playing tourist for the day?"

He shook his head. "No. I'm a professor."

"Oh?"

For a moment he looked unsure, then he stuck out his hand. "Dr. Thatcher Torrey, professor of history at George Washington University."

She grasped his hand and shook. "I'm Vickie Harris. Just a park ranger." She grinned. "No fancy title needed."

Thatcher laughed. "Sorry. I guess it sounds awfully pretentious to introduce myself as a doctor, doesn't it?"

"Not at all. Believe me, if I'd gone through all that schooling, I'd include it, too."

He shrugged. "I guess I'm in work mode right now, with school starting soon and all."

"I understand all about work mode. Normally, I hate to be up in front of people, but since it's part of my job, I can handle it. I go into ranger mode and am fine."

"Ranger mode, huh?" He smiled again. "I've always thought being a park ranger would be an interesting job. Do you enjoy it?"

"I love it. I started out as a seasonal ranger at Shiloh National Military Park in Tennessee."

"Shiloh, home of the Bloody Pond." He grinned. "Don't forget you're dealing with a history professor."

"Very good, Dr. Torrey." She returned his smile. "I've been working along the National Mall for the past five years." She motioned at the large statue of Lincoln. "There's something magical about the monuments here."

"Are you well versed in the history of Abraham Lincoln?" he asked.

She cocked her head and looked up at him. Was he going to ask her to speak to his classes? She'd had to do that sort of thing before and had found being in the classroom wasn't her thing. "Honestly, I've spent the majority of my time at the Washington Monument, but these past several weeks I've been stationed here a good bit. I've been learning more about Lincoln's life and legacy." She shrugged. "It's pretty interesting stuff, but being a history guy, I guess you already know that." She took a deep breath. It was time to bite the bullet and ask him for a date. Here's hoping the lack of a ring on his finger meant he was available. "I was wondering. . . ," she began, but he'd already started speaking.

"Could I maybe buy you dinner one night later this week?" he asked.

She felt her face flame. That hadn't gone as planned, but maybe it would placate Kristy. After all, accepting a dinner date from someone she met on a ranger program was definitely out of character. She normally liked to make sure she knew someone in common with a potential date so she could check to see what other people knew about them. But it was time to throw caution to the wind. "Sure," she said, trying to keep her voice steady. "What do you have in mind?"

"How about tomorrow night? Say sixish? If you don't mind getting a little touristy, I love Johnny's Half Shell. It isn't too far from Union Station."

She nodded. "I like that place."

Thatcher pulled out a card from the pocket of his khaki cargo shorts. "Here's my card. If something comes up, just call me. My home number is there, and you can leave a message if you need to."

"Okay. Thanks." She was suddenly unsure. *It's just dinner. No need to collect references for that.* Besides, they'd meet at the restaurant. It wasn't as if he were picking her up or anything.

"It was nice to meet you, Vickie. I'll see you tomorrow at six."

She watched him walk down the stairs and merge into the crowd. He was handsome. A little older than she was used to, but maybe that was okay. And he had a PhD, so he must be intelligent. She couldn't wait to call Kristy tonight and tell her she'd managed to get a date without having to do the asking. Turning thirty was suddenly looking up.

CHAPTER 10

Well, that had worked out better than he could've ever planned. When Thatcher had made the impulsive decision to visit the Lincoln Memorial to get some inspiration, he hadn't thought about park rangers having knowledge of the slain president. But as soon as he'd heard Vickie start talking, it had made perfect sense to him. He needed someone to help him on his quest for the documents, and who better to do it than someone who already had a working knowledge of the subject? Plus, it worked better that she wasn't an academic. There would be no question as to who was in charge of the quest and who was assisting.

Hopefully, John would have news for him once he got back to the office. If he could find out some of the details about what exactly Clark was after, that would at least point him in the right direction. And tomorrow night over dinner, he'd attempt to convince Vickie Harris to help him. He wondered if he should offer to pay her. Probably. Otherwise, what would her incentive be? And who knew how much time it would take? For all he knew, she could have a passel of kids waiting on her at home. A glance at her left hand had told him she wasn't wearing a wedding ring, but in this day and age, that didn't seem to mean a whole lot.

He finally arrived back on campus. Summer classes were over, and they were still a couple of weeks away from the date when students would start arriving back for the fall semester. The small number of people he passed on the way to his office was a welcome change from the bustling activity of the Lincoln Memorial. If he had to go there every day, he'd probably have a nervous breakdown.

Amanda Joyner poked her head into his office no more than a minute after he'd collapsed in his chair. Amanda was the department secretary, but everyone knew she ran the place. She'd been around forever and knew all the ins and outs of university politics. Amanda also wrote mystery novels on the side, and whenever anyone crossed her, she threatened to kill them off in her next book. "Thatch, you've had a couple of phone calls," she said with excitement.

"Okay." He looked blankly at her. "What's the problem?"

She stared back at him with wide eyes. "It was the same woman both times. I'm not sure what she wanted. She didn't leave a name or message." She peered at him. "Were you expecting a call?" she asked, lowering her voice like they were sharing a secret.

He shook his head. It figured that some woman would call while he was out. If he'd been in, no one would've known. But when he was out, his calls rolled over to Amanda. He glanced at her cat-who-ate-the-canary grin. "I wasn't expecting a call." His voice was gruff. "It was likely a helicopter parent of one of my incoming freshmen." Every year they got worse. At this point, it wouldn't surprise him if he had to start putting more chairs in his classroom in case parents wanted to observe their kids in college. It was out of control.

She raised an eyebrow. "If you say so. I was hoping maybe you'd finally found a lady friend." Her broad smile spoke volumes.

It was beyond him why his personal life was ever the topic of conversation around campus. He'd dealt with quite a few rumors through the years, but none had ever had any merit. Since when was it a crime for a man to be single and in his late thirties? "I'm certain. But thanks for your concern." He grinned. "Have you decided on your next victim?"

Her mouth twisted into a smirk. "I haven't written the murder scene yet, but after that faculty meeting the other day, I'll bet I know who gets your vote to be the victim." As usual, Amanda never missed anything that went on in the history department. "If it makes you feel any better, I can vouch for you. I'm the one who goes over all the course evaluations. Yours are as high as anyone else on staff. Higher than most."

"Thanks. That's a rumor I might need you to spread around." He chuckled.

"No problem." She winked and spun on her heel, leaving him alone.

He sighed and flipped on the computer. A ton of work-related e-mail messages to wade through waited for him. Everything was electronic now, from turning in class syllabi to end-of-semester grades. Even John gave him a hard time about sounding like a grumpy old man when it came to technology. But Thatcher couldn't help but worry about the detrimental effect it was having on society. As a historian, he tried to look at things from a global view. And in his opinion, although people were constantly connected what with their Blackberries and iPhones, they were connected on a much less personal level. There was less interaction. It drove him crazy when he had to call an 800 number and couldn't reach a real-live person. Sometimes it seemed that what was being touted as "progress" might be just the opposite.

His students were prime examples. They could win contests for sending the fastest texts, but many of them had a hard time carrying on a conversation. There had to be a balance.

A rap at the door pulled him away from his thoughts. "I've got news." John looked gleeful as he closed the door behind him.

"That makes two of us," Thatcher said. "And I met up with a park ranger today who I think might be able to help me, or at least be able to point me in the right direction."

John looked sheepish. "I wish I had time to help, man." He shook his head. "Megan would kill me, though."

Thatcher laughed. "I don't want to get you in trouble with the wife. Besides, Avery will only be young once. I wouldn't dream of keeping you away from her."

"I know. Her favorite word right now is *daddy*, and it makes me melt. I swear it's the most beautiful sound I've ever heard."

Thatcher nodded. "I would imagine so." He cleared his throat. "So, what's your news?"

"Well, it might not pan out. But you know the guy I told you was playing racquetball the other day with Clark's grad assistant?"

"Yeah."

"He and I have a game scheduled for later today. I'm going to try to dig for some dirt. You know how those grad assistants like to talk about what they're working on. I'm hoping to slip in some questions about Clark and see if he falls for it."

"Nice." Thatcher grinned. "See, even if you don't have much spare time, you can still pitch in."

John made a face. "It if keeps Clark from becoming department chair, I'm in. And I'm in no position to go after the chairmanship myself, what with just starting a family." He nodded at Thatcher. "So that means I'm throwing all my weight behind you." He stood. "By the way, Amanda was all in a tizzy earlier looking for you."

"She already stopped in. Said a 'mysterious' woman called for me twice." Thatcher emphasized the word by making quotation marks with his fingers.

John raised his eyebrows. "You're not holding out on me, are you? Besides, if I remember correctly, you've already had your one allotted dinner date for the year."

"That isn't a hard-and-fast rule. It's just worked out that way these past few years."

"Whatever. Your outlook on the female species mystifies me. Didn't you ever consider settling down?"

"A lifetime ago. Some of us were meant to walk through life alone. I'm like a lone wolf."

John rolled his eyes. "If the right woman ever comes along, you'll be in as much trouble as the rest of us. So who was the mystery woman, anyway?"

"Didn't leave her name. Probably a parent."

John nodded. "Probably." He opened the door then turned to face Thatcher. "I'll let you know how racquetball goes. And if I don't see you again, good luck with the park ranger."

Thatcher nodded and watched his friend leave. He'd conveniently left out the part where the park ranger he was meeting happened to be female, attractive, and smart. After all, he was planning to ignore that part himself and focus only on business. That outlook had served him well these past years, and he saw no reason for it to change now.

CHAPTER 11

Katherine steeled her nerves and tapped on the hospital room door. She'd spent a sleepless night, alternating between worrying about her mom's health and wondering what she should say about the cards and letters. In an odd way, she knew it was good to have something to distract her from the reality of the diagnosis.

"Come in," her mother called.

Katherine squinted as she stepped inside the room. The shades were pulled up, and early morning sunlight streamed into the room. She pulled the door shut behind her. "Good morning." She held up a bag and a coffee cup. "I stopped at Starbucks on my way here." She set the bag on her mom's bed and handed her the cup. "Blueberry muffin and a tall mocha. The breakfast of champions."

Her mom smiled. "You're my most favorite daughter."

"Very funny." Katherine perched on the bed. "Unless you've got another daughter stashed away somewhere, I'd better be." Her face clouded over as she thought about the cards and letters she'd read yesterday. Did her biological father have another daughter? Did she have brothers and sisters out there she didn't know about?

She felt her mother's eyes on her and looked up to meet her gaze. There were certainly a couple of elephants in the room this morning. It was time to tackle the first one. "So. Has the doctor been by this morning?"

Her mother nodded. "Yes. It looks like I'm going home tomorrow." She took a sip of coffee. "Please don't worry. I know the news wasn't the best yesterday, but I'm going to fight. You know that."

Katherine nodded. "I know."

They sat in silence for a long moment. Finally, her mom set her coffee cup on the table. "Katherine, I'm sorry. I can't imagine what you must be thinking right now."

Katherine shook her head. "Don't be sorry, Mom. Just tell me the truth about him."

"We shouldn't have gotten married in the first place. We were so young. Younger than you are now." She got a faraway look in her eyes as if she were looking deep into the past. "Eddie was so smart. Just being around him, you knew he was destined for big things. And I. . .well, I was a little bit wilder back then. I always liked to test the limits, you know?" She eyed her daughter. "Thankfully you didn't inherit that particular wild streak. My mother always said it would serve me right if I had a daughter who behaved just like I did." Her face twisted into a smile. "I like to think that instead I had a daughter who got the best parts of me and the best parts of her father and none of our glaring flaws."

Katherine shook her head. "I'm sure you weren't that bad."

Her mother sighed and brushed off a stray morsel of muffin from the sheet. "I got pregnant with you the night of our senior prom." She shook her head. "I don't know what came over us. I think we were giddy with excitement that school was almost over and our 'real' lives were about to start. The prom was magical, and afterward. . .well, things got out of hand. It was the first time for both of us." She sighed. "I didn't tell you before now because I didn't want you to turn out to be one of those girls who justified sleeping with your boyfriend because you found out your mom had when she was your age."

Katherine couldn't help but grin. "Mom, you've made your feelings about that very clear. I think I learned about the birds and the bees way before any of the other girls in my class."

Her mother laughed. "I wanted you to know all the facts and how I felt about the matter." She locked her gaze with Katherine's. "Anyway, by the time I found out I was expecting, it was time for graduation. Your father and I weren't even seeing each other anymore. Honestly, I think we both felt a lot of guilt over what happened prom night and we just couldn't get past it." Her brown eyes clouded over. "Telling my parents was so hard. They were disappointed, to say the least." She glanced over at Katherine. "Looking back now, I can say that you were the single best thing ever to happen to me. But at that time, it was really difficult. Our parents put a lot of pressure on us to marry." She sighed. "I didn't want to marry Eddie. We weren't even in love. We'd only been on a few dates. But I gave in."

"What about him? Did he want to marry you?" Katherine couldn't imagine going through something like that right out of high school.

"He said it was the right thing to do. For him, right and wrong were always black and white, you know? He had so much integrity, even at a young age. I think he thought it was his duty to marry me and be a father to you."

"If that was how he felt, I don't understand why things turned out how they did. What happened?"

"I was so unhappy. We had a quick wedding the week after graduation. My mom wanted me to walk down the aisle before anyone knew. As if that would make it okay somehow." She shrugged. "She got her wish, though. Most people assumed you were conceived on our honeymoon."

Katherine barely knew her grandparents. She could count the times she'd seen them on one hand, but from what she knew of them, they were very proper. She could only imagine that having a pregnant and unwed daughter must've been their worst nightmare.

"We tried to make it work but were both miserable. At first, it was okay. Kind of like an adventure. But suddenly, we were grown-ups with jobs and bills and responsibilities." Her mother gave a wistful smile. "He started college, and I found a job working at the front desk of a hospital." She grabbed Katherine's hand. "The one thing we had in common was that we already loved you. It was a tough situation, but we were honestly happy to be bringing you into the world. From the moment I felt you move inside me, I knew I'd been put on earth to be your mother."

Katherine managed a tiny smile. "So what happened next? Was he there when I was born?"

Jane nodded. "He sure was." She grinned at the memory. "He was more nervous than me, I think—always fearful he'd do something wrong. He made the head nurse teach him how to change your diaper so he'd know just the right way."

"But how did things change so quickly?" Katherine knew that only two years after she was born, her mother had married Mike.

"Once we were home from the hospital, the enormity of the situation hit me. I was married to a man I didn't love and who I was sure didn't love me. I wanted out." She shook her head. "So I did some pretty awful stuff."

"What do you mean?"

"At first, I'd leave you with my parents and go out with my friends. They were living it up in the dorm. When I'd go visit them, I'd pretend like I wasn't a wife and mother." She looked pleadingly at Katherine. "But I loved you so much. You were always taken care of." Her mother shook her head. "I tried to make Eddie unhappy so that he would leave me, but he never would. I tried everything." She paused. "And then I ran into an old boyfriend from junior high. He worked with me at the hospital, and we always had the best conversations. I fell hard for him, even though I had a husband and child. When your dad found out, he was devastated. As usually happens in such cases, things soon fell apart with my old flame. But by then, the damage was done with your father. I didn't see that I had many options, and to tell you the truth, I was terrified of losing you. So I withdrew all the money from our savings account, packed the car, and hit the road with you. I drove until we reached California." She took another sip of coffee. "I'd just turned nineteen. Can you imagine? Nineteen."

"How have you kept all this from me for all these years?" Katherine was amazed. Her mother had lived an entire life that she'd never known about.

Her mother's face was sheepish. "When you hear a doctor tell you that nothing can be done for you. . .I think it makes you want to share all your secrets." She managed a tiny smile. "Besides, these are things you need to know. It makes me feel better knowing that you're going to know my whole story."

"What happened once we got to California?" Katherine tried to imagine leaving her family and friends, driving across the country with a newborn, and starting over. No wonder her mother was as strong as she was. She'd had to grow up fast.

"In hindsight, it wasn't the smartest thing to do. I left everyone I'd ever known, including my parents. But I was determined. I cleaned houses for a living so I wouldn't have to put you in day care. I'd take you with me and leave you in your little bouncy seat. But you didn't care. You were always such a happy baby." Her mom reached over and tucked a stray hair behind Katherine's ear. "Your dad finally tracked us down, though. It was the angriest I'd ever seen him. He demanded we come back home with him. But by then, I'd met Mike. Your dad finally agreed to a divorce but wanted visitation rights."

"He did? I thought he never wanted to see me." That was the story Katherine had always been told.

Her mother inhaled sharply. "This is the part that I have to apologize for. I should never have told you that he wasn't interested in being your father. The truth is he was crazy about you. But he was so young." She shook her head. "Whenever you'd go spend time with him, you cried more than he thought was normal. He didn't know what to do with you. I think he tried just about everything. One week while you were with him, he even bought you a puppy, thinking maybe it would make you happy."

"Easton. I saw a picture in the box." Katherine drew her brows together. This was so complicated.

"I tried to explain to him that you were fussy because you didn't know him, but he didn't believe it. He thought it meant he was bad at being a father. And then, right after Mike and I got married, he came to the house to see you. You clung to Mike and didn't want anything to do with Eddie. I think it hurt him so much he couldn't deal with it. He didn't realize that you were just scared. So when Mike wanted to adopt you so we could live as a family, Eddie agreed to it." Her mother sighed. "From that point on, your dad would send cards and letters, but he stopped visiting. Eventually, he gave up on seeing you."

"Just like that." Katherine shook her head. "It sounds like he must not have wanted to be my dad too bad. Otherwise, he would've done more than just send letters and cards." She didn't point out that she'd never actually received them, because her mother knew that all too well.

"I shouldn't have hidden those from you all that time. At first, I tried to tell myself it was for the best."

"The best?"

"It was in your best interest not to be torn between two

families. I guess in my mind, when Eddie relinquished his visitation rights, I convinced myself it was like he was saying he didn't want to be part of your life." She paused. "But I knew better than that. He wrote those cards and letters steadily. I think he was hoping that once you got a little older, you'd want to meet him."

"But since I didn't know he was sending them, it never crossed my mind," Katherine finished. A year ago, she'd have been furious about this discovery. But now, coupled with the news of yesterday, it was a little easier to take. "Have you talked to him over the years?"

Her mom shook her head. "No. We haven't spoken since Mike legally adopted you eighteen years ago." She sighed. "I guess you saw all the checks. He sent checks to both of us throughout the years. I never cashed any of them. I felt too guilty. He wasn't getting to know you and to raise you like I was, and I knew that was my fault. So I didn't think it would be right to take his money." She grabbed Katherine's hand. "Can you forgive me?"

It was so much to digest. And at this point, even knowing the truth didn't seem to help much. It wasn't like they could go back in time and change anything. "Of course. You were doing what you thought was best." Katherine raised an eyebrow. "If you weren't sick, would you ever have told me the truth?"

"I'd like to think so. Like I said, the news from yesterday prompted the decision, but it is something I've thought about a lot, especially now that you're grown. The decision about whether to have him in your life shouldn't be up to me anymore."

Katherine furrowed her brow. "What are you saying? You think I should meet him?"

Her mother nodded. "That is exactly what I'm saying. I have no idea if he's married or if he has children. But the fact that up until last year he was sending you cards and letters tells me that you've never been far from his mind. Or heart." She cupped Katherine's face. "Will you at least think about it?"

Katherine nodded. She would think about it. But she was pretty sure she knew what her decision would be.

CHAPTER 12

V ickie looked at her reflection in the full-length mirror. When she'd first seen the pale blue dress hanging on the rack, it had reminded her of something straight out of the '50s. And as was often the case, as soon as she'd tried it on at the store, she'd had to have it. The fitted bodice and full skirt made her feel as if she'd just stepped out of an old movie. With Dawn's assurance that it was the perfect color to set off Vickie's dark hair and porcelain skin, she was sold.

There was nothing she enjoyed more than wearing pretty, feminine dresses. Although she'd never admit it to her mother, that was the one drawback to being a park ranger. Even though the female ranger uniform came with a skirt option, it was still made from the same green polyester material as the uniform pants. So while it was a little more ladylike, it was also highly impractical and not exactly the height of fashion. Plus, the required shoes were the ugliest she'd ever seen, and with the skirt on, the shoes were more visible. No thanks. She'd stick to the pants.

So it was no wonder that any occasion to dress up a bit thrilled her. Vickie had always been somewhat of a fashionista, and she had a closet full of nice things. Sometimes she'd even wear a dress and heels just to get groceries. It made her feel prettier to be dressed nicely.

She slipped into some strappy heels and took one last look in the mirror. She'd already applied her makeup, so a dab of tinted lip gloss was all she needed to complete her look. She stepped back and took a deep breath. She was finally ready for her dinner date with the professor.

The nerves didn't hit until she stepped off the Metro at Union Station. She normally delighted in the beautiful old train station with its elaborate columns and statues. But today, she may as well have been walking through an empty tunnel.

What would they talk about? She should've thought of some conversation topics beforehand. Politics? No. That might lead to a disagreement. Family? She knew better. Work. Work was always safe. Unless he hated his job or something. That was a chance she'd have to take.

She turned the corner and relaxed her pace, hoping the slower tempo would help return her heart rate to normal. No such luck. As soon as she spotted him standing out front, waiting for her, the pounding was back.

"Hey there," he said, smiling down at her. "I'm glad you could make it." He was dressed in khaki shorts and a red polo shirt. Not dressed up, but he'd at least made an effort to look nice.

"Hi." She was suddenly self-conscious. Was her dress too much? "Have you been waiting long?"

He glanced at his watch. "Nah. You're right on time." He ushered her into the restaurant, and they were quickly seated.

"I haven't been here in a long time," she said, once they'd placed their drink orders. "What do you normally order?"

Thatcher opened the menu. "The catfish is great. Or the crab cakes." He smiled. "Everything is delicious. I guess it depends on what you're in the mood for."

A moment later, the waitress was at their table. "Are you ready?" she asked.

Thatcher nodded and met Vickie's gaze. "You go ahead."

She'd always hated this part. Ordering dinner on a first date could be tricky. What if she ordered something a lot more expensive than what her date wanted to spend? Or even worse, what if she ordered an entrée that came with more food than his. Then she'd feel like a complete pig. "I think I'll have the appetizer portion of the crab cakes." She met Thatcher's curious gaze and shrugged. "I had a late lunch."

"How about you?" the waitress asked, her pen poised.

"I'd like the grilled halibut." He closed his menu and handed it to the waitress.

Vickie met his gaze. "So, have you lived in DC long?"

"I grew up in Virginia. I have a little fishing cabin there still." He gave a one-sided grin. "But I've been teaching at GWU for the past thirteen years. First part-time, then adjunct, then finally a full-fledged professor." He took a drink of tea. "How about you?"

"I'm originally from Brentwood, Tennessee. It's right outside of Nashville," she explained.

To her surprise, he nodded. "I'm familiar with Brentwood. I actually got my PhD from Vanderbilt."

Her eyes widened. "So you're a Vandy guy? Wow. My mom would be impressed."

He laughed. "Not you, but your mom? I'll take that, I guess."

"It's just that my mom had her heart set on me attending there. When I opted to go elsewhere, it nearly broke her heart." She shrugged. "But I know how tough the academics are there. I had several friends who attended."

"So where did you end up?" he asked.

"I went to a small Christian school. You've probably never heard of it." She smiled. "Only *my* mother would be disappointed that I chose a school where I could draw closer to God. Most people's parents would've been glad. I'm happy with the decision though."

"That's what matters." He looked at her seriously. "And did you? Draw closer to God, I mean."

Vickie nodded. "I think it certainly helped to strengthen my faith. And I met some friends I wouldn't trade for anything." She couldn't help but notice the faint stubble on his face. He was a lot more rugged than most men with whom she'd accepted dates. When she'd described him to Kristy, her friend had declared she was dating Indiana Jones. "But the younger, cuter one," Vickie had said. "Like from the first movie." Even so, she wondered again how old he was and wished there were a tactful way to find out. "So, what did you think of Tennessee?"

Thatcher squeezed some lemon into his tea and stirred. "I loved Nashville. Even though I didn't get out much because I was so busy studying."

"I can imagine. What's your area of expertise within the history department?"

"I wouldn't say I'm an 'expert' or anything, but World War II is probably one of the topics I'm most interested in. I teach a class on that topic every spring."

"Have you been to the World War II memorial along the National Mall?" Vickie had only given a ranger talk there a couple of times, but she'd enjoyed the studying she'd done on the topic.

Thatcher made a face. "Only once. It's a little too crowded for my liking."

She smiled. "I guess there are a lot of people around. But that's what makes my day exciting."

"I see." His eyes twinkled. "Crowds must help you stay in 'ranger mode.' "

Vickie's mouth turned upward in a grin. "Right."

The waitress arrived at their table, her tray laden with steaming platters. It smelled delicious. Vickie watched as Thatcher moved his tea out of the way so the waitress could set his food on the table. This was going well. Sure, it was standard get-to-know-one-another conversation, but she felt a tiny spark. Just talking to him made her feel giddy.

"Can I get you anything else?" the waitress asked.

Thatcher raised his eyebrows at Vickie. She shook her head. "I'm fine, thanks."

"Me, too."

The waitress smiled and walked off, leaving them alone. Thatcher cleared his throat. "Um. Would you like for me to give thanks for the meal?"

She couldn't help but smile. How many times had she complained to her friends that it was almost impossible to find a guy who shared her faith in God? "Yes, please," she said, bowing her head.

Thatcher said a quick prayer of thanks for the food and asked God to watch over them and their families. "Amen," he said, raising his head and meeting her eyes. "Dig in."

Vickie took a bite of her crab cakes. "These are delicious." She was surprised at how comfortable she felt. Normally she hated eating in front of a date because it made her feel self-conscious. But with Thatcher, she already felt at ease.

"I'm glad you think so."

They ate in silence for a moment; then Thatcher put his fork down. "Listen, Vickie. Let me get right to the point of why I asked you here tonight."

She looked into his brown eyes and smiled. He liked her. She could tell. She thought of her mother's admonition on her birthday about men who were interested in booking the second date during the first one. "Yes?" She was already anticipating their second date. Maybe something a bit more romantic. Theater maybe. She looked expectantly at him.

"I'm sure you thought it was a little odd for a strange man to approach you at the Lincoln Memorial and ask you to dinner." He shifted in his seat. "And honestly, I don't normally go around inviting random women to join me for a meal."

She smiled. "Well, I don't normally go around accepting dinner invitations from strange men, either, but I made an exception for you."

"I'm glad you did." He sighed. "Look, I know you've probably got somewhere to be later, seeing how you're all dressed up, so I'll cut to the chase."

Vickie was confused. Why would he think she had somewhere else to be? "Oh. . .no," she started, but he cut her off.

"The reason I asked you here tonight was to talk to you about a project I'm about to be working on." He met her eyes. "I could use some help and thought that even if you aren't available, you might know of someone who is."

The realization began to hit her. He'd only asked her here tonight to discuss a project? "What are you talking about?" she asked.

"I know this is going to sound crazy, but after I listened to you talk about Abraham Lincoln, I knew I had to talk to you further."

"If you had questions about my ranger talk, you could've just asked me yesterday." The mixture of anger and humiliation was too much for her to take. "That's the typical protocol. Not the next evening over dinner."

"I knew this discussion would take some time, and I didn't want to pull you away from work." He sighed and raked a hand through his hair. "There's a rumor going around that some letters exist that have never been found. Letters that were written by Abraham Lincoln himself. Finding them would be a huge historical find." He grinned. "A real history-in-the-making kind of moment."

The term *shell-shocked* didn't begin to cover it. He'd asked her to dinner to discuss Abraham Lincoln? "I don't understand what this has to do with me. I don't know anything about these rumored documents."

"I'm looking for someone to assist me. If the letters exist, I want to be the one to find them." He drew his brows together. "It's kind of important to my career."

"You're asking me to be your assistant?" The giddiness she'd felt earlier had been replaced by an icy chill in the pit of her stomach.

"I'd pay you, of course." He grinned. "I know it's a lot to ask, especially considering that you don't know me from Adam. But when I listened to you speak yesterday, you seemed so passionate about the history of the monument. I thought you might think it was sort of fun to go on a hunt for lost documents. Kind of like the *National Treasure* movies, only hopefully without our stealing anything or kidnapping the president." He chuckled.

Vickie forced herself to return his smile but kept silent. She was finding this turn of events a little hard to process.

"I have no idea how long it will take. Or where the search should even begin. But I did want to throw the offer out on the table." He cleared his throat. "Of course, you're welcome to think it over."

"That does sound interesting." She kept her voice even. There was no need for him to know she was upset. Or that she'd misinterpreted his dinner invitation for a date. "But I'm not sure I have the time to commit to such a thing."

"Oh. . .I understand. And believe me, it won't hurt my feelings at all if you have to decline." He smiled. "It's just business."

"Right. Just business." She was silent for a moment. She needed to get out of there.

"Tell you what, how about you think about it for a couple of days? You have my number. Call and let me know what you decide. If you come on board, we can work out the details of your pay." He looked at her with wide eyes. "I would absolutely pay you fairly. Hourly or a flat fee, whichever you prefer. And in the meantime, hopefully I'll find out a little more about these mysterious letters so I can go ahead and start mapping out a research plan."

She stared at him for a long moment. It was amazing. It was like he had no idea that there was even the possibility that his asking someone out to dinner might've been misconstrued as a date. "Sure. I'll think about it." She snatched her wallet from her purse and pulled some bills out. "Thanks for thinking of me for your project," she said, standing. "I'll be in touch." She tossed the money onto the table. "That should cover mine."

"You don't have to—" He half rose from the table.

"I insist," Vickie said. "Enjoy the rest of your food." She turned on her heel, wanting nothing more than to be out of there. *Don't look back. Just keep going.* She reached the door and made it onto the sidewalk. For a split second her heart raced as she imagined him bursting from the door and stopping her. But a quick glance at the door told her he was still inside, likely enjoying his halibut. How could she have been so stupid?

CHAPTER 13

Thatcher gazed out the window and watched Vickie walk away from the restaurant. She sure was in a hurry. Maybe she had a hot date to get to. He hadn't picked up on it when he'd seen her in her ranger uniform, but seeing her all dressed up made him sure she was one of those young professional types who always had some sort of event or gala to fill their evenings. Probably had a huge circle of like-minded friends, and they stood around at parties in their fancy clothes and talked about fancy things. He was glad he'd never entered that world. Nope. He was happy just the way he was, working hard and fishing in his spare time.

"Sir?"

He looked up. How long had the waitress been standing there? "Yes?"

She motioned toward the half-eaten crab cakes. "Is your girlfriend finished with her food?"

Thatcher jerked his head up to meet the waitress's gaze. "My what?" he asked, his voice ringing with surprise.

The older woman sighed. "Your gir–l–friend." She said the word slowly, using more syllables than necessary. "You know. The pretty lady who joined you for dinner."

He shook his head. "That was just business. She isn't my. . . I mean we aren't. . ." He looked at the waitress again. "It was business," he said firmly.

"Whatever you say, mister. But I've been working here a long time. I can read people pretty well. And your *business* partner sure did spend a lot of time primping in the bathroom earlier. For it to be just business, I mean." She waggled her eyebrows at him and moved on to the next table.

Primping? He'd noticed she was gone for a few minutes right after they ordered, but he hadn't thought much about it. Thatcher stared at the bills Vickie had thrown down on the table and the realization washed over him. Had she thought this was a date? He'd been so focused on the Lincoln papers, he hadn't even given a thought to how a dinner invitation might come across to a woman he didn't know.

The impertinent old waitress swept past his table again. "Excuse me, ma'am?" he called.

She turned on her heel, smacking her gum. "Yes, hon?"

He cleared his throat and motioned toward Vickie's crab cakes. "What you said earlier, about her being my girlfriend. Well, uh, do you think she thought this was a date?"

The waitress raised a drawn-on eyebrow. "I don't know, darlin'. Did *you* ask *her* to have dinner with you?"

He nodded. "Yeah. I asked her to meet me here for dinner. But I never said anything about it being a date."

She shook her head. "Did you know this woman? I mean, are you friends? Have you known her for a while?"

"No. I met her yesterday."

"You just met her yesterday, and you asked her to join you for dinner." She drew her brows together. "That sounds like a date to me. When a man asks a woman to have dinner. Unless you have an established friendship already. . .it's a date."

"But I wanted to discuss a project I'd like her help on."

"Did you tell her that yesterday when you invited her?"

Thatcher winced. "No, I guess it didn't occur to me that I needed to clarify the situation."

The woman let out a low whistle. "Seems to me that you might've misread some signals there." She motioned toward Vickie's empty seat. "And her early exit tells me she might not be too happy about it."

He sighed. Women were still a mystery to him after all these years. Despite many attempts from friends and colleagues to fix him up, he'd always managed to decline. And with the exception of the annual faculty dinner, he rarely dined with a woman. He should've known he'd mess up in this situation. Why hadn't he explained things to Vickie yesterday? "Thanks." He pulled his wallet from his pocket and removed some money to cover his portion of the bill.

The waitress picked up the crumpled bills Vickie had left behind and held her hand out in Thatcher's direction.

He placed his money in her outstretched hand. "Keep the change." He grinned. "Your insight is worth a lot."

The woman's weathered face lit up as she smiled. "I do what I can." She winked. "And I think you might want to apologize to your *business* associate." She nodded at him one last time and walked off.

Thatcher left the restaurant and began to walk aimlessly. He needed to clear his head, and it was a nice evening. How could he have been so stupid? Of course she'd thought he was interested in her. And to tell the truth, he had found himself having a nice time with her. But then the small talk had made him nervous, so he'd jumped right in about the documents. What a dummy.

She had looked especially nice, though. He'd noticed as soon as she walked up. But it hadn't occurred to him that she might've gotten fixed up for him. He'd just assumed she must have plans later.

He crossed Constitution Avenue and slowed his pace. The Capitol loomed to his left, and he couldn't help but stare. He'd grown up near DC and been on plenty of field trips to the area, but he always felt a reverence when he saw the Capitol, especially when he glimpsed the American flag flying out front. He made his way over to the reflecting pool and sat down on one of the concrete steps, the Capitol in front of him. This was one of his favorite spots to run, but that was always in the early morning hours. He couldn't remember the last time he'd seen the building at night. It was a majestic sight to behold as darkness began to fall. The lights illuminated the building in a way that made it almost glow.

Thatcher stretched his legs out in front of him and leaned back on his hands. He needed to apologize to Vickie. It was the right thing to do, and there was no way around it. As someone who'd spent the better part of his life avoiding confrontation, that wouldn't be fun. Or maybe he could forget it. Chances were he wouldn't hear from her again. It wasn't like they ran in the same circles or anything. So really, he could just drop it. Chalk it up to his awful track record with the female species.

He felt better now that he had a plan. But he still needed a research partner. Maybe the grad student John played racquetball with would be interested. He rose to his feet, and with one last glance at the Capitol, Thatcher set off in the direction of the nearest Metro station. Home sounded good about now.

CHAPTER 14

Vickie had cooled down some by the time she reached her apartment but could still feel the sting of embarrassment. She couldn't bring herself to call Kristy and explain the fiasco she'd just experienced. Instead, she slipped on her favorite pajamas and headed to the couch. Few things happened that an old movie wouldn't cure, and if this turned out to be one of those things, at least there was a fresh tub of chocolate ice cream in the freezer that would do the trick.

The blinking red light on her answering machine caught her attention as she settled onto the couch. Her friends made fun of her for keeping a landline, but she liked the security of having a backup in case something happened to her cell phone. She pressed the blue button and the machine sprang to life.

"Hi, Vickie. Sorry to bother you at home." Her supervisor's voice filled the living room. Janet Stevens was easy to work for as long as you didn't question her decisions. Thankfully, Vickie was usually happy to go with the flow. "Remember the shift change we discussed a couple of weeks ago? I know I said I would let it be up to you, but something's come up. I need you to switch beginning immediately. Tomorrow you can work your normal schedule, but Thursday, you'll be on the ten-to-eight shift. I know Mondays through Thursdays will be long days, but I'm sure you'll enjoy having three-day weekends. Thanks for understanding, Vickie, and have a great night." The machine clicked off.

Vickie stared at it in silence. What had just happened? She should've known better than to put off giving Janet an answer. If she'd have only gone to her last week to let her know she wasn't interested in switching shifts, the shift change might've gone to someone else. She sighed. The movie alone wasn't going to fix this day. She headed to the kitchen, Jake at her heels.

She put an extra large scoop of chocolate ice cream into a dish. This day called for chocolate. She'd just put the container back in the freezer when a knock sounded at the door. For a moment, she had to fight a flutter in her stomach. Maybe Thatcher had somehow tracked her down and was coming to tell her what a fool he'd been. She half smiled to herself as she crossed the living room. Her overactive imagination had always found a way to conjure up romantic scenarios with whoever her current love interest was at the time somehow swooping in and rescuing her. Wouldn't she ever learn?

"Who is it?" she called from the dining room.

"Dawn."

Vickie opened the door and ushered her friend inside.

Dawn was still dressed for work, in a black, pin-striped sheath dress with a thin belt at the waist. Black heels and an oversized bag completed the look. "I just wanted to stop in and see what was new with you." Her blue eyes were lit up with excitement.

"Whoa. It looks like you're the one who has news to tell. Do you want some ice cream?" Vickie asked, holding up her bowl.

"No thanks." Dawn smiled broadly. "And I guess I do have something to tell." She followed Vickie over to the couch and sat down. "Back when I was in college, we called this perma-grin."

She motioned at her face and laughed.

"What happened? Another date with the detective?" Vickie hadn't heard many details since the night she'd fixed them dinner, other than that they'd had a nice time.

"Oh, a whole string of dates." Dawn giggled. "I can't remember what all I told you, so stop me if I repeat myself."

"Um, you didn't tell much. If I remember correctly, you said you liked him and didn't want to jinx it by giving me details until you knew if he was as good as he seemed."

Dawn's smile grew wider. "He's even better than he seemed." Her blue eyes danced. "His name is Jason Redd. As you know, he's a detective with the police force." She took a breath then continued. "He's originally from Alabama, and he has an accent even thicker than yours."

Vickie grinned despite herself. The hint of a Tennessee twang in her voice was often the source of ribbing from coworkers and visitors who attended her programs. Anytime she'd spent a few days back home, her accent became more pronounced for a short time. "So you've found a real Southern gentleman right here in the city?" she teased.

"I know. I would've thought if either of us would find that, it would be you." She reached down to pat Lloyd, who'd sauntered in to see what the fuss was about. "Anyway, he also helps to coach a Little League team on weekends. And he even plays on a church league softball team." She giggled. "He wants me to come watch him play sometime soon."

"I can't believe you've fallen for a sports guy. That isn't like you." Dawn's taste in men had always been more in line with Vickie's: suit, tie, and perhaps golf as a hobby.

"I know. But he's so sweet. And intelligent." She leaned back against the couch. "I'm smitten."

In all the years they'd known each other, Vickie had never known Dawn to be smitten with a man, or at least not enough to admit it. She'd always been able to take them or leave them, instead focusing on her career and seeing dating as something to do to pass the time. But it looked like all that had changed. "I'm glad you like him. Who knew a setup could turn out so well?"

"So true. I'm going to have to send his aunt a thank-you note." She shrugged. "I guess sometimes you can meet the right person when you least expect it."

Vickie couldn't keep her eyebrows from raising in surprise. "The right person? You really think that?"

"It's stupid, isn't it? I know it's soon. But we have so much to say to each other. Every restaurant we go to we end up closing down because we're talking. And then we end up sitting outside on the steps, talking more. I've been dating for a long time, you know." She looked at Vickie. "And with Jason, everything feels so natural."

"Wow. That's great." Vickie shook her head. "I can only imagine."

Dawn gave her a sideways glance. "I'm sorry. I'm going on and on, and look at you." She motioned toward Vickie. "Pajamas before 9:00 p.m., a heaping bowl of ice cream, and"—she glanced at the TV—"*Sleepless in Seattle*. Someone must've had a bad day. What gives?"

Vickie sighed. "Oh no. You're fine. I like hearing about your life. And I am really happy for you and Jason." She rubbed her eyes. "It's just been a tough week."

"How so?"

"First I had a birthday dinner with my parents, which wasn't so much of a celebration as an evening listening to all the ways I'm a failure at life. Then I made this stupid promise to Kristy that I'd get out of my comfort zone and ask out the next available man I met."

"Hang on," Dawn interrupted. "*You* are going to ask someone on a date?"

Vickie rolled her eyes. "Yes, I was, thank you very much. I can be unpredictable."

Dawn snorted. "Of course you can. So did you? Ask someone out?"

"I was going to. Yesterday morning, this man attended my ranger program at the Lincoln Memorial. We started talking after it was over. He's a professor of history at George Washington University. And he's really handsome. I think he's a little older than me because his hair has some gray in it. Plus he has a kind of distinguished air, like he doesn't care what people think about him."

"This sounds promising. So what happened?" Dawn asked.

"I was getting all psyched up to ask him to have coffee with me, when he asked me if I wanted to have dinner."

Dawn let out a squeal. "Yea! When's the big date?"

Vickie rolled her eyes. "Do you see this bowl of ice cream? Don't you think if I were all excited about an upcoming date I'd be doing something more constructive with my time, like picking out the perfect outfit or shopping online?"

"Did he call and cancel?" Dawn asked, her brow furrowed.

"Nope. We met for dinner tonight. And come to find out, it wasn't a date after all."

"I don't understand."

"Yeah, neither do I. It seems that after listening to my talk yesterday about Abraham Lincoln, he only wanted to ask me to be his research assistant on a big mysterious project."

"What did you say?"

"That I'd think about it. I said whatever I had to in order to leave. I left him sitting there with his fish, like I had somewhere else I needed to be. He even said he'd pay me. The nerve." Vickie threw her head back against the couch and sighed. "And once I got home, I had a message from Janet. It seems that I've been switched to the four-day shift." She grimaced. "I'm sure you'll enjoy having three-day weekends," she said, mocking Janet's high-pitched voice.

Dawn gave her a tiny grin. "I don't want you to get mad at me for saying this, okay? But I sort of think you should take Mr. Professor up on his offer."

Vickie opened her mouth to protest, but Dawn cut her off. "No, really. Listen to me. You love stuff like that. Solving puzzles and researching history. Remember last year when you took that genealogy course and traced your family tree?" She shook her head. "Now I would think that was some sort of punishment, but you had a blast. And now you have three-day weekends to fill. If I know you, you'll fill them with some sort of activity." She looked pointedly at Vickie.

"So maybe I was already considering salsa lessons." Vickie managed a smile. "But I'm mad at this guy. I totally thought it was a date, but he was all, 'It's just business,' and it didn't seem to even occur to him that I was a female."

"I'm sure it occurred to him. But really. I doubt he meant to tick you off. Maybe he's one of those clueless men who have no idea how to act around women."

"Okay, fine. I'll give you that he didn't seem malicious or anything." Vickie let out a loud sigh. "I just felt so stupid because I kept thinking how well the date was going, and all he wanted to talk about was Abraham Lincoln."

Dawn burst out laughing. "I'm sorry. But this is something that would happen only to you."

Vickie twisted her face into a grin. "Yes. I'm quite aware of that." She picked up her bowl of half-melted ice cream from the coffee table. "You are right about one thing, though. It would be kind of interesting to work on his project." She shrugged. "Plus, instead of me shelling out money for salsa lessons, I'll get paid."

Dawn nodded. "See. There's always a bright side."

Vickie hoped she was right.

CHAPTER 15

Young lady, I am still your mother. I don't care if you are twenty." Katherine's mom rarely raised her voice, but she was clearly not in the mood for an argument today.

Katherine perched on the couch where her mother was reclining. "Mom, I think taking some time off from school makes sense. I can be here when you need me, plus I'll be able to work more hours."

Her mother wore a stony expression. "I know these past weeks have been difficult for you. But Katherine, just because I'm not in treatment right now doesn't necessarily mean that I'm on my way out. I'm going to pursue some alternative treatments. And who knows? Even Dr. Matthews says my condition could improve, and I know what a downer you think he is."

Katherine bit her lip. She was trying to remain optimistic along with her mother, but sometimes it was hard. Every night when she and Blake talked on the phone, he advised her that it would be best if she'd accept the situation as it was and not cling to false hope. "That is even more reason for me to be more available to you. If I'm not in school, I can be here to take you to doctor visits or whatever you need. Cook you lunch, clean the house. You know."

Her mother smiled broadly. "Oh, honey. What would I do without you? But don't you know it would make me feel a million times worse if I knew you were dropping out of school to play nurse for me? I'm not even in need of a full-time caregiver. I can manage just fine on my own." She patted Katherine's hand. "And if it ever gets to the point where I can't, I can hire a home health nurse."

Katherine stood and started pacing behind the couch. "No," she said firmly. "I know that you're the mother and I'm the daughter. But I'm also an adult." She eyed her mother. "Even if you don't always want to accept that. Remember, when you were my age, you were on your own and raising a child."

Katherine's mom leaned her head back against the pillow. "Somehow I knew you'd use that against me at some point."

"I'm just saying." Katherine sat back down and turned toward her mother. "Okay, fine. Let's come up with a plan that makes us both happy."

"See? You can be a grown-up. Bargaining and negotiating just like your grandfather."

Katherine grinned. "Thanks." She brushed a stray hair from her eyes. "How about if I agree to stay in school, but I live here instead of in the dorm?"

Her mother wrinkled her forehead. "Oh, honey. I don't want you to give that up. You had so much fun last year."

Katherine shrugged. "But this would make me feel better. I can be here every day with you to make sure you're okay. I'll still take a full load. And I can do stuff around the house."

"But would you be happy?"

"Mom, let's face it. It's a little hard to be truly happy right now. But at least this way, maybe I wouldn't worry about you so much." She managed a tiny smile. "And you know how I hate the cafeteria food."

Her mother met her eyes. "I admit, it would be nice to keep you here a little longer. Having you back under my roof for the summer has spoiled me." She sighed. "Okay, tell you what. If you promise that you will still be involved with some of the social stuff on campus and that we'll talk about it again at the end of the semester, I'll agree."

Katherine grinned and embraced her mother. "That sounds good to me. Now you get some rest, okay? I'm meeting Blake for lunch. You want me to bring you anything?"

Her mother looked up at her. "Where are you going?"

"In-N-Out Burger. Your favorite."

"I haven't had much of an appetite lately, but if anything could bring it back, it might be one of their burgers." She smiled.

"Great. I'll bring one to you soon. I won't be gone long. Probably just an hour or so."

"Be careful," her mom called as she left the room.

"I always am," Katherine yelled back as she closed the door behind her.

"You're really not going back to the dorm?" Blake asked, once they were inside the restaurant and Katherine had filled him in on the conversation she'd had with her mom. "I can see that Jane would love that, but are you sure?"

Katherine jerked her head up. "For your information, she tried to talk me out of it. But I insisted." It seemed like these past months as she'd spent more time with her mother, Blake had grown increasingly intolerant of their close relationship. He was one of those people who thought parents were people you should only see on holidays, and he'd never tried to understand or appreciate the closeness she and her mother shared.

"Easy there, tiger. I was only asking." Blake drew his brows together. "But I hope you've thought this through. You realize that this is like taking a step backward in your independence."

Katherine rolled her eyes. "What is wrong with you? Do you not get that my mom is really sick? And she might need me? That is far more important than my independence or whatever. Besides, I'll be saving a lot of money by not living in the dorm or having a meal plan on campus. Surely the numbers guy in you can appreciate that."

He threw his hands up. "You've got me there. The money-saving aspect of the plan is a good one." He sighed. "I only wish that it didn't mean that your mom would be able to track your every move."

"You know it isn't like that. She just likes to know where I'm going." Katherine sighed. "We've been having this same argument for the past year. Can't you try to understand that this can be a scary world and my mother likes to make sure I'm safe? It isn't that she doesn't trust me or whatever, it's just that she doesn't sleep well unless she knows I've made it in for the night."

"Fine. I guess I just think that those apron strings have to be cut sometime. Otherwise, you'll be an old lady, still having to call and check in with your mom."

Her eyes filled with tears. "I can't believe you'd even say something like that. I only wish that I could still be able to check in with my mom when I'm an old lady. You can be a hateful, hateful person sometimes." She got up from their table and went to order her mom a burger. He could be so selfish and insensitive. She glanced back at the table and could see the remorse on his face. He probably hadn't thought before he'd spoken. Because surely he wouldn't say something so hurtful on purpose.

CHAPTER 16

The arrival of students on campus always marked a hectic time of year. Many members of the faculty and staff volunteered to help the new students move into the dorm, and Thatcher was always a willing volunteer. It had been a hot day in DC, and by the time the last student had moved in, Thatcher was ready to collapse. He made his way to his office to check his e-mail one last time before heading home. Buster was probably chomping at the bit to play, and to tell the truth, Thatcher could use some playtime as well.

He collapsed into his chair and scanned through his e-mails. It looked like most everything could wait until Monday. Only a weekend separated him from the first official day of classes.

"Hey, man." John stuck his head in the door. "I thought you might still be here."

Thatcher leaned back in his chair. "Long day."

John nodded. "I didn't get here until a couple of hours ago. Megan's parents are in town, and we had a few things planned this morning."

"Oh yeah? Anything fun?"

"We went and did a few touristy things. Washington Monument, Lincoln Memorial. You know the drill." John took a seat across from the desk.

At the mention of the Lincoln Memorial, Thatcher sat upright. "Did you happen to catch any ranger talks?"

John grinned. "Nah. Why? Was your friend working today? What did he say the other day when you asked him about helping with the research?"

"Actually, it was a she I asked to help with the research." Thatcher cleared his throat. "Her name's Vickie."

John raised his eyebrows. "I see. The other day when you said you'd spoken to a park ranger, I guess I just assumed it was a guy." He looked curiously at Thatcher. "So? Is *she* on board?" he asked with emphasis.

Thatcher grimaced. "Do you want to know how stupid I am?"

"Always."

"When I first talked to her at the Lincoln Memorial, I didn't think to tell her about the project. There were so many people around, and I wanted to get out of there. You know how I hate crowds." He shrugged. "So instead, I asked her to meet me for dinner. I just figured it would take too much time to explain, plus I thought maybe if I bought her dinner it might butter her up a little bit and she'd be more likely to agree to help."

John's eyes widened. "How old is this Vickie person?"

"I'm terrible with guessing ages. You know that. Especially women. The female students in my freshman history classes look like they're twenty-five and most of them aren't a day over eighteen." He paused. "But I'd guess that Vickie is probably in her late twenties or early thirties."

"Is she cute?"

Thatcher wrinkled his forehead. "Why do you care? It isn't like you're a bachelor."

"No, but you are."

"Whatever, man. I messed up. I think she thought I'd asked her for a date. So when I started explaining why I'd invited her, she kind of looked angry. Then she put money on the table to pay for her food and walked out."

John let out a low whistle. "You really have a way with the ladies." He laughed. "Sorry. But what, exactly, makes you think that she thought it was a date?"

Thatcher sighed. "Well, first of all, she was all dressed up. In this blue dress and heels." He shrugged. "I figured she had someplace to be later. But when I said that, she kind of got a funny look on her face. I didn't think anything about it until she was gone and the waitress asked me where my girlfriend was."

"Yeah?"

"Yeah. It was this old-lady waitress, and she really made me feel awful. Said that when a man asks a woman out to dinner, it's a date unless they already have some kind of a friendship. Then she told me she saw Vickie 'primping' in the bathroom. Women don't primp like that unless they think they're on a date. . .do they?"

"I agree that you need help in the figuring-out-women department. But I don't know the answer here. Maybe she just likes to look nice."

"Maybe."

John grinned. "But I think I'm inclined to agree with the waitress. It sounds like your park ranger friend didn't realize it was a business meeting." He scratched his head. "Even so, what did she say to your offer? You think she might be willing to help out even though you kind of messed up?"

Thatcher shook his head. "Nah. She said she'd think about it, but I'd bet just about anything I never hear from her again."

"Too bad. Hey, I may know someone who could help you. For the right price, of course."

"That'd be good. And this time, I'll ask over the phone. No more dinner invites." He managed a smile.

John chuckled. "Good idea, buddy."

◎⊚

Thatcher opened the sliding door and stepped onto his patio. It was little more than a square of concrete, but he loved sitting in his chaise lounge and watching his dog run around the tiny yard. "Sorry about the small space, Buster boy. We'll go out to the cabin tomorrow morning, and you'll have two whole days to play." The old fishing cabin had been in Thatcher's family for years. His grandfather had left it to him when he'd died, declaring that his grandson who loved fishing as much as he had should be the new owner. Since then, it had provided Thatcher with a welcome retreat from the crowded city. It wasn't a long drive, but it was far enough away from the traffic and noise that he felt like he'd gone to another country.

Buster ran over to where Thatcher sat, dropped a chew toy in his lap, and looked at him expectantly.

Thatcher laughed. "You certainly communicate well when you want to. Here you go." He threw the toy, and it bounced off the fence and landed in the yard. The dog happily ran to retrieve it.

Thatcher heard the phone ringing from inside the house. For a moment he considered letting the machine get it but thought better of it. He stepped inside and grabbed the phone just before the machine picked up. "Hello."

"Could I speak to Dr. Torrey, please?" a female voice asked.

"Speaking." He tried to place the voice but couldn't. For a split second, he considered the upside of having caller ID, something he'd always made fun of.

"This is Vickie Harris. From the National Park Service." Her voice was indifferent. Almost as if she'd never met him in person.

"Oh. Hi, Vickie. It's nice to hear from you again. Did you

think of someone who might be interested in being my research assistant?" he asked. Should he offer an apology for the other night?

"That's why I was calling. I've recently found out that I'm going to be working a different shift than normal for the park service. So I'm going to have three-day weekends."

He didn't know where she was going with this. "Oh? That's nice."

"Since my work schedule has changed, I'll have some extra time. So if you're still in the market for an assistant, I'm available."

"Oh, that's great news." He was torn. Although it was great news that he'd have someone knowledgeable helping with the research, it also happened to be someone whom he'd managed to upset. Would that make things uncomfortable between them? "I didn't expect to hear from you again after the other night."

Vickie was silent.

"I mean, I'm not sure what you thought about me asking you to dinner and all, but I'm really sorry if I gave you the wrong impression." His voice wavered.

"I'm not sure what you mean. It was obviously just business." She paused. "I apologize for rushing out like that, but I needed to be somewhere."

He was puzzled. So the waitress had been wrong? "Okay, great. Um, are you free sometime later next week? Maybe we can get together and map out a plan. And I'll come up with a couple of options for payment. We'll hopefully find one that works for both of us."

"I'll be working late hours Monday through Thursday. I get off at eight. Is that too late for you?"

"Nope. A lot of times, I'm still at the office then anyway. Especially if I've found time to sneak home during the day and check on my dog."

"Fine. How about Tuesday night? Say we meet around eight fifteen?"

"Where?"

"Tell you what. How about we meet at the Washington Monument? I'll be working there that night. Some benches run all the way around the monument. I'll meet you on the side that faces the Lincoln Memorial."

"Sounds perfect." He chose not to express his distaste for the National Mall. Besides, now that they were nearing the end of August, maybe there wouldn't be so many people out.

He hung up the phone and went back outside. He couldn't wait until tomorrow. A day fishing and relaxing was just what he needed before his busy schedule kicked in next week—including Tuesday night's meeting with Vickie.

Even though he didn't want to, he felt a tiny pang of regret. There'd been something flattering about thinking someone like her could be interested in someone like him.

CHAPTER 17

Vickie had only worked her new schedule for a short time, but she could already tell it was going to take some getting used to. Last night when she'd finally gotten home, she'd been exhausted. But that made her enjoy the first day of her three-day weekend even more.

She'd spent a few days thinking about Thatcher's project and Dawn's advice that she should work with him. Dialing his number had been tough, but she was proud of herself for going through with it. Especially when he'd tried to make a bumbling apology. She'd almost felt sorry for him. Almost. And saying that she'd had somewhere she needed to be was true. She'd needed to be home in her pajamas, not on a faux date.

She looked again at the calendar in her kitchen. Normally, she loved looking at the brightly colored pictures of Tuscany scattered around the edge of the calendar. But now all she could focus on was today's date and what it signified. She knew there was another phone call she had to make today, and it wasn't going to be an easy one.

Exactly a year ago, her friend Ainsley Davis's husband, Brad, had been killed in an accident. Ainsley had worked as a park ranger at the Grand Canyon, and Brad had served as a firefighter. As would be expected, the loss had been devastating. Brad and Ainsley had been married for five years, and the day of his accident had been the day they'd learned Ainsley was finally pregnant.

Vickie stared at the phone. She knew nothing she could say to her friend would make the hurt go away, but she also knew that making the phone call was important. She hit the speed-dial button and listened to the ringing.

"Hello." Ainsley's voice was shaky.

"Hey." Vickie carried the phone into the living room and settled onto the couch. "I thought I'd check to see how you were doing today."

Ainsley sighed. "I didn't know it would be so hard. You always think of anniversaries as being happy occasions. But this particular one is almost more than I can bear."

Vickie's eyes filled with tears. "I'm so sorry. I've been praying hard for you lately, that you could somehow find some peace today."

"Thanks. I know that you and Kristy both keep me in your prayers, and I can't tell you how much that means to me."

"Are you still staying at your parents' house?" Ainsley had moved back in with her parents after Brad's death and had decided to remain there for the duration of her pregnancy. But Faith would be four months old soon.

"I'm still staying with them. I guess that seems crazy, huh? I'm a grown woman with a child." She sighed. "But I'm terrified of being in a house alone. Isn't that silly? Ever since Brad's accident, I've been surrounded by people. I guess I'm afraid of what will happen when that isn't the case anymore."

"Well, I know your parents love having you and Faith." Vickie knew Ainsley's family well enough to understand that they'd probably be thrilled if she never left. Her friend had one of those large, tightly knit families that Vickie had always admired. They'd offered Ainsley a tremendous amount of support over the past year.

"They do. And with the basement addition, it's kind of like having my own little apartment. Dad turned into quite the handyman before Faith was born and added a bathroom and a little kitchen area. So it really is nice, plus I don't feel like I'm imposing on them too much. And they've all been such a help with Faith."

"Is she finally sleeping through the night?"

"Yes, thank goodness. I was beginning to think it would never happen. But she's turned into such a good little sleeper. And you know I've always had insomnia, so she must've taken after her daddy. . . ." Her voice trailed off.

"I hope you're getting some rest, too." Ainsley had always been a troubled sleeper, even years ago when they'd worked together as seasonals at Shiloh. It hadn't been unusual to get up in the night and find her in the living room, reading or watching TV.

"I'm trying. And I'm about to start back to work, which will either be really good or really bad." She laughed. "I guess it could go either way. It will be good to get back to a routine, but I hate the thought of leaving Faith, even for just a few hours. I'm just thankful there is a national park near Flagstaff that had an opening. I'm going to work there for awhile and hope that something might open up at the Grand Canyon." She heaved a great sigh. "This was not part of our plan, you know. Brad and I always figured that once we had children, I'd stay home. I always thought about homeschooling our kids so I could put my education degree to use."

Vickie was silent. She'd known that was their plan, and she was so sorry for her friend's pain. "It might not be the easiest thing to hear, but remember that God has His own plan for you.

And I have no doubt it is a great one.'"

"You're right. But it's hard sometimes."

Vickie sensed that a change in topic was needed. "Have you talked to Kristy lately? It sounds like their wedding plans are finally coming together."

"She actually called earlier today." Ainsley laughed. "She was really proud of herself and said that you hadn't had to remind her to call."

Vickie chuckled. Kristy was not big on planning or on remembering dates. So for years, they'd fallen into a pattern where Vickie would call or e-mail her reminders about important occasions. "Funny. I talked to her a couple of days ago. It looks like next month we're going to be hitting the beach for a wedding. You are going to be able to come, aren't you?"

"I wouldn't miss it. And Faith will be old enough to travel then. I can't wait for you guys to meet her."

"I can't wait to meet her, either. And to see you. I can't believe the three of us haven't been together since your baby shower last March."

"I know. Hopefully by the wedding date, I'll have lost the rest of my baby weight. I haven't seen the dresses yet, but if you get any input, please make sure she chooses one that is 'new-mommy friendly.' "

"Will do." Vickie chuckled.

They said their good-byes, and Vickie clicked off the phone. She sank back onto the couch and thought about what she'd said to Ainsley. God did have His own plan for each of them. Why was that so hard sometimes? Vickie had spent years trying to be patient and trying to understand what that plan was. But she knew that often she was guilty of plunging ahead, trying to forge her own path with little regard for what He might want. Why was it so easy for her to remind Ainsley but so hard for her to accept in her own life?

She picked up her Bible from the coffee table and flipped to the fifth chapter of 1 Peter. She read and then reread verse seven: *"Cast all your anxiety on him because he cares for you."* So often she was tempted to worry, and instead of casting her anxiety on God, she let it eat away at her. It was so easy to focus on her problems rather than focusing on God. She sighed. It was time to make some changes.

CHAPTER 18

Blake leaned down to kiss her good-bye, but Katherine turned her face. His lips landed on her cheek instead. His insensitive words still rang in her ears. Even though she could excuse them away, she couldn't help but realize she'd been making excuses for his behavior for some time now.

"Thanks for lunch." She smiled. "I'd better get this to Mom. Maybe it will jump-start her appetite." She climbed into her car and started the engine.

Blake tapped on the window and motioned for her to roll it down.

"Yeah?" she asked.

"I'm sorry. About before. You know that, right?"

She nodded. "I know." She sighed. "Look, I've got to go before Mom's burger gets cold. I'll talk to you later."

"Okay." He waved to her as she pulled out of the parking lot.

Ten minutes later, she was in the driveway. The FOR SALE sign served as a reminder of the poor housing market. As their real estate agent had said a few months ago, if their house had been on the market only a year ago, it would've been snapped up immediately.

Although it was hard for Katherine to think of selling the only home she'd ever known, her mom had been adamant about going ahead and listing it. Almost as soon as she'd gotten the original diagnosis, she'd decided it was time to downsize. "I want to simplify my life," her mother had said. And even though it was hard to digest, Katherine had gone along with her decision.

She walked up the path to the front door, clutching the bag. Hopefully the burger would do the trick.

"Katherine, is that you?" her mom called from the living room as she opened the door.

"Yep." She walked into the room, expecting to see her mother resting on the couch. Instead, she was sitting at the desk in the corner, ruffling through some papers.

"Is everything okay?" Katherine asked worriedly.

"From the look of those red-rimmed eyes, I think I should be asking *you* that." Her mom rose from the desk and walked over to where Katherine stood in the doorway.

"Just a stupid fight with Blake." She handed the bag from In-N-Out to her mom. "Not a big deal."

"Honey, I hate to say this. Because I like Blake."

Katherine shot her a look.

"I *do* like him. I just don't like him for *you*." Her mother chuckled; then her face turned serious. "It sure seems to me that you come home upset an awful lot of the time."

If her mother knew that many of their fights were about her, Katherine knew how bad she'd feel. "I know." She sighed. "To tell you the truth, I've been thinking about ending it with him. But I'd need a clean break, you know?"

Katherine's mother nodded. "I know exactly what you mean, honey."

ை

The next morning when Katherine walked into the kitchen, her mother was already seated at the table, drinking a cup of coffee and writing on a notepad.

"Good morning." Katherine pulled a coffee cup from the cabinet.

"Morning." Her mother didn't look up from her notepad.

Katherine took her coffee and sat down across from her mother. "What's going on?" she asked.

Her mother put the pen down and looked at Katherine. "I have an idea."

"Why do I not like the sound of that?"

"I know it's going to seem like it's out of the blue, but it isn't. It's something I've been thinking a lot about since I first learned of my condition."

"What's on your mind?" Katherine took a sip of coffee and tried to prepare herself for whatever was coming.

Her mother sighed. "You know how I put the house on the market when I first got sick?"

"Yeah. And Mom, I understand. I'm on board. I think a smaller place would be a good idea."

"That wasn't really my only reason for putting it up for sale."

"I don't follow." Katherine drew her brows together. "What was your other reason?"

"Now that you know what brought me to California in the first place, I think it's time you know the rest of the story." Her mother ran her finger around the rim of her coffee cup. "The truth is that, all these years, I haven't been able to forgive my parents for forcing me to marry Eddie. So when I moved out here, it was partly to punish them." She shook her head. "I know I keep saying how I was so young and stupid then, but I want you to understand that that is really the only excuse I have. I did you a great disservice as your mother by cutting you off from the rest of your family."

"Don't say that. I think you did a great job." In recent years, even before she learned about the cancer, Katherine's mom had begun to apologize for her mothering skills. "I think I turned out remarkably well." Katherine grinned.

Her mother laughed. "I'll give you that. But seriously, I do regret that you don't know your family. And even more, I regret that they don't know you." She sighed. "I've been thinking a lot, especially lately, that I might like to go back home for a while." She glanced up at Katherine. "What would you think of that?"

Katherine raised her eyebrows. "Really? Like for a vacation?"

Her mother shook her head. "I was thinking more like long-term." She reached across the table and patted Katherine's hand. "But I want to talk to you about it first."

"School hasn't started yet. So I could stick to what I mentioned and take the semester off from classes."

"Or you could transfer."

Katherine considered it. She hadn't really made any great friends at college, mainly because she'd spent all her time with Blake. But a temporary relocation would give her an easy way to get out of that relationship. She glanced at the hopeful look on her mom's face and knew there was no way she could say no. "Can you promise me something?"

Her mother nodded. "What's that?"

"This isn't one of those things where you want to get your affairs in order and make peace with your loved ones, is it? Because I'm afraid then you won't fight as much as I want you to." Katherine couldn't stop her eyes from filling with tears. She couldn't believe she'd voiced her fears.

A weak smile stretched across her mother's face. "I wish you wouldn't worry so much. I do want to make peace with my loved ones, but not so I can stop fighting." She looked at Katherine with wide eyes. "So are you on board?"

Katherine slowly nodded. "It could be nice to start over in a new place."

"I'm going to call the real estate agent. You remember that couple who was interested in the house a few weeks ago?"

"Yes."

"I wonder if they might be inclined to purchase if we brought the price down a bit." She rose. "Keep your fingers crossed."

"Mom?"

Her mother stopped and turned to look back at Katherine. "Yes, honey?"

"Do they know? Your parents, I mean. Do they know you're sick?"

"They know. And they've offered for us to stay with them for a while if we so choose." Her mother plucked the phone from the receiver and walked into the living room.

Katherine sat at the table and looked out into the backyard. She couldn't remember ever feeling so unsure about things. The constant knot of worry in her stomach had only grown in the months since her mom first got sick. In some ways, the thought of being around family was comforting. Then she wouldn't feel like she alone was responsible for taking care of her mom. But on the other hand, there would be added stress on her mom, and Katherine wasn't sure if she was strong enough to withstand it. She also sensed a niggling worry that she wouldn't feel at home with her grandparents. She sighed. Life was difficult sometimes.

She reached over and slid the notepad her mother had been writing on across the table. It looked like her mom had been making a pros and cons list about moving. Katherine smiled. Every major decision she could remember her mother making had included a list of the pros and cons. She glanced down over the list and her breath caught. The first word underneath both columns was her biological father's name.

CHAPTER 19

Aside from three-day weekends, the other perk to Vickie's new schedule was getting to sleep in a little. Although she had never been much for lounging around, she did allow herself an extra thirty minutes of sleep. Just having some extra time around her apartment felt nice.

But by nine, she was completely ready for work, the cats had eaten, and she'd straightened the apartment. And she still had another hour before she had to be at work. This would take some getting used to.

Ten minutes later, she emerged from the Metro and stepped out onto the National Mall. There was no point sitting around her apartment with nothing to do. Instead, she made her way to one of the park benches scattered along the walking path and pulled out her phone.

"Hello," Kristy's sleepy voice answered on the fourth ring.

"Oh. Sorry. Did I wake you?"

"Umm. Kind of. But that's okay. . .I had a lot to do today anyway."

"I figured since you were off today you'd have some wedding

stuff going on." Kristy's days off were Sunday and Monday.

"I do, actually. Mom and I are going to Memphis to look for a wedding dress."

"Ooh. That sounds fun. I hate it that I can't be there."

Kristy laughed. "Believe me, so do I." The years they'd lived as roommates, Kristy had relied on Vickie to serve as her fashion advisor. Even though they were now separated by miles, it wasn't unusual for Kristy to call for advice or even to send cell phone photos of outfits to get Vickie's opinion.

"Are you going to send pictures?"

"Of course. So keep your phone handy today."

Vickie watched a couple walk by, hand in hand. She couldn't stop the pang of jealousy from hitting her. They looked so happy. "I will."

"So, I think we have some unfinished business." Kristy sounded more awake now.

"What do you mean?"

"Your little birthday promise went unfulfilled." Kristy paused. "I know the guy ended up asking you to dinner, but seeing how it wasn't even a date, I think we need to get back to the original plan." Vickie had finally filled Kristy in on the situation, including her decision to assist Thatcher with his project.

Vickie groaned. "I was really hoping we could let that drop. Don't you think it was humiliation enough that I misinterpreted his invitation?"

"Nope. I think we'll just chalk that one up to a failure to communicate." Kristy giggled. "Besides, I've been to DC. I know it's a city filled with cute men who fit your criteria."

"Right. If it is a city filled with men who fit my criteria, can you tell me why I've lived here for five years and not met any of them?"

Kristy was silent. "Maybe the timing wasn't right." She sighed. "Vick, are you sure you don't want to sign up for online dating? At least that way, you know the guys who have profiles are actually interested in finding someone to date."

"Umm. . .or someone to kill." Vickie rose from the bench and began walking toward Survey Lodge. She'd have a few extra minutes to check her e-mail before heading to the Washington Monument. "I don't want to go that route yet. Hey, maybe there'll be a cute guy on one of my programs today."

"I'm thinking maybe you should look elsewhere for a date. Not only did the last guy you met on a ranger program turn out to be a dud, but chances are, they'll be tourists only in town for a day or two." She paused. "Hey, how about Dawn? Didn't you say she was dating a new guy? Maybe he has a friend."

Vickie thought about her options. Even though she hadn't had to go through with asking Thatcher out the other day, her face flamed at the thought of what would've happened if she had. Maybe asking Dawn to set her up was the best idea. It was certainly better than online dating, which, despite her protests, was starting to look more and more attractive. "That's a good plan. I'll talk to her this week and see what she thinks. I'm not sure if she's met his friends yet or not. But I do know that he plays on a softball team on weekends."

"Great. Okay, I've got to go get ready. My wedding dress isn't going to buy itself."

"Talk to you soon. And I'll have my phone ready to see pictures."

They said their good-byes as Vickie stepped inside the lodge to get ready for her day.

⊚⌒⊚

"If you'll step into the elevator, we'll ride back to the entrance of the monument." The next evening, Vickie stood outside the elevator doors at the top of the Washington Monument. She ushered the visitors inside the elevator, and once the allotted number of people were inside, she stepped in. "As we travel the five hundred feet to the bottom, we're going to slow down to see a few of the memorial stones on the interior walls of the monument." She pressed the button to begin the journey to the bottom.

"If everyone will face outward, keep your eyes on the elevator windows." The elevator slowed down and the lights dimmed so the passengers would better be able to view the stones. "There are 195 memorial stones embedded into the interior wall of the Washington Monument," she explained as the visitors oohed and ahhed at the views. "The stones came from all fifty states, many major cities, civic organizations, and foreign countries. The only stipulation was that each stone had to be fashioned from a material native to the place it represents." She paused. "For example, the stone from Arizona was made from petrified wood."

"Cool," said a teenage boy who stood near Vickie. "Why are some of the stones different sizes?" he asked.

"It was up to each entity to decide what their stone would look like."

The elevator sped up for a few seconds then slowed again so the passengers could view a new set of stones. "The memorial stone from New York is the largest in overall mass, but Baltimore has the tallest stone," she said. "And if you'll notice, most of the dates on the stones you see now that we're toward the bottom are in the 1850s. Construction on the monument was stopped in 1858, and the monument remained unfinished for the next eighteen years. If you look at the monument from the outside, the top and bottom sections have a visible difference in color. So it is very easy to see where they stopped working in 1858."

"Do you ever take visitors down the stairs?" a woman in the center of the elevator asked.

"Not anymore. But there are 896 steps from the bottom of the monument to the upper level. We stopped doing walk-down tours a few years ago because of safety reasons."

They reached the bottom of the monument, and the doors opened. "Thanks for visiting the Washington Monument. Have a wonderful evening," Vickie said as the passengers filed into the small room that led to the exit. She was thankful that was her last tour of the night but had a sinking feeling in her stomach. It was time to see Thatcher for the first time since their disastrous dinner.

"Good night," she called, passing by the security guards who were working the security screening checkpoint at the monument's entrance.

"Night, Vickie," one of them responded.

She stepped out into the warm night air. It would be fall before long, so she knew she should enjoy the warmth while she could. She hoisted her backpack and walked around the base of the monument. Even though it was after eight, throngs of people still milled around. Many people thought it was best to visit the National Mall after the sun went down because the monuments were illuminated. She had to admit, it was a pretty awesome sight.

Vickie spotted Thatcher as soon as she turned the corner. He was perched on one of the stone benches, facing away from the monument toward the Lincoln Memorial, so she wasn't in his line of sight. He must've come straight from school, because he had on khaki pants and a blue dress shirt. She didn't think classes had begun yet but figured faculty meetings were probably in full swing.

She made her way over to where he was waiting, trying to quell the apprehension in her stomach. What if this had been a terrible idea?

As if he felt her presence, he turned in her direction, and his face lit up with recognition. "Vickie." He stood up from the bench. "Thanks for meeting me."

CHAPTER 20

For some reason, the entire time he was waiting for Vickie, he was on the lookout for a girl in a blue dress. But when she walked up, he was thankful to see that she was wearing her ranger uniform. There was no question that this was a business meeting, and it made him feel much more at ease. "How was work?" he asked.

"Good. Long day, though." She smiled. "I'm still adjusting to working these ten-hour shifts." She motioned up at the Washington Monument. "But this is my favorite site to work, so all in all, I can't complain."

He grinned. "Don't you get sick of saying the same things over and over?"

She wrinkled her smooth forehead. "Do you get tired of teaching the same topics to your classes each year?"

"Point taken." This girl was smart.

Vickie grinned, revealing even, white teeth. "I'm always amused at the questions people come up with. They certainly keep me on my toes." She shrugged. "Besides, we're encouraged to develop our own ranger talks, and with so many monuments to cover, it's easy to switch things up."

"I guess I hadn't thought of it like that." It sounded a lot like teaching. Funny, he'd never thought teaching had anything in common with being a park ranger. But it did made sense. They were both trying to share a knowledge of history.

"Did you have anywhere in particular in mind for our meeting tonight?" she asked.

"Not really. I guess we can sit here if you want."

"Actually, I need to swing by Survey Lodge for a second. It isn't far from here. Is that okay? It won't take long, and then we can walk toward the other end of the mall while you explain the project."

"That sounds great." He always felt more comfortable, even in his classroom, when he was able to walk around rather than sit in one place.

She picked up her backpack from where she'd dropped it. "Ready?"

"Lead the way." He fell in step beside her once they reached the sidewalk.

"Excuse me," an elderly man said to Vickie as they passed him on the sidewalk. "Can you tell me where the nearest restroom is?"

Vickie gave him directions then turned back to Thatcher. "So, are you ready for classes to start?" she asked as they continued walking.

He shook his head. "Will you think badly of me if I say no?" He laughed. "People think teachers have it so great, having summers off. But it seems like they get shorter and shorter." He shrugged. "I had several projects around the house I wanted to get to but didn't. To tell you the truth, I probably spent a little too much time at my fishing cabin." *And loved every minute of it.*

"I guess that would be nice. If you like that sort of thing."

"What, you're not a fan of fishing?" He glanced over at her profile and was struck by how perfect it was. Her slightly upturned nose and full lips would've been at home on any movie star.

"Let's just say that I don't do a whole lot of outdoorsy activities."

He burst out laughing. "If that's true, isn't it a little ironic that you're a park ranger?"

"I know. Everyone has this image of park rangers being outdoorsy people who love to hike and fish and be out in nature." She looked up at him and grinned. "Tell you what. I won't judge you for not being ready for school to start if you won't judge me for being a non-outdoorsy park ranger."

"Deal." He followed her into Survey Lodge.

"If you'll wait here for a minute, I'll be right back."

He watched her hurry off then turned to look at the assortment of maps and brochures that were on display. Her career choice impressed him. The variety of monuments and memorials along the National Mall was vast. She must be very intelligent to be knowledgeable about each one.

"Okay, I'm ready."

He turned toward the sound of her voice. She'd changed out of her ranger uniform into a pair of khaki shorts and a green tank top. Her shoulder-length dark hair was pulled back into a low ponytail. "You changed?" As soon as the question left his mouth, he knew how stupid he must sound. Clearly she'd changed.

"I brought a change of clothes with me. Believe me, if we're going to be along the mall, you don't want me to still be in uniform. Otherwise we'd never be able to have a conversation because of the questions." She smiled.

"I didn't think about that. I guess you're right." He held the door open for her to walk through.

"Just like that man earlier wanting to know where the restroom is, we'd get questions about the nearest Metro, the nearest refreshments, and the list would go on."

"Don't you ever get sick of talking to people?"

She nodded. "Sure I do. But as long as I have that uniform

on, it's part of my job." She led him back to the path where they'd come in. "How about we walk toward the Lincoln Memorial? It's pretty cool at night."

He nodded. "Okay."

They walked in silence for a moment. "Okay, tell me the story behind this research project," Vickie said as they were waiting to cross Seventeenth Street. "Did you find out more information?"

"A little bit. I'm still trying to find more, though." They strolled slowly past the World War II Monument. It was a large, open monument, different than most of the others along the mall. In the center were bubbling fountains, and the sound of rushing water filled the air. Thatcher stopped near one of the large archways. "Can you tell me any interesting tidbits about this monument?" he asked.

Vickie laughed. "I guess I only *thought* I was getting out of answering questions by changing out of my uniform."

He couldn't tell if she was mad or not. "Oh. You don't have to tell me. We can keep walking."

She stopped and touched his arm. "Don't be silly. I was kidding." She pointed to the large stone archway they were next to. "See that? There's one on each side of the memorial. One for the Atlantic and one for the Pacific. To symbolize the war was fought across two oceans."

"How about all the pillars?" There were a number of stone pillars that formed two semicircles surrounding the archways.

"There are fifty-six of those. One for each state, territory, and of course, the District of Columbia." She pointed at the nearest one. "See how each is inscribed with the name of the state? And that circle on each one is a wreath of oak and wheat." She met his gaze. "To emphasize our industrial and agricultural strength during the war."

He was impressed. "For the first time, I'm starting to doubt my career choice. I think your job seems fantastic."

She laughed. "It is fantastic, most days." She paused. "Shall we keep going?"

"Yes, let's." He followed her to the dirt path that was right beside the reflecting pool. The Lincoln Memorial loomed large ahead of them, and the great statue seemed to glow.

She waved her hand in the direction of the rectangular reflecting pool. "I can't tell you how many times a year I see someone pretend to be Forrest Gump right here."

Thatcher burst out laughing. "Is it awful that I always think of that scene when I'm here? I'm always tempted to yell, 'Jenny!' in my best Gump impression."

"Well, you might be able to resist, but you'd be surprised at how many people don't have your self-control." She giggled. "Stuff like that makes my job interesting, though."

They walked in silence for a moment. "So, back to the project," he said, telling himself he wouldn't get off track again. "One of my colleagues has reason to believe that there are a series of letters written by Abraham Lincoln that have never been found."

"Letters? To whom?" she asked.

"Have you ever heard of a woman by the name of Ann Rutledge?"

Vickie shook her head. "I don't think that name sounds familiar." She stopped. "But if you're going to tell me that you want me to help you prove that Honest Abe was a philandering cheater, I don't think I can be involved."

He couldn't help but chuckle at the adamant expression on her face. "No. Nothing like that. Do you think I'd want to go down in history as the man who tried to give Lincoln a bad name?"

She looked relieved. "Good."

They resumed their walk. "Ann was a young lady who Lincoln met when he was in his early twenties. Way before Mary Todd was even on his radar, if that makes you feel better about things."

"It sure does." She grinned up at him.

"Anyway, there has always been a rumor that Abraham and Ann were secretly engaged and that he considered her his true love. But then she was stricken with a fever and died suddenly."

"That's terrible."

They stopped at the bottom of the stairs leading up to the memorial, where the huge stone figure of Lincoln sat, illuminated in lights, stoically keeping watch over the mall.

"Do you want to walk up?" he asked.

"Yes. I'll show you my favorite, supersecret spot." She smiled over her shoulder at him. "Come on." Vickie motioned for him to follow.

They climbed up the steep stairs until they reached the very top. Instead of going inside where the statue was, Vickie turned to the right and walked all the way to the space between the last two columns.

"It's so quiet over here." He was amazed. Just a few seconds ago, the air had been filled with the sound of voices and laughter of the people milling about. But now it was almost silent. Even though they weren't far away, it was as if they'd somehow stepped through a kind of sound barrier.

"I know." She sat down and let her legs dangle over the edge of the concrete. "Sit down," she said.

He sat down beside her, next to a large column.

"I'll let you have my favorite seat." She smiled at him. "If you lean against that column, the groove fits your back just like a seat back."

He shimmied a little closer to the column. She was right. It was perfect. "Nice."

She sighed. "Look out there. Isn't it beautiful?"

From their perch, they could look out and see the reflecting pool, the Washington Monument, and the Capitol in the distance. It was a breathtaking sight—one he would have missed if he hadn't met Vickie here tonight.

CHAPTER 21

Even though Vickie had resolved to keep Thatcher at a distance, here she was, showing him her favorite place in the city. Had she no shame? She glanced over at him as he took in the view. Oh well, it was too late now. But after this, she'd make sure their relationship was strictly professional. "This is my favorite place. I come here a lot and just sit and think and watch people. Sometimes I bring my Bible to read." She smiled. "No one ever bothers me. In fact, it's rare that anyone walks over here. It's like my own little sanctuary right here in the middle of the crowds."

"You may have some competition for the spot now that you've shown it to me." He grinned at her, and his brown eyes sparkled.

"I should've known better than to share my secrets."

He laughed. "I'm kidding. To tell you the truth, prior to the day I met you, I hadn't even stepped foot at the Lincoln Memorial for several years."

She glanced at him. "How about the other monuments? Do you ever visit them?"

"Sometimes I jog here along the paths, but that's always before seven in the morning and rarely during prime tourist season."

He motioned in the direction of Lincoln. "Okay, now that we're settled, let me get on with my story."

She nodded. Each time their conversation veered away from the project, he'd find a way to steer it back. He must really want to make sure she knew he was only interested in her as a research assistant. That was fine. "Please do."

"After Ann's death, a lot of people thought that Lincoln went over the edge for a little while. He sort of went into hiding, and those closest to him said he was so devastated he never fully recovered."

"Poor man."

"Exactly. And for years, scholars have debated how her death helped to shape him into the man he became," he said, looking over at her.

For the first time, she noticed a tiny scar on his left eyebrow. She wondered how he'd gotten it but pushed the thought away. Too personal.

He sighed. "The problem is that there has never been any actual evidence the relationship between Ann and Abe existed."

"So, these letters. . ." Her voice trailed off. "Where might they be?"

"*If* they even exist—which we don't know for sure—they could be anywhere."

"But they'd have to be hidden pretty well, right? Otherwise they'd have been found by now."

"Exactly. And I'm not really sure if you and I should first set out to find them or set out to prove that they don't exist." He raked his hand through his shaggy hair. "I'm inclined to say maybe we should go through some of the research that's been done in the past to see what we can find out about the Abe/Ann relationship as well as any mention of the documents." He looked at her. "And then we can go from there."

She couldn't hide her excitement. "What do you think the odds are that the rumor is true?"

He shrugged. "Honestly? I have no idea. Like I told you the other night, Abraham Lincoln isn't my area of expertise."

Vickie leaned back on her hands and looked over at him. "What did you mean the other night when you said this was important to your career?" She sat upright. "I guess it seems odd that someone who doesn't even consider himself to be a Lincoln scholar would take on such a task."

Thatcher examined his hands. "It's something I want to do."

He was hiding something. Her instincts told her as much. "But why?" she asked, pressing the issue. If there was one thing she wanted in a partner, business or otherwise, it was honesty.

He leaned his head back against the column and sighed. "I guess you may as well know the story." Thatcher sat up and looked at her, his brown eyes serious. "Basically, I've taken a lot of flack lately within my department." He sighed. "Once upon a time, I was considered one of the best professors on campus. And I don't mean that in a braggart sort of way. I've devoted my life to my work, and I've always tried to go above and beyond to make sure my students are prepared for whatever lies ahead of them, whether it be graduate school, a doctoral program, or just life itself."

Vickie watched the emotions dance across his chiseled face. He was very passionate about his work. Although she didn't know if he was dating anyone, she wondered if he'd sacrificed his personal life for his professional one. If so, it made her very sad. "That sounds admirable. What's the problem?"

"The problem is that the number of history majors is declining. I guess since I'm one of the longest-standing professors, they consider me partially to blame." He looked sheepish. "At this time last year, everyone who knows anything about our department would've said I'd be the next department chair."

"And now?" She was starting to get the full picture.

"Let's just say that any security I felt with the position is gone. To make it worse, one of my colleagues despises me. He muddies my name any chance he gets and is trying to schmooze his way into consideration for the position."

She slowly nodded her head. "So you're trying to beat him to the punch."

"Something like that." He grinned at her. "So, what do you say? Are you in?"

She thought for a second. This could be nothing but a gigantic wild-goose chase and a major waste of time. On the other hand, it could also be fun. She wasn't one to just sit around her apartment and do nothing, so even if she opted not to work with Thatcher, she'd end up filling her time with something. At least this project would be interesting. If nothing else, she might learn information to add to one of her ranger talks. Finally she met his gaze. "I'll do it. But I must warn you, with this new work schedule, I'm really only available Friday, Saturday, and Sunday after church."

He nodded. "That's fine. That will work well for me. I'm loaded with classes this semester, but on Fridays, I'm through before lunchtime. We'll have to just make a short amount of time count each week until we're through."

She smiled. "Sounds good."

"So how about we get together again Friday? I'll see if I can find a list of some of the Lincoln works we should consult. Maybe looking through those will give us an idea of where to start."

"Friday sounds good. Where and what time?"

He furrowed his brow. "I don't know. I'd rather stay away from campus. I don't want anyone there to get wind of our project." He glanced over at her. "Do you have any ideas?"

"How about this? Once you get the list of works we're going to consult first, see which ones are in the library on campus. You can go ahead and check some of them out, and then we'll already have some materials to start with."

"Makes sense. We just need a place we can spread out and work."

Vickie thought for a second. Normally it would take more than three meetings with someone before she'd dream of inviting them into her home. But she felt comfortable with Thatcher. "Why don't you come to my apartment once you're through with classes? I'll fix lunch, and we can work as we eat."

An odd expression flashed across his face. "Oh no. I mean, I don't want you to go to any trouble."

Why had she even suggested it? "It's fine. I mean, if you're not comfortable with that, you can eat beforehand." She looked at him. "Unless you just don't want to come to my place."

He cleared his throat. "Actually, I'd appreciate it. That would be fine." He rose to his feet from where he'd been reclined against the column. "Lunch will be great."

"Okay." She slowly got to her feet. It was amazing. Did he have a split personality? One second he was all business, with a serious expression, and the next he was all smiles and warmth. "How about straight-up noon?"

"Perfect."

She pulled a notepad from her bag and quickly scribbled directions. "Here are directions to my place and my phone number. Just call if you're going to be late or if something comes up."

They made their way down the stairs and paused at the bottom of the memorial.

"Are you headed to the Metro?" he asked.

She nodded. "You?"

"I'm going to walk instead."

"Oh. Okay then. See you Friday." She headed toward the Metro without another look back. She walked slowly at first, just in case he decided to come after her and walk her to the Metro. But after two blocks, she realized that wasn't going to happen. *It's just business.* She had a feeling she'd be reminding herself of that a lot over the next few weeks.

CHAPTER 22

The past few days had been a hectic flurry of activity. Katherine hadn't dreamed things would move so fast. The couple who'd initially been interested in their home had made an offer once the asking price was lowered. "It isn't enough to hurt us," her mom had said. "We can at least take comfort in that."

So now they were trying to decide what items would be necessary for the next few months while they were at Katherine's grandparents' house in Maryland. Everything not deemed absolutely necessary would go into a storage building. The one thing that gave Katherine a little peace was that they'd hired a moving company to handle packing and moving those things. But still, trying to pack her entire life into just a couple of suitcases was difficult. And she had no idea what to expect at her grandparents' house. Would she have her own room? She didn't want to bother her mom with endless questions, so she tried to convince herself it was just an adventure.

Katherine sank down onto her bed and stared at the walls around her. The room still looked the same as it had when she was a child. Sure, toys had been replaced with books, and instead of *NSYNC posters, framed copies of famous paintings covered the walls. But even so, the room was the same. She leaned her head against the wall and scanned the furniture. The desk was the one she'd used for homework during elementary school all the way through her senior year of high school. On it sat a framed picture of her and Mom on the cruise they'd taken to celebrate graduation. There were the team pictures of her softball and basketball teams from junior high.

This had been a good home. A happy home. The thought that she'd not have it to come back to was nearly more than she could bear. As soon as the SOLD sign had been placed out front, it occurred to Katherine that she was essentially homeless. It was not a good feeling.

A gentle knock at the door caused her to jump up and grab the nearest item. She could at least pretend to be packing. "Come in."

Blake poked his head inside. "Hey. Your mom said you were up here packing. I thought you might want to take a little break."

She nodded. "Sure. Come on in."

He walked in and closed the door behind him. "Guess your mom's rule of always leaving the door open when I'm in your room can be broken, all things considered."

She twisted her mouth into a smile and nodded. "Guess so." She sank into the old recliner that had been the one she'd been rocked in as a baby.

Blake took a seat on the bed and leaned back against the wall. "Are you sure about this?" he asked, not meeting her eyes.

She wasn't sure if he was referring to the move or to the declaration she'd made yesterday that they should see other people while she was away. She decided to address the move. "It's what my mom wants. I think she needs to go back to her home and face her family." She played with a strand of her wavy dark hair. "Plus, I want to meet them, and I want to do it while she's with me." Her eyes filled with tears, and she looked up at him. "I'm aware of what's probably her reasoning behind all of this, you know. Even though she denies it. I'm not stupid."

Blake wrinkled his forehead. "I don't think you're stupid. But I'm glad you see this move for what it is."

"It's been keeping me up nights ever since the house sold. I'm worried that as soon as she's made her peace and seen to it that I have a family to support me, she won't have much of a reason to fight."

He nodded. "Kate," he said, using his pet name for her, "I think you need to put those thoughts out of your mind. You're getting the chance to spend a lot of quality time with your mom over these next months." He scooted down on the bed until he was next to the recliner. "And you'll be surrounded by people who love you. Try and enjoy it." He grabbed her hand. "I'm sure it's hard though."

She gestured around the room. "I guess I didn't realize how attached I was to this place. It's all I've ever known." She sighed. "But it looks like I'll be able to enroll in school. I've already talked to a college not too far from where I'll be living."

"At least you won't lose any time."

"Not too much, anyway. Especially since I'm still getting my basics." She managed a smile. "But I'm not taking a full load this semester. I'll only have to go to classes a couple of days a week. The rest of the time, I'll just be with Mom, visiting family."

"How about your biological father? Have you made any decisions there?"

Katherine shook her head. "I'm not sure where he is exactly. But I don't want to just waltz into his life and claim my place as his daughter. I'm probably going to do a little detective work first."

Blake raised one eyebrow at her. "Detective work?"

"Don't look so shocked. I want to know who he is before I decide whether to meet him. You know—is he married, does he have kids, where does he live, what does he do for a living. . .all that stuff."

"Can't Jane just tell you the answers to those questions?"

"I don't know. Probably not all of them. But I think it makes her sad to talk about. And I don't want her to be sad. So I'm just going to handle it on my own."

"Of course you are." Katherine knew her independent streak had always worn on Blake.

She met his brown-eyed gaze. "About us. . ." She trailed off and sighed. "I've been thinking a lot about this. I know yesterday I told you we should see other people. But I'm afraid I might've made that sound like I thought we'd get back together when I got back here." She looked down at her hands. "To tell the truth, I'm not sure if I'll ever come back."

He reached out and brushed a strand of hair from her eyes. "I had a funny feeling you were going to say that."

"Do you hate me?" she asked. Even though she knew in her heart that Blake wasn't the guy for her, it was still hard to know that they wouldn't see each other for a while. Maybe ever.

"How could I? You're doing what's best for you." He stood. "I hope your mom gets better."

She folded herself into his waiting arms, thankful that he'd at least had the decency not to put her through an ugly breakup. He could be sweet when he wanted to be, and even though it had turned out to be not as often as she would have liked, she was glad he'd acted right tonight.

"Good-bye, Kate." He leaned down and kissed her on the forehead then turned and walked out of the room.

She sat back down in the recliner and wiped away a stray tear. The suitcase in the corner was nearly packed. Tomorrow she and her mom would set out on the reverse cross-country trip they'd made together all those years ago. Even though it was bittersweet, she knew the memories would last her a lifetime.

CHAPTER 23

Thatcher had made what he hoped was a decent list of books pertaining to the life of Abe Lincoln and was looking at the online card catalog to find out which ones were in the university library. With a click of his mouse, he could place the book on hold and it would be waiting for him at the desk. This was the extent of his appreciation for technology.

A rap on his door startled him. Only one person knocked with that pattern. Amanda. "Yes?" he called.

She poked her head in the door. "Is this a bad time?" she asked.

"Nope. Come on in."

She stepped inside, her curly gray hair sticking out in all directions. "Sorry to be the bearer of bad news. But I thought you might like to know that the committee Dean White formed is going to start meeting next week."

"And?" He leaned back in his chair, his hands behind his head.

"And your biggest fan sure does seem bound and determined to bring you down." She perched primly in the chair across from his desk. "Listen," she said lowering her voice. "I probably shouldn't even tell you this. I'm sure they could fire me for squealing." She grinned. "Except I'd love to see how long it would take for somebody new to figure out how things around here work."

She was right about that. He wasn't sure she was replaceable. "What do you want to tell me?"

"I think they're planning on asking a few of the professors to put together presentations this semester."

"I don't understand." He'd never been asked to put together a presentation before. But he had an inkling who might be behind it.

"Word through the grapevine is that there will be a couple of professors who will be asked to prepare in-depth research about the trends in teaching and learning and how those apply to the history department." She raised her eyebrows. "Basically, they're looking for some ideas about how to bump up enrollment by the beginning of the fall semester next year." She leaned toward his desk. "And do you want to know what I think?"

He couldn't help but grin. It was nice to have Amanda on his side. The older lady had taken him under her wing years ago, joking that he was like the son she'd never had. "What's that?"

"I wouldn't be surprised if the assignment of putting together these presentations didn't fall to you and Dr. Langston. And—now this is only my gut instinct—but I'd guess that the department chair position will go to the person who comes up with the most pleasing plan as judged by the deans and the vice presidents."

What she said made sense. But he would have to hope she was wrong. Where would he ever find the time to take on another project, in addition to the Lincoln papers and his full class load? He sighed.

"I'm pretty sure your friend Dr. Langston is somehow behind it. I'm not saying it was altogether his idea, but I'd feel safe betting that he at least planted the seed." She shook her head. "Why no one else sees through that man is a mystery to me." Amanda stood.

"And there's one more thing." She grinned. "I'm pretty sure that same lady called again. You know. The one who called for you a couple of times last week."

"Did she leave a message?" he asked. He made a mental note to check in with his sisters to see if either of them were trying to get in touch with him at work.

"No message." She shrugged. "But of course, I could be wrong. It could've been a totally different person."

"Probably so." He grinned. "I wouldn't worry about it." And he wouldn't, either. Unless it was an irate parent. Or some new plan Langston had cooked up to needle him. "Thanks for the heads-up about the presentations. Any idea when that assignment is supposed to come down the pike?"

"Soon, although I'm not sure when. Don't say I didn't warn you." She gave him a wink and left his office.

He sighed and turned his attention back to the book list. He couldn't worry about something that might not happen. But he could throw himself into the Lincoln project and hope for the best. Starting the next day at noon, it could have his full focus for the weekend.

For a second, his stomach jumped at the thought of tomorrow. Had he been stupid to agree to meet at Vickie's apartment? And she was fixing lunch.

Something about that situation seemed so personal to him. He'd be among her things and get a glimpse into her life. He couldn't remember the last time he'd been to a woman's house. It must've been last year when Dr. Evelyn Simmons, the professor of European history, had invited the faculty over to her house for a holiday party. John and Megan had dragged him along with them, despite his protests. He'd been mortified because everyone was part of a couple except for himself and Evelyn, who was at least fifteen years his senior. She'd had a little too much of her "special" holiday punch and made a pass at him at the end of the night. John and Megan still teased him about it, and to this day, he ran the other way when he saw Evelyn coming—although John assured him that she probably didn't even remember the incident.

Even so, that was nothing like tomorrow would be. It would just be him and Vickie. Compared to her, he felt so rough around the edges. She was so refined. He was afraid he'd spend tomorrow being terrified he'd use the wrong fork or spill something. Despite the fact that he was able to intelligently lecture his classes or participate in speaking engagements around the city on behalf of the university, ten minutes with Vickie, and he turned into a bumbling idiot. She was so well-spoken, so sure of herself.

Even though he was apprehensive, being an honest man, he had to admit he was also looking forward to tomorrow. And while the thought of Abraham Lincoln's hidden papers might have something to do with his anticipation, he couldn't deny that the chance to spend more time with a certain green-eyed park ranger was equally exciting. That was a foreign feeling to him.

CHAPTER 24

"So your this-is-not-a-date guy is coming over for lunch tomorrow?" Kristy asked, the confusion ringing through the line.

Vickie was on her way home from work Thursday night, and it was so nice out, she'd decided to walk the short distance to her apartment and catch up with her friend. "Yes. It looks like we're going to be friends. And the project he needs my help on will be interesting."

Kristy was quiet for a minute. "Hmm. Just be careful, okay? I know you kind of like this man, and it seems like he's made his feelings clear."

"Don't worry. I'm going to talk to Dawn soon and see what she thinks of a setup with one of Jason's buddies."

"Good," Kristy said. "I don't want you to wait around for something that isn't going to happen."

Vickie fought to hide her irritation. She wasn't stupid. But she also wasn't in the mood for an argument. "So, how are the wedding plans coming? I can't believe you'll be a married woman next month!"

"Pretty good." Kristy sighed.

"Oh no. What's the problem?" Vickie wondered if Kristy's family dynamics had anything to do with her dejected tone. Kristy and her sister didn't get along very well, and her dad had moved out of state, remarried, and rarely spoke to her. "Is your dad not coming?"

"Oh no, he's coming. He didn't even argue when I told him I wanted to walk down the aisle alone. I think his wife helped him to understand that being given away made me feel like a piece of property." She laughed. "I know I'm speaking to Miss Traditional, so I'm sure you'll think it's weird, too."

Vickie couldn't help but grin. "Nope. My motto for weddings is 'Your day, your way.' I just want you to be happy." She paused. "So are you?"

Kristy cleared her throat. "You know that I always dreamed of getting married at Shiloh. But after my almost-wedding to Mark on park grounds, I don't think it would be appropriate." She sighed. "It makes me sad. I mean, with Ace, the park played a huge role in our early relationship. It was where we met, fell in love, and even where we shared our first kiss. And you know he proposed near my favorite monument."

"I know. Do you really think he'd be opposed to the idea of holding the wedding there?"

"I don't want him to be reminded of my previous engagement any more than he probably already is."

"Does he ever mention it?" From what Vickie knew of Ace, he wasn't the kind of guy who had an irrational jealous streak. It was far more likely that he chalked Kristy's broken engagement up as a blessing rather than something to be upset about.

"Nope. He never mentions it. But still, I think it's just more appropriate to hold the wedding elsewhere."

"Worrying about what's appropriate is usually more my arena."

Kristy let out a tiny laugh. "I know." She sighed. "But I'm

afraid people would talk. A lot of the same people who were invited to mine and Mark's wedding will be invited to this one, too, and I don't want them to think, *Hey, haven't we done this before?* or whatever."

"I really think you should talk to Ace about it." Vickie walked up the stairs of her apartment building. She reached her door and held the phone with the crook of her neck as she fumbled with her keys.

"I know. You're probably right. Maybe I will." Kristy's voice was unconvincing.

"Okay, I'm inside. Thanks for talking me home." Vickie threw her bag on the couch and sank down beside it. "Whew. I'm exhausted."

"Well then it's lucky that you have a three-day weekend in front of you."

As they said their good-byes and Vickie tossed the phone onto the coffee table, she thought about her three-day weekend. Maybe Kristy had been right to caution her about this whole Abraham Lincoln thing. Vickie couldn't seem to think of anything but Thatcher.

ᥣᥣᥣ

Friday morning brought a fresh round of nerves for Vickie. Even though her relationship with Thatcher was purely a working one, she still wanted her home to look nice and inviting. There was nothing she enjoyed more than the role of hostess. Despite the differences she and her mother had, a love of entertaining was one thing they shared.

She'd decided a simple meal would be best for lunch, something that didn't require heating up the oven. Her gram's chicken salad recipe would be perfect. After a leisurely cup of coffee, she busied herself by chopping onions, celery, and pecans and pouring them into a large red bowl. She mixed in a large can of chicken, some mayo, and finally added a cup of dried cranberries. Vickie covered the bowl with plastic wrap and set it in the refrigerator to chill. There were croissants from a nearby bakery to go along with the chicken salad, and the fresh cantaloupe wedges she'd gotten from the farmer's market would make a yummy dessert.

She dusted the living room, taking special care to make sure all the pictures and framed artwork were dust free. A quick pass with the vacuum, and the room was spotless. She inspected the couch for any wayward strands of cat hair and was pleased to see that the roller she used on it each night was doing the trick.

Vickie knew that some of her friends thought she was a little too much of a neat freak. But it made her feel so calm when her house was clean. She couldn't imagine how anyone could relax around clutter. Kristy's house was always cluttered, and Vickie never understood how her friend could concentrate when there were out-of-place items around. They joked that they had taught each other the true meaning of patience when they shared a dorm room. It was almost as if there were a line down the center of the tiny space with one side neat and the other messy.

After showering and doing her hair and makeup, she pulled a yellow shirtdress from her closet. It was one of her favorites, and since it was sleeveless, she knew it was nearly time for it to be relegated to her off-season closet. One perk of living alone was that all the closets were hers. Given her extensive wardrobe, she needed them.

An hour later, the doorbell rang. He was nothing if not prompt. Vickie peeked through the peephole and saw Thatcher standing there holding a backpack and a briefcase. She opened the door.

"Come in," she said, standing to the side so he could come through the doorway. "You can set your things on the coffee table if you want to."

"Thanks," he said, putting the bags down. "I brought several books and have a list of more once we're through with these." He stood near the couch and looked at her. His crisp brown trousers and white button-down dress shirt were topped off by a tweed jacket.

"You can hang your jacket up if you'd like." Vickie pointed out a series of hooks behind the door where a set of keys and a raincoat hung. "There should be plenty of room."

"Thanks." Thatcher shrugged out of his jacket and hung it up.

"Have a seat if you want, and I'll get the lunch stuff ready." She motioned toward the plush navy couch. "The remote is on the coffee table if you want to turn on the TV."

He slowly sat down on the couch and began rolling up his shirt sleeves, revealing tanned forearms. "That's okay." He pulled a thick book from his bag. "I'll go ahead and get started." He fished around in the bag and came up with a steno notebook and pencil.

"Okay. I'll call you when it's time to eat." She paused at the dining room and threw a quick glance over her shoulder. He was already hard at work, probably wishing he was at the library.

CHAPTER 25

As soon as Vickie exited the room, Thatcher glanced around at his surroundings. The room was painted a warm yellow with ornate white crown molding. The navy couch and matching recliner held yellow throw pillows that exactly matched the wall color. He glanced up at the artwork hanging over the couch. He wasn't an art expert, but he was pretty sure it was a reproduction of a Van Gogh that showed an outdoor café. Her living room was simple but tasteful.

Two large white bookshelves sat on either side of the TV. The shelves were full of books, mostly classics, but he also spotted several Dean Koontz and Mary Higgins Clark titles. Vickie hadn't struck him as a suspense reader, but the more he got to know her, the more he realized she might be full of surprises.

A series of framed photos caught his eye, and he rose from his spot on the couch to get a better view. In the first one, Vickie and two other girls, one redheaded and the other blond, stood smiling in front of a cannon. All three wore park ranger uniforms. He guessed it was her stint at Shiloh when she was in college. Except for her hairstyle, she'd hardly changed over the years.

The next one was more recent. Vickie and an elderly woman were perched on a porch swing. Vickie's head was thrown back in laughter and the older woman grinned mischievously at the camera. Thatcher couldn't help but wonder what she'd said to make reserved Vickie laugh like that.

The third and final photo was of a couple dressed in formal attire. Her parents? He peered closely. Even though Vickie didn't bear much resemblance to the woman with the upswept blond hair and icy blue eyes, he could see that they shared the same petite stature.

"Are you hungry?"

Her voice startled him, and he jumped, embarrassed to have been caught looking at her photos. "Sorry. I was just looking at your bookshelf."

She grinned. "It's fine. Look all you want." She walked over to where he stood and pointed at the middle photo. "That's my gram. If you like the food today, you'll have her to thank. She taught me everything I know about cooking." She paused and pointed at the blond woman in the next photo. "And if you don't like it, you can blame my mom. She thinks cooking is something you should hire someone to do."

He laughed. "I'm sure it will be delicious."

She tilted her head toward the other room. "Come on, then."

Thatcher followed her through an arched entryway and into the next room. The walls in the combination dining room and kitchen were painted a deep red. He took a seat at the rectangular cherry dining table. A bowl of some kind of salad and a platter of croissants lay in the center of the table. "Wow, placemats and everything." He met her eyes. "I guess I'm more of a TV-tray kind of guy," he said sheepishly.

Vickie flashed him a smile. "I don't blame you. I have dinner in front of the TV way too much." She gestured at the table. "But I loved the finish on this table, and even though it's larger than

I need, I couldn't resist buying it. So I jump at any chance I have to use it." She stepped around the kitchen counter and picked up two red plates. "I hope you like chicken salad," she said, holding the plates up. She set the plates down on the table. "Is tea okay? It's sweet though, in case that makes a difference to you. I also have bottled water."

"Sweet tea sounds great." He watched as she poured two glasses and brought them to the table. She put his glass in front of him and took her seat. "Dig in," she said, passing him the bowl of chicken salad. "There are croissants, but if you don't like them, I have some plain wheat bread."

"Croissants are fine. Makes me feel like I'm back in France." He couldn't help it. He wanted her to think he was cosmopolitan. He may not be as well traveled as some, but he'd at least crossed the water once.

"Ah, *mais oui*." She grinned as she plucked a croissant from the platter. "So you've traveled to France?"

He nodded as he heaped chicken salad onto his croissant. "Only once. It was during graduate school. I went to Normandy to see the D-Day beaches."

"Aren't they incredible?" Her green eyes widened. "And the American cemetery there is such a moving sight. I really think the only thing that I've ever seen that comes close is Arlington."

He passed her the chicken salad. "I wish every American could visit Normandy." He shook his head. "As the Greatest Generation dies off, I'm worried that we as a people will forget about the sacrifices that were made."

Vickie nodded. "I know what you mean." She daintily scooped some chicken salad onto her croissant and set the bowl back in the center of the table.

"Would you like for me to offer thanks?"

"Please do." She bowed her head.

He said a quick blessing, thanking God for the food and the

hands that prepared it. He hoped Vickie wouldn't notice that his voice shook a little. Even as a small boy participating in vacation Bible school, praying out loud had always made him feel self-conscious.

"This is delicious," he said after his first bite.

"I'll thank Gram for you the next time I see her."

He grinned. "The recipe might've come from Gram, but I think you're underestimating your culinary talent."

She looked pleased. "I've had my fair share of disasters, but I enjoy cooking."

They ate in silence for a minute.

"So let's discuss your fee," he said finally. "What are your thoughts?"

Vickie looked at him and narrowed her green eyes. "I haven't thought much about it."

Thatcher gave her a tiny smile. "I guess I don't have to tell you that I'm not exactly a millionaire. But I do want to make sure to pay you fairly for the time you put into the project."

"At this point, it's kind of hard for me to say. Since we really don't know how much time we'll spend working and all. Would it be weird to gauge how many hours I work and then decide?"

He thought for a moment. "Okay," he said finally. "As long as we have the fee determined soon, I'm okay with doing that." With one last bite, Thatcher finished his lunch. "Tell you what. I'm going to go ahead and bring the books I checked out in here." He motioned toward the kitchen counter. "I'll just set them out, and that way we can get started as soon as the table is clear." He slid his chair back from the table and went to collect the books. This was feeling far too much like a social call. It was time to get to work.

CHAPTER 26

After three hours of near silence, Vickie found herself going stir crazy. She glanced across the table where Thatcher was furiously scribbling on a notepad. She really had to admire his single-mindedness. He'd put on a pair of round, wire-rimmed glasses at some point, and she couldn't help but think how cute he was in them.

She cleared her throat, but he didn't even look up. Finally, she couldn't stand it any longer. "I think I'll put on a pot of coffee," she said, rising from the table.

He looked up as if he'd forgotten she was there. "Sounds good." He stretched his arms over his head. "Have you found anything interesting?"

Vickie filled the carafe with cold tap water and poured it into the coffeemaker. "I've found one scholar who was adamant that Lincoln was engaged to Ann Rutledge and that the relationship was a significant one. And I've found one who says there isn't any proof, but even if it happened, it doesn't matter." She grinned. "You think they cancel each other out?"

"I'm sort of in the same boat. I did find one that alluded to the fact that the two shared written correspondences, but there isn't a reference for that particular point." He sighed. "This might not have been the best way to go about it."

The aroma of coffee began to filter through the small space. Vickie felt more energetic already. "I don't know. I sort of think this gives us a good starting point." She pulled two mugs from the cabinet. "This way, we know what others have found out about the situation. I feel certain we aren't the first people to search for these documents." She shrugged. "It stands to reason that we can learn from those who came before us."

A broad grin spread over Thatcher's face. "I like the way you think. That's exactly what I tell my students. Learn from both past mistakes and past successes." He stood up from the table and walked over to the coffeepot where Vickie stood.

There was a tiny patch of stubble on his jaw where he'd missed a spot during his morning shave. She hid a smile. Something about that tiny patch was so endearing, the urge to run her fingers over it surprised her. She quickly turned away from him and focused on the brewing coffee. "Do you like cream and sugar?"

"Just a bit of sugar will do. No cream." He leaned against the counter and crossed his arms.

She scooped a teaspoon of sugar into his mug. "Here you go. Let me know if you need more sugar."

He took a sip. "Perfect. I needed a break." He grinned. "And some caffeine." Thatcher carried his mug back over to the table and sat down.

Just as Vickie was settled back into place with another volume about the life of Lincoln, a knock sounded at the door. She met Thatcher's startled gaze. "Sorry. I'll go see who it is."

She peeked through the peephole. Dawn and a muscular guy stood in the hallway, holding hands. She'd left Dawn a message last night to stop in the next time she had the chance. As she'd promised Kristy, she was going to ask about the possibility of a setup. But now certainly wouldn't be the time to ask. Vickie threw open the door. "Hi," she said with a grin.

"Sorry for the drop-in," Dawn said once the pair was inside. "But I got your message and wanted to see how you were." She flashed a dazzling smile. "And I also wanted you to meet someone." She turned toward the handsome man at her side. "Vickie Harris, meet Jason Redd."

Jason gave Vickie a nod. "Nice to meet you, Vickie. I've heard so much about you." He grinned. His tanned face and arms told Vickie that he spent a lot of time outdoors. His dark hair was closely cropped, and he had brilliant green eyes. She could definitely see why Dawn was so smitten.

"Likewise," Vickie said.

Dawn poked her head into the dining room then turned back with wide eyes. "I didn't know you had company," she hissed, grinning mischievously. "Don't you want to introduce us?"

Vickie hadn't planned on introducing them to Thatcher, but she supposed it would be rude not to do so now. Especially since he could probably hear every word of their conversation. She motioned for Dawn and Jason to follow her into the dining room.

Thatcher looked up from the thick book he was poring over and removed his glasses.

Vickie made the necessary introductions and exchanged amused glances with Dawn as the two men sized one another up then firmly shook hands.

"We're on our way to a Nationals game," Dawn said.

Vickie raised her eyebrows in question.

"Baseball," Jason said, laughing. "I take it you're not a fan?"

"My knowledge of sports is pretty much nonexistent." She grinned. "Other than the badminton class I had to take in college to fulfill my PE requirement."

Thatcher and Jason wore identical expressions.

"What? Badminton is a sport, right?" Vickie looked at Dawn for support. "Come on, back me up. It isn't exactly like you're a sports girl either."

Dawn held up her hands. "You've got me there. The whole reason we're going to a Nationals game is because I made the mistake of telling Jason that I'd never been to one."

Jason laughed. "I told her that it was a crime and that everyone needed to spend at least one summer night at the ballpark."

"He was apparently some kind of all-star baseball player in college," Dawn explained. "Although I have to take his word for it since he conveniently left his pictures and yearbooks with his mother in Alabama."

"You played college ball?" Thatcher looked interested. "Where'd you go to school?"

"University of Alabama."

"Roll Tide." Thatcher grinned.

Vickie and Dawn exchanged glances. "I'm sorry, what language are you speaking?" Vickie asked.

The men burst out laughing.

"I did my graduate work at Vandy, so I'm well versed in Southern sports teams," Thatcher explained to Jason.

"I miss playing baseball. I've been helping one of my coworkers coach his kid's Little League team, but it isn't the same as getting to play. I started playing on a church-league softball team a few weeks ago. It's pretty fun." Jason grinned at Dawn. "We've got a game tomorrow, and Dawn's going to come cheer me on."

Vickie cut her eyes at Dawn. What was going on with her? Dawn normally spent her weekends going to fancy dinners and the theater. And now she'd turned into a sports fan?

"Do you play?" Jason leaned against the kitchen counter and looked at Thatcher expectantly.

Thatcher nodded. "It's been awhile, but yeah. Last spring I got talked into playing in a student/faculty game. I guess that's the last time I was on the field."

Jason shrugged. "You should come out tomorrow afternoon. We can always use another player."

Thatcher met Vickie's gaze. "We have a lot of work to do tomorrow, so I'm not sure."

She could see the excitement in his eyes. "I'm fine with getting an early start tomorrow so your afternoon will be free."

"Great then. Here, let me write down the name of the field." Jason sat down at the dining room table across from Thatcher and began scribbling on a notepad.

Dawn grasped Vickie's arm and pulled her into the living room. "He's very cute," she whispered. "Don't tell me this is the man who had you all riled up the other night."

Vickie nodded. "One and the same."

"I knew I was right when I said you should be his assistant. Even if you aren't dating, he's still fun to look at." She grinned.

"What's with you and Mr. Sports? I didn't think that was your type."

The blush that crept across Dawn's face was priceless. Vickie had never seen her friend in such a state.

"I guess sometimes the right guy can make you forget you ever thought you had a type." Dawn winked. "You'll see."

Jason strode into the living room. "Babe, we're gonna be late if we don't go." He turned to Vickie as they reached the door. "Hey, you should come with Dawn tomorrow—so she'll have someone to sit with in the bleachers."

Dawn's eyes lit up. "Yes. You should. I'll call you."

Before Vickie could utter an excuse, they were gone. She slowly walked back into the dining room.

"I'm going to have another cup of coffee. Do you want one?" Thatcher stood at the coffeepot.

"Yes, please." She set her cup on the counter and watched him carefully pour the brew.

Jake peeked his head around the corner and seemed to decide it was safe to make an entrance. The cat preened and stretched his way to the center of the kitchen then collapsed as if the walk from the bedroom had been a great effort.

Thatcher looked down at the cat and grinned. "Hey, kitty." He met Vickie's eyes. "I've been here for several hours and didn't know you had a cat." He knelt down and scratched Jake behind the ears. "He must be a hermit."

"I have two cats. They tend to hide when people are around." She smiled. "This is Jake. Lloyd is a little shyer, but he'll probably venture out at some point."

Thatcher stood up and wrinkled his nose at her. "Jake and Lloyd? Those are unusual names for cats."

She shrugged. "Jake Ryan and Lloyd Dobler are characters in two of my favorite movies." She expected that he'd ask what the movies were, but he didn't. Instead he nodded.

"Ready to get back to work?" He handed her a thick book with Abraham Lincoln's face on the cover. "This might be just the one we need to put us on the right track."

She grabbed her coffee cup and settled back at the table. Back to work.

CHAPTER 27

What had gotten into him? Thatcher's life had been predictable for years. Now all of a sudden, he was agreeing to play in a pickup softball game instead of working. But Jason seemed like a nice guy, and the prospect of playing ball sounded fun.

He glanced across the table and considered asking Vickie what she thought. Would it seem to her as if he was trying to engrain himself into her world somehow? He sighed. No, that was silly. She probably wouldn't even come to the game, so it would be a nonissue.

"Problem?" she asked.

He looked up and saw her curious expression. "No. Just wondering if maybe I should call Jason and tell him I can't come tomorrow." He shook his head. "We have a lot to do, and I have some projects at the house I've been meaning to get to."

Vickie bit her bottom lip. "You seemed like you were pretty excited at the thought of playing. It's only for a couple of hours. Surely you can spare that." She grinned. "Then you won't have to go to the gym." She paused. "I mean, if that's the kind of thing you do."

"Nope. I'm not a gym rat. I prefer running." He put the pencil down and leaned back. "Okay, these days it's more like jogging. Right after I turned thirty-five, I had to have knee surgery. Since then, I've stuck to a slower pace." He grinned. "Old age setting in, I guess."

She laughed. "I wondered how old you were but didn't want to pry."

"Thirty-eight. Man, time flies." He looked curiously at her. "And you? Is it rude to ask a lady's age?" He knew it was rude, but for some reason, he really wanted to know how old she was.

"Since you shared yours, I'll share mine." Her green eyes gleamed. "That's my rule, anyway. I'm thirty. Newly thirty." She paused. "In fact, the day we met at the Lincoln Memorial was the day after my birthday."

"Happy belated birthday."

She smiled. "Thanks."

He shifted in his seat. "So, I guess maybe we should call it a day, huh? It's getting close to dinnertime, and I'm sure you have plans." That had slipped out. Would she think he was fishing to see if she had a date? Maybe he was. He did wonder about her status.

"My plans for the night include an old movie and probably a leftover chicken salad sandwich." She grimaced. "Exciting, I know."

Thatcher grinned. "Sounds good to me. Depending on the movie, of course."

"I'm a sucker for a good chick flick. The cheesier the ending, the better." She laughed.

He groaned. "I think I can safely say I've only watched a couple of those in my entire life." When one or the other of his sisters forced him to.

"What? Do you make your girlfriend go see action and war movies?" She cocked her head ever so slightly as she asked the question.

He shook his head. "I'm not seeing anyone right now." He cringed inwardly. *Right now?* What was that supposed to mean? That he was normally seeing someone? Because that was a joke. He cleared his throat. "How about you?"

A light pink blush crept over her creamy skin. She shook her head. "No one special."

"I guess it's best. Gives us more time to work."

"Yes." She nodded. "You're exactly right."

He closed the book in front of him. "I should be going so you can get to your movie." He picked up a stack of books from the table. "Tell you what. How about if we just work separately tomorrow? That way you don't have to get an early start just because I'm playing softball." He grinned. "I don't want to ruin your weekend or anything." If he were honest with himself, he knew he didn't want to work separately. But he'd gotten so little done today. He figured it had something to do with being on her turf. It threw him off of his game and kept him from concentrating. So tomorrow, he'd have to make up the progress he should've made today. Maybe he wouldn't have to keep reading the same sentences over and over if there was no one around but the dog.

Vickie nodded slowly. "Okay. That's fine." She nodded at the books on the table. "Do you want to leave a few here?"

"Sounds good. Maybe Sunday afternoon we can get together again? I'll call you." He paused. "Unless you think you might come to the game."

Her expression was unreadable. "Maybe. I'm not sure yet."

"That's fine." He shoved the books into his bag. "Either way, we'll talk tomorrow afternoon or night." He stepped to the door then turned back to look at her. "Thanks for lunch."

"You're welcome."

He closed the door behind him and headed down the stairs. Somehow he always managed to feel awkward around her. He did fine as long as they stuck to the business at hand, but when he delved into personal territory, he felt himself stumbling. And he didn't like it.

⊙◉

Saturday was a beautiful early fall day. The heat was warm, but not the sticky warm that had been present all summer. After a morning of playing fetch in the backyard with Buster and reading through several articles about Lincoln, Thatcher was suited up for softball. He just needed to find his glove and he'd be ready.

The front closet that kept his winter coats and jackets was full of old sporting equipment. He sorted through old tennis rackets and a set of flags his family used for the annual Thanksgiving flag football game and finally emerged victorious with his battered softball glove. He ran his hands over the weathered finish. He'd had this glove for at least twenty years.

The trouble with the past was that it was always present. As a student of history, he knew all too well the ways the actions of long ago could impact present day. He wasn't immune in his own life. Every now and then, he felt a familiar pang of regret. *Shake it off, Torrey. No good can come from playing what-if.*

Thatcher was still pondering the ways a person's history affected their daily lives when he arrived at the ball field.

Jason loped over, a black and green jersey in hand. "Hey, man. Glad you could come." He tossed the jersey to Thatcher. "Here you go." He jerked his head in the direction of the field. "Most everyone is here, and they're already warming up." He held up a tattered piece of notebook paper. "I'm going to put you in left. That okay?"

"Sure. Outfield is probably best." He grinned. "It's been awhile."

Jason pointed to the sparsely populated metal stands. "Looks like we've got some cheerleaders."

LOVE IS MONUMENTAL

145

Thatcher looked up into the crowd. Dawn and Vickie were climbing to the center of the stands. "Guess so." His stomach churned. It had been ages since he'd played, and now someone was going to watch him. But that was crazy. She wasn't there to see him. She was there to keep Dawn company in the stands. He'd bet she'd be here even if she'd never met him. At that disheartening thought, he jogged onto the field.

CHAPTER 28

I can't believe I let you talk me into this." Vickie settled beside Dawn on the hard metal bleachers. "I don't think I've been to a baseball game since I was in college."

"First of all, this is *softball*." Dawn laughed. "If you're going to be a superfan, you've got to at least get the sport correct." She propped her denim-encased legs on the bleacher seat in front of them. "Besides, I didn't exactly have to hold a gun to your head to get you here." She glanced over at Vickie. "Admit it. He intrigues you."

"Don't encourage it." Vickie frowned. "He's made it clear that he isn't interested. Last night he even asked me if I had plans, but then when he found out I wasn't busy, he told me to have a good night." When Thatcher had asked her if she had big plans for the night, she'd assumed that when she said no he would ask her to make some. Grab a quick bite, go see a movie—something like that. But he'd checked her calendar, seen that it was free, and then gone home to do a project around the house. Any man who was interested in a woman would've tried to make plans upon finding out she was available. She let out a loud sigh. "I'm hopeless.

Always falling for guys who aren't really into me."

"So now you're a movie?"

Vickie laughed. "Let's just say that movie could've been a biopic of my life." She looked over at Dawn. "Things with Jason seem like they're going really well."

Dawn let out a contented sigh and leaned back against the row behind her. "Better than I ever expected. He's home to me." She smiled. "I've always heard of people finding that, you know? Someone who made them feel so safe and warm that it was like going home. He's that person."

"Wow." She glanced over at Dawn. "So no bumps in the road?"

Dawn shrugged and pushed a strand of blond hair from her eyes. "Not to speak of. At this point, we haven't run into anything that's a deal breaker." She sighed.

"Do I sense a *but* somewhere in there?"

"It's probably nothing. It's just that Jason always talks about his mom and how she's such a great cook and keeps a spotless house. Sounds like she's some kind of Southern domestic diva." She grinned. "Now, for you, it would be like you were a long-lost daughter. But for me. . ." Her voice trailed off. "I'm not sure I can ever measure up."

"Has he ever said anything negative about you in that way?" Dawn ran a very successful event-planning business and was sought after in the city whenever something special was going on. But no one would ever accuse her of being domestic. To Vickie's knowledge, she'd never used her oven, and she hired someone to clean her apartment once a week.

Dawn shook her head. "Oh no. He'd never say anything about it. But we're flying to Alabama next weekend so I can meet his family. You know, once I arrived firmly in my thirties, I thought nerves were a thing of the past." She glanced at Vickie. "Not so."

"How firmly in your thirties are you?" Vickie clasped her

hands over her mouth. "I'm sorry. That just came out." She felt a blush rising up her face. She'd spent her entire life trying not to be tacky, and lately it seemed like that philosophy had gone right out the window.

Dawn laughed. "It's okay. It isn't really a secret, just something I don't go around publicizing." She looked at Vickie. "I'm thirty-six." She leaned over. "And if you want to know a little secret, I'm finding my thirties a lot better than my twenties were. Once you've dealt with having that three at the beginning of your age, I'm sure you'll feel the same way."

"Let's hope so." She glanced over at Dawn. "So you're nervous about meeting his family?"

"Just a little. I get the feeling his family is the kind that will think it highly unusual that I've never successfully baked a cake. Or a pie. Or a casserole." She laughed. "But I make a mean bowl of popcorn."

"That you do. But seriously, they'll love you. Don't worry."

Dawn smiled. "I hope you're right." She pointed at the field. "There they go. Looks like your man is in the outfield."

"He isn't my man. Just to get that point across to myself, I'm going to go out with a new guy soon. We met at church." She shrugged. "We'll see. He's sent a couple of e-mails so far, and the last one mentioned getting together in the near future." She raised an eyebrow. "So there. I'm not under any kind of false delusions about Thatcher."

Dawn was silent.

The umpire called the game into action, and the first batter stepped up to the plate. His bat made contact on the second pitch, and the ball careened to left field. Thatcher effortlessly held his gloved hand up and caught the ball.

Vickie leaped to her feet, clapping. She cast a sideways glance at Dawn, who stared at her with one eyebrow raised.

"No delusions, huh?"

Vickie quickly sat down. "None. Just cheering the team on." But she remained glued to her seat for the rest of the game, careful not to clap again until Jason hit a home run that ended the game.

The two women left the bleachers and headed toward the home team's dugout. Players streamed from the field. Jason jogged over and planted a kiss on Dawn's cheek. "Thanks for the support."

Dawn beamed. "I don't know much about sports, but that was a great hit at the end."

"Thanks." He grinned. "And here's the star outfielder."

Thatcher joined their circle. Wearing a baseball hat low over his eyes, he looked much younger than his thirty-eight years. He nodded at Vickie and gave her a slow grin. "I wouldn't say star as much as I would say lucky." He rubbed his right shoulder. "And I'm pretty sure tomorrow I'm going to be sore."

Jason chuckled. "Old age will get you every time, man." He turned to Dawn. "I'm starving. Anyone up for pizza?"

"Pizza would be great. How about Matchbox?" asked Dawn.

Vickie turned her head toward Thatcher, who still clutched his shoulder. She had the sinking feeling that he was racking his brain to come up with another home-improvement project that couldn't wait until tomorrow. His gaze locked with hers, and he opened his mouth to speak.

CHAPTER 29

"That sounds good to me," Thatcher said. He'd already eaten pizza for the majority of his meals this week, but who was counting? He nodded at Vickie. "Are you in?" He hated to be the third wheel. And even more than that, he looked forward to the chance to spend time with her without the pressure of carrying the conversation. At least if Jason and Dawn were there, his awkwardness might not be so obvious.

"Sure." She smiled. "It's been ages since I've eaten at Matchbox. I try to limit my pizza intake."

"Then it's settled. Can we go as is, or are you ladies going to insist we go clean up first?" Jason nudged Dawn.

"As is will be fine with me." Dawn smiled prettily. "There aren't many five-star pizza joints, so you shouldn't stick out too much."

"Let's go." Jason grabbed Dawn's hand and headed for the Metro.

Thatcher hung back for a minute.

Vickie stopped walking and glanced at him over her shoulder. "You coming?"

He hurried to catch up with her. "Thanks for coming to support us today."

"It was fun. I haven't been to a game in a long time. Besides, Dawn didn't want to sit in the bleachers alone."

Thatcher looked over at her. Was that her way of saying she definitely didn't come for him? "Yeah, I guess that wouldn't have been much fun."

"Nice catch out there, by the way," she said. "Really."

Throwing him a bone? Maybe. But he'd take it. "Thanks."

Fifteen minutes later, the four of them were seated in the restaurant.

"I'm starving." Jason rubbed his hands together in anticipation. "I could eat a whole pizza by myself, but I'll spare y'all the ugliness."

Dawn laughed. "Thanks."

They settled on a large pepperoni and a large cheese. Thatcher's stomach rumbled at the thought. He took a sip of his Coke. "So, did you get any work done this morning?" he asked Vickie.

She shrugged. "I found a couple of things." She picked up a straw wrapper and folded it into a tiny square. "One of Lincoln's former law partners gave a speech after his assassination where he discussed the relationship between Abraham and Ann. He claimed it was vital to the future character of Lincoln. But as seems to be the case everywhere we look, nothing backs his claims except speculation."

Thatcher thought for a moment. Were they foolish to think they could solve a historical mystery so many others before them had sought? The very idea that Clark could one-up him made him even more determined. If the proof was out there, he and Vickie would find it. "We'll just keep looking."

Dawn slapped her hands on the table, startling him. "Enough, Indiana Jones. Don't you two have anything to talk about besides history?"

Vickie let out a tinkling laugh. "Sorry if we're boring you. You seemed a bit preoccupied over there anyway."

Dawn raised an eyebrow but didn't respond. Instead, she directed her blue-eyed gaze at Thatcher. "So, Thatcher, why don't you tell us a little about yourself?"

He shifted uncomfortably. "Not too much to tell. As you know, I'm a professor of history. I grew up not too far from here in Virginia. I have a dog." He pressed his lips together. "That's about it. Nothing too interesting." His answer clearly wasn't enough for Dawn's liking.

She regarded him for a moment, her eyes narrowed. "You're single?"

He nodded. "That I am." Thatcher glanced over at Vickie, who was poring over the menu. Since they'd already placed their order, she must be bored with the conversation.

"Well that's a real shame." Dawn smiled sweetly. "For some reason, ever since Jason and I met, I've just wanted to see the whole world coupled up and as happy as we are."

Thatcher gave her a wry grin. "I'm glad you two are so happy." He cleared his throat, eager to extract himself from the conversation. He didn't like the look she had in her eye. He'd seen it before, and it usually ended with someone trying to fix him up. He looked at Vickie for help, but she was still fascinated by the menu. "So, Jason. Did you always want to be a detective?"

Jason grinned and shook his head. "Nope. I wanted to be a major league baseball player. I even played in the minors for a couple of years. But I had a pretty serious knee injury followed by a torn ACL, so I finally decided to go into something else."

"I'll bet your job is exciting."

"I enjoy it. My old man is a cop, so I sort of grew up around it." He leaned back. "I'm never going to be one of those guys whose job is his whole life, though." He put a hand on Dawn's shoulder and gave her a squeeze. "In my line of work, I get the chance to think daily about what's really important. No one ever went to his grave wishing he'd spent more time at the office, you know?"

Thatcher was quiet. This probably wasn't the time to tell them about the amount of hours he put in during a normal week and that if he didn't have Buster, he'd probably just live at the office. Instead he nodded. "That's true. It's nice that you've got your priorities in order."

"Of course, getting this workaholic to cut back so we can see each other some during the week was the real challenge." Jason planted a kiss on Dawn's cheek. "Thankfully, she finds me irresistible."

Dawn blushed.

Thatcher felt an unfamiliar pang in his stomach. Something about being in the presence of a couple so obviously in love caused him to have to acknowledge his loneliness.

The waitress set two steaming pizzas on their table.

"Wow." Vickie slapped the menu down and her eyes lit up. "I didn't realize how hungry I was until just now."

Jason said a quick blessing for the food, and they dug in.

"So, have you finally adjusted to your new work schedule?" Dawn asked Vickie.

Thatcher glanced at Vickie from the corner of his eye. Her hair was swept back in a ponytail, but one strand had escaped. His hand itched to reach out and tuck it behind her ear.

"Mostly. I was really tired at first, but I think I'm starting to get used to the longer days." She grinned at Thatcher. "Plus, now I have more time to devote to one of history's mysteries."

He laughed. "And I'm thankful to have your help."

"At least this prevents her from taking some kind of class," Dawn said, wiping her mouth daintily.

Thatcher caught Vickie's horrified look. "A class?" he asked.

Vickie rolled her eyes. "Sometimes I've been known to take

classes to fill my time." She shrugged. "I was considering a salsa class when you came along needing a researcher."

Dawn met his eyes across the table. "She's got a lot of unusual talents now. Cake decorating, genealogy, quilting—but that one didn't turn out very well." She grinned and continued, "Ballet, painting. . ." She trailed off. "And of course, who could forget belly dancing?"

Thatcher almost spit out his Coke. He looked at sweet, demure Vickie. "Belly dancing?" he asked incredulously.

Vickie, ten different shades of red, shot daggers at Dawn with her eyes. "Let's not make a big deal about that. It was a class of all women, and it was only for exercise." She was quiet for a moment; then a tiny smile broke through her embarrassment. "But I guess it does sound a little shocking."

"I'll say," Jason piped up, a mischievous grin plastered on his face.

The waitress arrived at the table, putting a halt to the conversation. "Is this separate checks?"

"You can put ours together." Jason pointed from Dawn to himself.

Thatcher froze. He didn't want to overstep his boundaries with Vickie, but he also didn't want to be rude. "You can put ours together, too," he told the waitress.

"You don't have to do that." Vickie placed a small hand on his arm. "At least let me give you some cash for my part."

He turned toward her, suddenly aware of how close they were in the booth. He could see a tiny freckle underneath her eye. "You made lunch for me yesterday. It's the least I can do." He nodded at her plate. "Besides, you only ate like two pieces." He grinned.

"Thank you," she said softly.

They stepped out of the restaurant into the night air. The chill took Thatcher by surprise. The day had been unseasonably warm, but now in just shorts and a T-shirt, he was cool.

Dawn shivered, and Jason put an arm around her. "This was fun," Jason said. "We'll have to do it again sometime."

Thatcher nodded. It had been fun.

"We're going to head to Jason's to watch a movie." Dawn directed her comment to Vickie. "Thanks for being a sports fan with me today."

Vickie grinned. "Have fun."

Hand in hand, Dawn and Jason strode off toward the Metro, leaving Thatcher and Vickie standing in front of the restaurant.

"My apartment is right around the corner," Vickie said. "So I'll just walk home. Thanks again for dinner."

"My pleasure. I'll call you later in the week, and we can discuss the project."

"Sounds good." She met his eyes for a moment. "Good night." She gave him a smile and walked away.

"Night," he called, rooted to the spot. A part of him wanted to stop her and offer to walk her home. But he didn't. Instead, he set out toward the Metro. He'd try to get a little more work done before bedtime. This day had become way too much of a social outing. It was time to get refocused.

CHAPTER 30

Katherine gripped the steering wheel and glanced over at her mother. One second Mom would be looking out the window; then she'd quickly stare straight ahead. It was as if she couldn't decide what she was supposed to be doing.

The past couple of weeks had been fantastic. Katherine and her mother had taken their time driving from California to Maryland. Any time either of them had wanted to stop and play tourist, they had. Of course, Katherine's mother tired easily, so that added to their stops. But now, they were nearly there. And Mom looked like she might crawl out of her own skin.

Katherine bit back a smile. "Nervous?"

"No point in trying to hide it, huh?" Mom leaned her head against the passenger window. "I'd be lying if I said I hadn't imagined what this moment would feel like. I never expected it to be under these circumstances, though."

Katherine was silent. It was so easy to wait until a crisis to realize relationships needed to be resolved. She was guilty of it, just in a different way. She couldn't help but think of how lately she'd been in a pattern of waiting to talk to God until there was a problem. Or how she prayed a lot harder when she was on an airplane than any other time. It was sort of the same thing. She resolved to learn from this experience. "I'm a little nervous, too. What if they don't like me?"

Mom reached over and patted her leg. "They will love you. And if you can forget all of the things you've heard me say about them over the years, you'll love them, too."

Katherine nodded. "I will. I'm excited about meeting the rest of the family."

"And from what I hear, they're pretty excited about meeting you as well."

The prospect of having aunts, uncles, and cousins was foreign to Katherine. She and her mother had a large circle of friends in California. Neighbors and people from her mother's work had stepped in and filled the roles normally held by family. While it had been hard to leave some of them behind, Katherine couldn't shake the excitement of getting to know her relatives. With one exception.

"Honey," her mother began. "I know this is going to be difficult for you. It is for me, too, just in a different way. If you ever feel like it's too much for you to handle, just let me know. We'll go check into a hotel or something." She smiled. "I know better than anyone that my parents, particularly my mother, can be a lot to take."

"I'm sure it will be fine." Katherine hoped her voice held more certainty than she felt. As excited as she was about meeting her family, she also knew it could be a disaster. But at this point, there was no turning back. The house was sold. She'd registered for classes and already explained that she'd be starting late.

Her mother pointed at a street to the left. "Here's the turn." She took a deep breath. "It's time to face the music."

Katherine slowed the car and turned onto a quaint street lined with brick houses and lush green yards. Ivy grew on some of the brick, a sure sign that this neighborhood had a history dating back many years.

"Right there, on the left. I used to say that was the house where dreams went to die." Her mother gave a strained laugh.

Katherine pulled the car into the driveway, thankful there weren't a lot of vehicles parked at the house. Too many new people at once would be overwhelming.

An elegant woman strode toward them. Her gray hair was cut in a sleek bob, and her pantsuit was expensively cut. She was smiling broadly though, making her less intimidating.

Katherine and her mother both climbed from the car.

"Katherine, dear," her grandmother said. "You've grown into a beautiful young woman." She gave her a quick embrace.

"Hi, Mother." Katherine's mom hesitantly stood next to the car, one hand still on the door handle. She looked as if she were considering climbing back inside the car from which she'd come. "You look great."

By Katherine's calculations, it had been at least a decade since they'd seen one another. Her grandparents had flown to California for a vacation when Katherine had been in elementary school.

"Jane." Grandmother stood, staring at her daughter. "I'm so sorry that you're sick. I wish you'd let us know sooner." She crossed to the passenger side and gave her a hug. "Your father is worried sick. He's inside, probably watching out the window." She gave Katherine a wink. "Probably afraid we'll get into an argument right here in the driveway," she whispered.

Katherine's mom gave a tiny smile. "Let's try not to argue at all during our visit."

Grandmother nodded. "I think that's a fantastic idea. Besides, now that the two of you are home where you belong, there's nothing to argue about anyway." She grasped one of Katherine's hands. "Come in and rest. You can unload your things later." Katherine and her mother exchanged glances. She had to admit, her grandmother was a force to be reckoned with. She wasn't the kind of woman who'd take kindly to someone not wanting to do things her way. As they stepped inside the spacious home, Katherine hoped they could manage to keep the peace for her mother's sake.

CHAPTER 31

Tuesday morning, Thatcher set out down Pennsylvania Avenue at a brisk pace. He had just enough time to get in a good jog before his first class of the day. He paused at the National Archives to read the inscription on the large statue out front. It reminded those who passed by to study the past. He couldn't help but consider his own history for a moment.

There were so many things in his past that he wasn't proud of he could hardly stand to count them. Going all the way back to high school, when he'd just been a shy, nerdy guy who was more interested in studying and learning to play the piano than playing sports or dating. The other day on the softball field, he'd heard Vickie clapping from the stands when he made a catch. He'd felt like an all-star from that moment on. It was amazing how a compliment or a glance from her could make him feel taller somehow.

But involvement with her would be too complicated. He'd spent so many years living a simple life that he'd convinced himself it was exactly what he wanted. And up until a few weeks ago, that had been enough. Something about seeing a couple revel in the newness of a relationship made him long for that kind of companionship.

He began to jog again, heading toward the Capitol. There was a problem with a relationship. He'd have to let someone through the wall. And let them find out all of his secrets. No way was he ready for that.

☺౨☺

"Dr. Torrey." Amanda stepped to the door. "Dean White wants you in his office, pronto."

He glanced up from the paper he was reading. "Oh yeah? What for?" He couldn't remember the last time he'd been summoned to the dean's office.

She placed a hand on her hip and regarded him with a raised eyebrow. "I have no idea. I'm only the messenger."

He doubted that was the complete truth. She always had at least an idea of what was going on. But he'd give her the benefit of the doubt. "If you say so." He tossed the paper onto his desk and grabbed a small notebook.

They exited the office. "I'll just take messages if you get any calls. Your secret admirer hasn't called lately." She grinned.

"I imagine my 'secret admirer's' son or daughter has adjusted just fine, and that is the reason she hasn't called lately. Give it until midterms when things get tough, and she'll probably start back."

She sighed. "Can't you at least let an old lady imagine that you have an admirer? Handsome professor like you." She got a faraway look in her eyes. "Maybe I should switch from mystery to romance."

"Well I'm certainly no hero." He gave her a wink as he began the journey down the long hallway toward Dean White's office. Thatcher paused at the door then lightly rapped with his knuckles.

"Come in," the dean said in a gravelly voice.

Thatcher pushed the door open. Clark Langston was already seated in one of the leather chairs across from the dean's desk.

"Afternoon, gentlemen," Thatcher said, taking a seat.

Clark glowered. "Hello, *Thatcher*," he said. "It's so nice to see you."

Thatcher flinched at Clark's sarcastic tone.

The dean sat up and slapped his hands on the desk. "Let's get right to it, shall we?"

The two younger men nodded.

"I know you've both got more than enough on your plates." Dean White's bushy white eyebrows seemed to be growing by the minute. "But I have an assignment I believe you're both going to want to put some extra time into."

Thatcher knew what was coming. He was thankful Amanda had warned him. He glanced over at Clark. His jaw was clenched in anticipation, and Thatcher suspected he'd also had an inkling this was coming. Knowing Clark, he probably already had his plan together and was using unsuspecting graduate assistants to do the hard part.

"You both know that we are displeased with our enrollment numbers. You also know that the department chair position will be vacated within the year." Dean White leaned back in his chair and pressed his fingertips together. "I'm interested in knowing what the department could look forward to underneath your leadership. You each have until the faculty meeting in January to put together a plan for how the department can grow and prosper under your direction."

Thatcher and Clark both nodded.

"That's all. I'm sure you have classes to prepare for and papers to grade. You've got roughly two and a half months to pull something together."

They stood to exit.

"And gentlemen." The dean paused. "Better make it good. I'd say your careers depend on it." With that, Dean White went back to his computer.

Thatcher followed Clark out the door. Once they were in the hallway, Clark turned abruptly to face him. "Some things never change, do they? You and I started competing more than twenty years ago." He sneered. "And here we are in one final competition."

"Look, Clark. Everything that happened was so long ago. Can't you just put it behind you? I have."

"Oh, I know you have. You think you can just ignore things and that means they don't exist." Clark frowned. "But you and I both know that isn't true." He leveled his gaze at Thatcher. "I, for one, am looking forward to this competition. May the best man win." With that, he strode off toward his office.

Thatcher watched him go. He hadn't forgotten the past. He just chose not to dwell on things he couldn't change. He'd spent enough time playing "if only," and it hadn't gotten him anywhere. Shaking his head, he made his way back down the hall and to his office. At least Clark hadn't gotten the best of him. Yet.

CHAPTER 32

"Explain to me how a professor of history doesn't have a card to use the Library of Congress," Vickie said the following Saturday as she and Thatcher walked along Independence Avenue.

He shrugged. "I never thought I needed one. I just use the school library for most things."

"But don't you think it might be helpful to your students to be familiar with, oh, I don't know, the *largest* library in the *world*?" She grinned.

Thatcher gave her a sheepish look. "It never crossed my mind."

"Our first order of business is to get you a card. The Reader Registration Room is in the James Madison Building." She pointed to a large building ahead. "Three buildings make up the Library of Congress. Surely you've been to the Thomas Jefferson Building. That's the main building where most tourists go."

He regarded her with raised eyebrows. "You know how much I love being surrounded by tourists. I guess I've probably been inside, but it was probably when I was in high school."

Vickie made a face. "You need to get over your aversion to crowds and tourists. That building is phenomenal. I go there sometimes just because it's so beautiful inside."

"You and I are very different people."

That was an understatement. "Yes, I suppose we are." They walked past an assortment of stone tables where several people were sitting, eating, and talking. "Here we are."

They went through security at the door. Entering any building in Washington meant going through airport-style security. The Library of Congress was no different. Once they were inside, Vickie pointed to her left. "The registration room is this way."

She waited while Thatcher filled out the appropriate paperwork and got his photo ID made. Soon he was finished. "Check it out." He held out his card and grinned. "I feel so official now."

"Officially a geek, you mean." She laughed. "It's okay, I'm like the geek queen. In fact, the day I got my Library of Congress card was practically a holiday in my world."

He chuckled. "Okay, what next?"

"While you were getting official clearance to be a Library of Congress reader, I was chatting with the nice lady at the desk. I told her we were doing some research on Abraham Lincoln. . . ." She paused as his face clouded over. "Simmer down. I didn't tell her what we were looking for. Anyway, she suggested we start at the Manuscript Reading Room. It should have any documents Lincoln wrote, like letters and speeches. How does that sound?"

Thatcher nodded. "Perfect."

"I'll have to check my bag." She pointed at a bag-check room. "They clearly think people are going to come in and steal important documents." She held up her oversized red bag. "I mean, do I look like a thief?"

He grinned. "If only everyone were as honest as you. I'll wait out here for you." He leaned against the wall just outside the bag-check door.

A moment later, bag checked and claim ticket in hand, she sauntered over to where Thatcher stood. "Ready?"

He nodded. "Lead the way."

They walked into the Manuscript Reading Room. It was tomb silent, and an older gentleman peered at them from behind a desk. Vickie plastered on her best smile as they stepped up to the desk. "We're hoping you can point us in the right direction," she said quietly, motioning at Thatcher. "He's a history professor, and I'm a park ranger. We're doing some research about Abraham Lincoln and wondered if any of his letters and papers are housed here."

The man was silent for a moment as he pushed his glasses up on his nose. "Yes. More than twenty thousand documents associated with President Lincoln are here. But you can only see them on microfilm to ensure their preservation." He cleared his throat and leaned forward. "Actually, the entire Lincoln collection is also available online. You might be better served to use that outlet because it is easy to type in search terms and such."

Thatcher and Vickie exchanged glances. Online would be perfect. That meant they could access the documents any time and from any place.

"Thank you, sir." Thatcher nodded at the man.

Once Vickie had collected her bag, they stepped out into the October sunlight. "That's a welcome turn of events." She smiled.

"Although I'm a little sad that I don't get to use my card." Thatcher twisted his mouth into a grin. "Maybe some other time though, huh?"

"I still think your classes should be familiar with the LOC. Especially your upper-level ones."

"The LOC? Are you trying to flaunt your familiarity?" He laughed. "We're equal now. Both of us card-carrying members. Although maybe you're right about my classes."

"Of course I'm right." They paused at an intersection, waiting for the light to change.

"Hey, we're close to one of my favorite spots in DC. You've

shown me yours; now let me show you mine." He glanced down at her. "Unless you have someplace to be right now."

She tried to keep the surprise from registering on her face. All the time she'd spent with him, he'd kept her at arm's length. The fact that he even considered showing her his favorite place in the city was astounding. "Sure. I mean, I don't have anywhere to be. So lead the way."

They set out along Capitol Circle, the pathway that led around the Capitol. Thatcher walked so fast Vickie struggled to keep up with his pace. Finally, she couldn't take it anymore. "Hey," she gasped, stopping to put her hands on her knees. She tried to catch her breath. "I know I don't have anywhere to be, but what gives? Did you suddenly remember an appointment you were late for?" She tried to mask her panting.

He was a few steps ahead, but he stopped and turned around. "I'm sorry." He walked toward her, uncertainty painted on his face. "I guess I didn't realize how fast I was walking." He nodded at her legs. "Plus, my legs are a lot longer than yours."

Vickie's face flamed. "Thanks for pointing that out. Not only am I out of breath, but I also have short legs."

He stammered. "I. . .uh. . .I didn't mean that." He sighed. "I just meant that obviously my stride is longer than yours because you're so short."

Vickie couldn't help but laugh. "Really, stop." She held up a hand. "Have you always had such a knack for saying the wrong thing?"

Thatcher joined in her laughter. "Pretty much." He glanced at her, his brown eyes thoughtful. "Are you ready now? I promise to slow down."

"Yes. Let's go." They set out at a much slower pace, this time side by side. "Isn't that better?" she asked after a moment.

He shrugged. "Yeah, I guess it is. I think the words 'leisurely stroll' just haven't entered my vocabulary." He looked over at her. "Until now."

"Well then, I guess you should be thankful for my short legs." She giggled.

"Uh-uh. No way. I'm not getting involved in another conversation I'm sure to mess up." He pointed ahead. "And anyway, here we are."

They'd arrived at the west side of the Capitol where the large reflecting pool sat. It was similar to the one on the other end of the National Mall, near the Lincoln Memorial.

She followed Thatcher to a step and they sat down. "This is your favorite place?"

He nodded. "Surprised?"

"Considering your apparent hate for all things touristy, yes."

Thatcher motioned around them. "Not a lot of tourists over here. Check out the business suits and the joggers. Most of these are locals. The tourists are at the other end of the mall, near all the monuments."

"I guess you're right." She leaned back on her hands. "So what gives? What makes this your super-favorite place?"

"Look around. I love the energy. The majesty of the Capitol. The people rushing around on their way to something important. I guess I like to just sit here and take it in."

"Why do you have such an aversion to tourists?" Vickie glanced over and met his brown-eyed gaze.

He shrugged. "I feel suffocated by all the people. Especially in the summer. And in the spring when the cherry blossoms are in bloom." Thatcher nudged her. "Come on. Admit it. They get on your nerves a little bit too, don't they?"

Vickie shook her head. "Nope. First of all, remember what my job is? If there were no visitors, there'd be no need for park rangers."

"Okay, I guess I didn't think of it that way."

"But it's more than just job security. I love to see them, especially the families with kids. I'm thankful they're here to learn a little bit about American history rather than just at an amusement park or at the beach."

"What do you have against amusement parks and beaches?" he asked, his tone teasing.

She cut her eyes at him. "You make me sound like an ogre. And I'm not. I'm all for vacations full of sunburns and Mickey Mouse." She grinned. "But come on, Mr. History Teacher. I'd think you of all people would be happy there are still people interested in learning about the past. I mean, think about it. This is a city where you can learn about anything from the three houses of government to the Vietnam War. And in one stop, you can see Seinfeld's puffy shirt, Dorothy's ruby slippers, *and* Abraham Lincoln's stovepipe hat. Is this a great city or what?"

Thatcher nodded. "You've got me there." He looked thoughtful. "Are you up for a little field trip next Saturday?"

Why did she not like the sound of that? "What do you mean?"

"My poor dog needs to get out in the country and run. He's all cooped up during the day, and my backyard is kind of small." He shrugged. "I was thinking maybe you might want to get out of the city on Saturday. We could do our research from my fishing cabin. Especially now that we know we can access the Lincoln papers online." Thatcher grinned. "What do you say?"

Vickie couldn't think of a single reason why she should decline. She knew she was probably playing with fire, spending even more time with someone she was a little infatuated with. But she'd just have to get over it. It was research and nothing more. "That sounds great to me."

CHAPTER 33

It was only a forty-five minute drive to Thatcher's fishing cabin, provided there was no traffic. But once he, Vickie, Buster, and all their assorted items were loaded into his old pickup truck and on their way, it seemed like the trip was never-ending. "Buster, stop licking her." Thatcher leaned over and pulled the dog toward him. "Sorry." He glanced over at Vickie.

She laughed. "That's okay. He's just being friendly." She wiped the doggy kisses from her cheek.

"Sit, boy," Thatcher commanded, keeping his eyes on the road. At least driving kept him from worrying too much about what she must be thinking about his old truck. The inside was clean, but it was certainly not a luxury vehicle.

Buster promptly curled up between Thatcher and Vickie, his head resting on her leg.

Thatcher stretched his hand out to pat the dog, but it landed on top of Vickie's hand just as she was reaching out to rub the dog's soft fur. They both pulled back as if Buster was a hot stove. "Sorry," he said.

"Don't worry about it."

He was silent. Maybe it had been a bad idea to invite her to his cabin. But he'd been over to her house a couple of times now to work, and he didn't want her to feel like he expected her to always be the hostess. "We're nearly there."

"It's beautiful country. I love getting to see the fall colors."

A few minutes later, they pulled into the driveway of the rustic cabin. "It might not look like much from the outside, but I've completely renovated the inside."

Thatcher reached over and clipped a leash onto the dog. They climbed out and made their way up the path leading to the door. It was a beautiful fall day. The sky was a brilliant blue and the warm sun offset the cooler air.

He unlocked the door and took the leash off the dog. Buster went bounding through the house, happy to be at his second home. "After you," Thatcher said, holding the door open for Vickie.

She stepped inside. "These floors are beautiful." She entered the living room, her attention still focused on the gleaming floors. "I refinished them a few years ago. They're the original floors that my grandfather put in. I inherited the place from him." He motioned down the hallway. "Feel free to look around while I put Buster outside." The dog was already eagerly waiting at the back door. "I think he lies around all week, dreaming of the weekends when he can spend time out in the country."

She laughed. "Probably so."

Thatcher walked through the kitchen and opened the door. "Have fun, buddy," he called. Buster hit the backyard at full speed and began running laps around the yard. Thatcher grabbed a plastic bowl from the cabinet and began to fill it with water.

"This is a great place. Very manly. But still inviting." Vickie leaned against the door frame, watching him.

"I'm glad you like it." He'd never brought a woman to his cabin, at least one who wasn't related to him. Her presence made him a little uneasy. He set the water outside for Buster and came back in to find her running her hands along the wooden cabinets.

"These are great. Did you refinish them, too?"

He nodded. "The kitchen and bathroom are the only two rooms I made many changes to. I completely gutted both of them and started from scratch." He nodded toward the cabinets. "So those were custom made to match the wood of the floors."

"Cool. I wouldn't even know where to start with a renovation like that."

He gave her a sheepish grin. "Don't judge me for this, but I got hooked on those home-improvement shows a few years ago. So I got a lot of tips from watching them."

"I love those shows. But I'd never have the patience to do any renovations like that."

He met her gaze. "I've seen your place. It looks like it belongs in a magazine."

Vickie sat down at the kitchen table and pulled her laptop from her bag. "That's different. I didn't have to do much work. Decorating is easy."

"That's the way I feel about renovating. Looks like we'd make a good team if we ever ended up with an old house together."

She glanced up at him, obviously startled.

He cringed. Where had that come from? Was she afraid that he'd lured her out here under the guise of their project to work his masculine wiles on her and convince her to move into an old house with him? He backpedaled. "My sisters helped me decorate this place. I was completely out of my element when it came to selecting wall colors and fabrics."

"So do you have a large family?"

Thatcher crossed over and took the seat across from her at the table, silently thanking her for letting his foot-in-mouth moment go unmentioned. "Yeah. Two brothers and two sisters. I'm right smack in the middle." He looked at her. "How about you?"

"It's just me. No brothers and sisters. My dad's an only child, too. So no real family on his side. Mom has a sister, but she lives in Texas so I don't know my cousins very well."

He furrowed his brow. He'd grown up surrounded by family. "Sounds lonely."

Vickie looked up from her computer. "I guess. My parents traveled a lot when I was young. I practically lived at my grandparents' house, especially in the summer. My mom's parents." She grinned. "They were wonderful, though. My gramps passed away last year, and now Gram lives alone." Her face grew sad.

"I'm sorry."

She looked up at him. "He was a Christian. That always gives me comfort. For years and years, he never mentioned God. Gram would be at church anytime the doors were open. But for most of the time I was growing up, you couldn't drag Gramps there."

"So what changed?"

"He never really said. One Sunday morning about ten years ago, he got up and put on his best suit. Told Gram that it was time for him to straighten up. And he did. From that day forward, he gave himself to God. He'd pray before every meal and invite his buddies to services." She grinned. "He even started leading singing sometimes on Wednesday nights."

"Wonder what made him have such a change of heart."

Vickie sighed. "I thought about it for a long time, trying to figure out what it was that finally got through to him. Even though I don't know for sure, I suspect he knew all along that was what he should be doing. He was just too stubborn to do it. I think it had to be his own decision."

"I guess a lot of us are that way. We know the path we should be on, but sometimes we try out another one just out of stubbornness." Thatcher shook his head. "I can't tell you how many times I've stumbled along, trying to forge my own way, trying to totally ignore God. And you know what always happens?"

She met his gaze. "What's that?"

"Inevitably, I get knocked down. And there I am, calling out for Him to help me even though I've tried to veer off on my own."

Vickie nodded. "I understand that feeling. Lately I feel like my whole life is just serving as one big reminder that I'm not the one in charge." She grinned. "It seems to be a lesson I have to learn over and over again."

CHAPTER 34

Normally, Vickie was put off by men who wore what she considered to be feminine colors. But today, Thatcher looked especially cute in his faded jeans and buttery yellow polo shirt. So cute, in fact, that she had to fight the urge to flirt with him. But since flirting had never been her strong point, she managed to keep her one-liners to herself. At least thus far. "So are you ready to get started?"

Thatcher nodded. "I suppose so. How about if you start on the LOC online database, and I'll sift through some of these books?"

"Perfect." She quickly found the correct Web page and typed in some search terms. They sat in silence for quite some time.

"Whoa." Vickie sat upright. "Check this out."

Thatcher rose from his chair and came to stand behind her so he could see the screen.

She pointed to the section she was reading. "In 1928, *The Atlantic* published a series of letters between Abraham Lincoln and Ann Rutledge. It looks like they caused quite a stir." She felt his breath on her neck as he leaned closer to the screen.

"It looks like four months later they were proven to be

forgeries." He pointed out a section at the bottom of the screen. "What would possess someone to do that?"

"Money. Fame. I'd guess there are plenty of reasons. But the fact that those were fakes doesn't necessarily mean there aren't real ones out there somewhere. I'd guess that a lot of times rumors are based, somewhat at least, in truth."

He nodded. "Let's hope that you're right."

The ringing of her cell phone caused her to jump. She fished the phone from her bag. "I need to take this. It's my friend Kristy, and she's getting married next weekend."

"Sure." Thatcher walked back to his seat and picked his book up.

Vickie hit the button and greeted her friend. "Are you ready for a wedding?" She stepped outside onto the patio and sank into a green plastic chair. Buster came over and nuzzled her until she patted him.

"There's a tiny snag." Kristy's stress came through loud and clear. "It seems that late October is still hurricane season in the Gulf."

"Oh no. Is there one forecast?" Vickie had been so caught up with working and researching lately that she hadn't even thought to check the weather for her upcoming beach trip.

"I'm no hurricane expert, but I've certainly become familiar with the terms these past couple of days. Apparently there is something called a 'cone of uncertainty' that shows the potential places the particular storm can hit. And wouldn't you know it, Gulf Shores happens to be in the cone next week."

"What are you going to do?"

"Ace and I have talked about it at length. We've decided that even though there's a chance the storm will turn and hit somewhere else or even weaken before it reaches the shore, we don't want to risk it. We're going to have a church wedding instead. The church my mom attends is available, so I guess we'll do it there."

"I'm so sorry. I know you were looking forward to a destination wedding." Vickie was also sorry for herself. She'd really been looking forward to the beach.

"Can you go ahead and change your plane ticket for Tennessee? The good news is that since there's a storm forecast, it shouldn't cost you anything to switch it."

"Not a problem. Are you sure you're okay?"

"I don't know that I have a choice. I want to marry him next Saturday even if we have to do it at city hall. If I have to spend even another week planning the wedding, I think I will explode into a million pieces."

"I don't blame you." Vickie absently stroked Buster's soft fur. "Try not to worry about it. You're marrying the love of your life. It doesn't matter where it takes place."

"You're right." Kristy sighed. "Okay, I've got lots more calls to make. Let me know once you have your flight information. I can come pick you up from the airport."

"Sounds good. I'll call Ainsley later, and we can try and coordinate so you'll only have to make one trip."

Vickie snapped the phone shut. She could only imagine what it would be like to have to scrap wedding plans and start over with only a week to spare. Actually, that sounded kind of fun to her, but she'd always enjoyed planning and coordinating. Kristy, not so much.

"Everything okay?" Thatcher stepped out onto the patio. "You were just staring into space looking all lost."

Vickie laughed. "Everything's fine. Just a change of wedding plans." She filled him in on the situation.

"I'm sure it will go off without a problem." His mouth quirked into a grin. "I always say that most weddings are too much about the wedding anyway, and not enough about the marriage. And who knows? Maybe this little glitch will end up making it even more special." He sat down on the top step, and Buster ran over to him.

"Okay, that sounded suspiciously like something a secret romantic would say. I totally wouldn't peg you as that."

Thatcher drew his head back in mock horror. "What? I'm as romantic as the next guy."

She snorted. "Umm. . .that pretty much means not at all." She grinned. "Let's just say that the average guy isn't all that creative with his efforts."

"Maybe the average guy is just scared."

"Of?" She caught his gaze and held it.

He shrugged. "Looking stupid. Getting hurt. You probably know the drill."

"But if you never take a risk, you might never know how wonderful it could be."

"Are you speaking from experience or just hope?"

She bit her lip. "That's irrelevant." She sighed. "Anyway, I'm sure my friends will be fine." She managed a tiny grin. "And I can be a good maid of honor just as easily in Tennessee as I could have been at the beach."

He nodded. "I'm sure you can." He motioned toward the house. "You ready to get back to it?"

She stood and followed him back inside, kicking herself mentally. He'd given her the perfect opportunity for them to get to know each other better, and she'd changed the subject. But she hated to admit to him how inexperienced she was with love. The next time such an opportunity presented itself, she would have to take it. Vickie settled at her laptop and glanced over at Thatcher. He was already engrossed in a book. Any moment of getting to know one another had passed.

CHAPTER 35

The plane touched down right on time at Memphis International Airport. Vickie always selected a window seat when she flew, and by the time she'd booked today's flight, the only one available was at the back of the plane. She tried to stay patient, waiting on all the passengers ahead of her to collect their luggage and exit. She'd resolved to put Thatcher out of her mind for this trip. She'd spoken to him on the phone earlier in the week, and even though he'd sounded happy to talk to her about what was going on with her during the week and share a little about his week, he still managed to steer the conversation to their project. But she didn't want to dwell on her growing confusion. This weekend was about Kristy and Ace.

Finally it was her turn to deplane. She slid across the row of three seats and lugged her red bag over her shoulder. She'd checked her suitcase but liked to have a few incidentals with her just in case. She'd been the victim of lost luggage too many times.

Vickie made her way off the plane and into the busy airport. The thick smell of barbecue filled the air, and she inhaled sharply.

Only in Memphis would even the airport aroma be that of the local specialty.

Just as she descended the escalator that led to baggage claim, she spotted Ainsley standing next to the baggage carousel. It had been far too long since she'd seen her friend. She quickened her step. "Ainsley."

The tall young woman with long, wavy red hair turned at the sound of her name. Her face lit up in a smile. "Hi." She leaned down to give Vickie a quick side hug. "I can't believe we're finally here."

Vickie pointed at the baby sleeping in a sling that was draped across Ainsley's front. "And I can't believe you have a baby." She peered closely at the tiny form. "She's beautiful. I can't wait to get my hands on her."

"Thanks." Ainsley gently caressed the tiny form. "She's been a good little traveler. Just look at her sleeping, even through the noise." She motioned at the flower-printed sling. "And this thing has been a lifesaver. I can't believe I almost left it." She laughed. "If Faith is fussy the day of the wedding, do you think Kristy will get mad if I just wear it down the aisle, baby and all?"

"I think she'll be so happy to be marrying Mr. Right that she wouldn't notice if we wore our park service uniforms and did cartwheels at the reception."

Ainsley made a face. "You know how much she loves being a ranger. Let's not mention the uniform thing, lest she decide that sounds like a cute idea."

Vickie burst out laughing. "Oh, I see my luggage. I'll be right back." She rushed to the carousel and pulled her large navy suitcase from the moving belt.

"Do I need to carry your luggage?" Vickie asked once she was back with Ainsley.

"No. I think I can manage." She'd attached the diaper bag to the top of her suitcase and was able to roll them together. "I pack light, remember?"

"I didn't know how much extra stuff you'd bring for Faith."

"Not too much. Kristy's mom has an extra car seat and a few other things that she's used when her grandkids have stayed with her. She's supposed to have dropped off anything she thought I might use at Kristy's house."

Vickie pulled out her cell phone. "Speaking of which, have you talked to her?"

"No. I'd just gotten my luggage when you got here."

"I'll call to see how far away she is." She punched a button. It was only an hour and a half drive from Shiloh to Memphis. But knowing Kristy, she was probably running late. Especially considering all the last-minute things she was likely doing as a result of moving the wedding location. "Hi," Vickie said into the phone once Kristy picked up. "Two women, a baby, and a bunch of luggage are waiting anxiously for your arrival."

"Are you at the curb already?" Kristy asked.

"Nope, we're still at baggage claim."

"Then I'm one step ahead of you." Kristy laughed. "I just pulled up out front." She paused. "I don't think this security lady is going to let me leave my car though, so I hope you guys can manage."

"We'll be fine. Earth Mother has some kind of kangaroo contraption to hold her baby so her arms are free."

Ainsley burst out laughing. "You can only hope that when you get to be a mother you're as hip as me."

Vickie grinned and snapped the phone closed. "You're right." She paused to let Ainsley go ahead of her. "Besides, by the time I have children, you'll be an expert so you can tell me what to do."

"I don't know about that." Ainsley pointed to her right. "There she is."

They slowly made their way over to the SUV. Just as they reached it, Kristy jumped out.

"I'm so excited to see you guys," she squealed, hugging Vickie first and then Ainsley. "And look at this precious baby. She's perfect."

"Thanks," Ainsley said, grinning. "I kind of like her."

Kristy opened the back door of the vehicle. "I borrowed Sarah's car seat for you."

While Ainsley got the baby situated, Kristy and Vickie loaded the suitcases into the car. Five minutes later, they were pulling away from the airport.

"Thanks, you guys; I know changing plans was a hassle," Kristy said, once they were on I-40. "And I also know coming to Tennessee isn't the same as a few days at the beach would've been."

Vickie glanced over at her friend. "It works for me. I'm just glad to be together." She turned to the back. "And to finally meet Little Miss, of course." She settled back in her seat and the three of them kept up a constant stream of chatter about the upcoming wedding.

◎◎

Vickie looked into the full-length mirror in Kristy's hallway. They were about to leave for the wedding rehearsal at the church, followed by dinner at Hagy's Catfish Hotel, Kristy's favorite restaurant.

"You look great," Kristy said, stepping out of her bedroom.

Vickie had settled on a slim black skirt, red twinset, and black heels. It was dressy but not too much. "Thanks." She turned to look at her friend. "And so do you. You're every bit the beautiful bride."

Instead of her usual ponytail, Kristy's medium-length blond hair fell loose around her shoulders. She wore a dark purple wrap dress that accentuated her trim figure. "Are you sure? This is a little out of the norm for me."

"It's perfect." Vickie grinned. "Are you nervous?"

Kristy was silent for a moment. "You know, I thought I would be. I mean, you know how I am." She gave a tiny laugh. After being left at the altar, trust hadn't come easily to Kristy. But she and Ace had worked through those issues and seemed happier than ever.

Vickie nodded. "I know."

"But it's weird. I'm not nervous at all. Just excited." She leaned against the door frame. "And I'm so glad you and Ainsley are here." She lowered her voice. "How do you think she's doing, really?" she asked, nodding toward the living room where Ainsley was feeding Faith.

"It's hard to tell," Vickie murmured. "I'm hoping that once we get home tonight, we'll have time for a good talk."

Kristy nodded. "Definitely. It's my last single-girl night." The corners of her mouth turned up in a huge grin. "And you're not getting off the hook, either. We want to know what's been going on in your world." She raised an eyebrow at Vickie.

"What? There's nothing going on in my world."

"So you say. But you've been acting funny lately, and I want to know why."

Vickie looked at her watch. "You'll have to wait a bit for the inquisition. It's time to rehearse your wedding."

CHAPTER 36

Once she'd finished her fried catfish, Vickie glanced over at Ainsley, who cradled a sleeping Faith in her arms as she tried to eat her own dinner. Vickie held out her arms. "I haven't gotten to hold her nearly enough," she told Ainsley as she took the baby.

"I'm glad for the help." Ainsley smiled. "It's nice to have two hands to eat my dinner."

Vickie pulled the baby toward her and inhaled. "Seriously. They should bottle this smell." She closed her eyes and smiled. "Although I'm pretty sure my biological clock just went into fast-forward." She paused. "But don't tell my mother I said that."

Ainsley laughed. "Uh-oh. Is she giving you a hard time?"

"Let's just say that my thirtieth birthday was less than a celebration."

"Oh no." Ainsley took a sip of her water.

Vickie looked down at Faith's angelic face. "How do you not just stare at her all the time? She's so sweet."

"Thanks."

The clinking sound of a fork on a glass got everyone's attention. A hush fell over the room as Ace stood up. "We'd like to thank everyone for coming to be with us during this special time." He gazed down at Kristy and grinned. "Even though we could be on a beach right now, Mother Nature just didn't agree with that plan. But I hope everyone is enjoying their time here at Shiloh."

"We're just happy to see you two finally tie the knot," an older gentleman called out. Vickie thought he'd been introduced earlier as Ace's uncle. "It doesn't much matter where it happens."

Ace smiled broadly. "Our sentiments exactly." He held out his hand to Kristy and pulled her up from her seat. "We do want to thank our parents, especially, for everything they've done for us."

Kristy nodded and smiled her agreement. "Thanks to each of you. If you are here this weekend, it is because you are someone very important to us, and we are so blessed to have such wonderful people surrounding us as we begin a life together." She gazed at Ace, the love in her eyes apparent to everyone in the room, then looked back at the crowd. "The next time I see all of you, it will be the happiest day of my life."

Ace leaned over and gave her a spontaneous kiss on the cheek. Everyone applauded and cheered.

Faith began to stir at the noise. "Should I take her out where it's quieter?" Vickie leaned over and asked Ainsley.

"No. She'll be fine." She grinned. "She'll have to eat again soon anyway, so it's inevitable that she'll wake up."

As the crowd began to depart, Kristy walked over with her mother.

Nancy O'Neal's hair was as red as it had always been. She wore a gray pantsuit with a smart royal blue scarf tied around her neck. "Hi, girls," she exclaimed, hugging first Vickie and then Ainsley. "I wanted to come over and say hello and of course see this beautiful baby." She peered at Faith. "I can't believe you're old enough to be mothers. It seems like just yesterday you were college freshmen."

They laughed.

"It's been twelve years since our freshman year," Kristy said. "I guess we're not spring chickens anymore."

Nancy laughed. "What's that they say? Thirty is the new twenty?" She grinned.

"Sounds good to me." Vickie shifted Faith to her other arm.

"I want you girls to make sure Kristy gets some sleep tonight, okay?" Nancy asked. "You know how grumpy she can be when she stays up too late."

Vickie and Ainsley laughed. Kristy was notorious for falling asleep early. And her mother was exactly right. On the few occasions she managed to stay up late, she was a bear the following day.

"Don't worry, Mom." Kristy grinned. "I promise to be in bed by eleven."

"Good," Nancy said. "Now I know you three are going to get ready at your house tomorrow. I'm not going to bother you. But I do have a surprise."

The three girls looked at her expectantly.

"A limo is going to come pick you up to take you to the ceremony. I thought it would be fun for you."

Kristy grinned broadly. "You didn't have to do that." She paused. "But I'm glad you did."

"Did I hear someone say limo?" Owen Branam, a big burly man walked up, holding the hand of a petite woman. "That's awfully fancy for these parts." He chuckled. "Look who we have here. Two of my favorite seasonal rangers of all time." He grinned. Owen had been working as a ranger at Shiloh for the better part of twenty years. When Vickie, Ainsley, and Kristy had worked as seasonals, Owen had helped train them.

"Owen!" Vickie exclaimed. "It's so good to see you."

"It's been a long time," Ainsley piped up.

"I want you to meet my beautiful wife." He put his arm around the woman at his side. "This is Dorothy Branam. My better half."

Vickie remembered how devastated Owen had been several

years ago by the loss of his wife. Kristy had played matchmaker between Owen and Dorothy and had been ecstatic that it had worked out so well. "Nice to meet you, Dorothy." Vickie smiled and shook hands with the older woman.

"Kristy told me that you'd volunteered to hold Faith during the wedding," Ainsley said. "Are you sure you don't mind?"

Dorothy's blue eyes lit up. "Oh, I'm glad to do it." She patted Owen on the shoulder. "And Owen will be there to help me. He loves babies." She grinned. "I'll come and find you before the ceremony begins."

"I really appreciate it," Ainsley said.

"I told her she could just carry Faith down the aisle, but she said no." Kristy laughed.

Owen peered at the baby in Vickie's arms. "Well, she's prettier than any bouquet I've ever seen."

Ainsley beamed. "Thanks." Her hazel eyes sparkled.

"I'm going to go tell Ace good night." Kristy flashed them a grin. "I'll meet you at the car." She hurried off to where Ace was standing with his parents.

They slowly strolled out of the restaurant and onto the wooden deck that overlooked the Tennessee River. "The weather is perfect," Vickie proclaimed. Even though it was October, Indian summer was hanging on. "Tomorrow should be a beautiful day for a wedding."

"That it should," Ainsley agreed.

They made their way out to the car and waited on the bride-to-be.

◎◎

"Wow, I'm tired," Vickie said, once they were back at Kristy's. Ainsley had fed Faith and put her to bed in the borrowed Pack 'n Play, and everyone had changed into their pajamas.

Kristy sat on the couch, scrutinizing her eyebrows in a little round mirror. "I think my stylist took a little too much off the left brow." She turned to look at Vickie and Ainsley. "Do I look uneven?" She raised her eyebrows and smiled at them.

They burst out laughing.

"Put the tweezers down and step away from the mirror. You don't want to over-pluck and look funny in your wedding pictures." Vickie plopped down on the couch and took the mirror out of Kristy's hand.

"You don't look uneven, anyway. You're just paranoid," Ainsley said from her place in the recliner. "Hey, I meant to ask you earlier, where's your dog?" Kristy had a Cavalier King Charles Spaniel who'd been her constant companion for the past several years.

"I thought it would be best if Sam stayed with Ace tonight." She grinned. "Otherwise, he'd be in the guest bedroom, mesmerized by Faith." She laughed. "He loves babies."

"Speaking of babies. . ." Vickie's voice trailed off, and she looked at Ainsley. "How's mommyhood?"

Ainsley played with a wavy strand of her dark red hair. "I love it." She gave them a tiny smile. "I just love her so much. More than I ever realized would be possible."

"How's everything else?" Kristy asked.

Ainsley was silent for a moment. "Okay." She took a deep breath. "I don't want to spend much time on this. Promise?" She looked from Kristy to Vickie.

They both nodded.

"Things aren't going very well." She shook her head. "I don't know who I am anymore. Before Brad's death, I was on a specific track. I was a wife, and we were planning to be a family. And I guess I don't really know how to be me now that I'm not part of that."

Vickie didn't know what to say. She couldn't imagine how devastated Ainsley must be.

Ainsley took a breath and continued. "You don't have to tell me that I'm not moving through the grief like I should. I know it. It's like I know what I should do, but I don't feel like it yet. I haven't even been back to the Grand Canyon since the day of the accident. And you know how much I loved it there." Her eyes filled with tears. "I need you to hold me accountable for something."

Vickie and Kristy exchanged confused glances. "Anything. What is it?" Vickie asked.

"I've been putting off going to a grief counselor. Can you believe it?" Ainsley shook her head. "Because I didn't want to hear what they'd have to say. So I've decided to give myself a deadline."

Vickie raised her eyebrows in question. "A deadline?"

"This will be Faith's first Christmas. And because of that, I want us to stay at my parents' house for a little bit longer." Her hazel eyes filled with tears. "Every time I imagine the two of us moving into our own place and having a pitiful little tree and me being so sad. . .well, that's not the kind of first Christmas I want her to have. You know?"

Kristy nodded. "Of course. I think it's fine for you to stay there for as long as you need."

"That's just the problem," Ainsley said. "I'm afraid I might never feel like I'm ready to leave. So I've decided that by the end of January, I'm going to start talking to a grief counselor and see if maybe I can learn to be myself again." She looked at Kristy and Vickie. "But I might need you guys to gently remind me of my deadline." She gave them a tiny smile.

"I can put it in my planner right now." Vickie smiled. She never went anywhere without her daily planner.

Ainsley looked down and rubbed her finger on the stuffed arm of the recliner. "There's one more thing."

Kristy propped her feet up on the coffee table. "Name it."

"This one will entail a little more effort from you two." She glanced over at them. "But I need to know I have something to look forward to. So I was thinking that maybe we could plan a trip. Sometime next summer?" She looked at them expectantly.

Vickie sat up. "I'm in. Name the destination."

"Me, too. You know I'm always up for a trip." Kristy nodded.

"Thanks. I think that'll help me get through the next few months. Knowing I have fun plans. By then, Faith will be old enough for me to leave her with my parents for a few days." She looked glum. "You know how Brad and I used to travel any chance we got?"

Kristy and Vickie both nodded.

"Well, this is the first trip I've taken in over a year." She sighed. "I had to practically hog-tie my mother to keep her from coming with me. She wasn't sure I could handle it." She glanced at them. "And I'm not going to lie. Traveling with a baby wasn't easy." She paused. "And I had to muster up every ounce of courage I have just to get on the plane. Anyway, I'm hoping that planning a fun trip will help me get some of my life back."

"Of course. And by the way, you're welcome to come and visit me in Washington anytime you want," Vickie said. "I mean that. I have an extra room that is always available."

"Thanks." Ainsley smiled. "Okay. Enough about me and my problems." She glanced at Kristy and wiggled her eyebrows. "How about you, Miss Bride-to-Be? Any last-minute jitters?"

Kristy shook her head. "Nope." She paused. "Well, maybe a tiny one. But it isn't really a jitter—more like a bad memory." She picked up a pillow from the couch and pulled it to her. "I guess I keep remembering the feeling of standing there in my wedding gown, knowing Mark wasn't coming." She gave them a tiny smile. "And before either of you say anything, I'm not worried about Ace not showing up. I know without a doubt that he is the man I'm supposed to be with." She sighed. "But it makes me feel guilty somehow that he knows I almost married someone else. Does that even make sense?"

"I guess," said Ainsley. "But instead of feeling guilty, I think you should be thanking God that Mark backed out, even if it was difficult for you at the time. I'm certain that is how Ace looks at it."

Vickie nodded in agreement. "I've never seen any indication that Ace might hold that against you. So I think you should let go of that guilt." She met Kristy's blue-eyed gaze. "Besides, what you went through with Mark helped make you who you are today. After your relationship with him, you were able to take stock and figure out what you really wanted."

Kristy nodded. "True. It did help me put a lot of things into perspective." She gave them a tiny smile. "So you don't think I should feel guilty?"

Vickie shook her head. "That's all in the past. I think you need to leave it there." She remembered what Thatcher had said about learning from the past mistakes and successes.

"Amen," Ainsley said. "You said it at the rehearsal dinner. Tomorrow will be the happiest day of your life so far. You should just enjoy it."

"I guess y'all are right." Kristy turned to Vickie with a gleam in her eye. "And that brings us to you. Don't think you're getting off the hook."

"No doubt," Ainsley agreed. "You've been awfully evasive lately. What in the world is going on in DC?"

Vickie had known she wouldn't be able to avoid questioning. And her friends were right. She had been purposefully quiet lately about her personal life. "Okay, fine. I'll tell you." She bit her lip, trying to figure out where to start. "You know how I've been spending a lot of time with the professor lately?"

Kristy laughed. "Every time you call him that, all I can think of is *Gilligan's Island*."

A soft chuckle came from Ainsley's direction.

"Very funny, you two." Vickie couldn't help but smile. She'd taken to calling him *the professor* because it seemed less personal. Guess that plan hadn't worked. "Let me start over. I've been spending a lot of time with Thatcher lately." She sighed. "And I think I've developed a little crush on him."

Ainsley and Kristy exchanged a glance.

"What? What was that look?" Vickie sat upright.

"I was afraid you were going to say that." Kristy was suddenly enthralled with the remote control. She turned it over and over in her hand.

Vickie narrowed her eyes. "What do you mean you were afraid?"

"Hasn't he made it clear that this is just a professional relationship?" Ainsley asked gently. "We just don't want to see you get hurt."

Kristy drew her eyebrows together. "Like last time."

CHAPTER 37

Vickie felt like she'd been punched in the gut. She shouldn't have said anything about Thatcher. But they were her best friends. She wanted to be able to have everything out in the open. "What do you mean?"

"Remember Joe Calhoun our senior year?" Kristy asked.

"That was totally different. I can't believe you'd even bring him up."

Ainsley raised her eyebrows. "How was it different? You two worked on your senior history project together. You had a mad crush on him but never acted on it."

"You were hung up on him for like a year," Kristy piped up. "You drove me crazy with your planning and scheming so you'd run into him in the student center." She looked at Vickie. "Remember?"

Vickie wrinkled her nose. "That was a long time ago. It wasn't the same."

"Fine. Then how about that guy you met right when you moved to DC? The one who used to live in your building. What was his name?" Kristy asked.

"Kyle Dakota." Vickie's voice was low. "Do we have to go there?"

Kristy nodded. "I think we do. Because this is starting to be a pattern. You and Kyle were inseparable, remember?"

Vickie nodded. "Endless dinners, movies, and road trips. I remember."

"I never met him," Ainsley said. "But I remember hearing you gush about him. You were totally crazy about him."

"And I never told him." Vickie shrugged her shoulders. "He probably didn't feel the same way, anyway."

Kristy jerked her head up. "That's just the point. He was content to hang out with you over dinners and movies. He didn't mind asking you to pick up his mail when he was out of town. But he wouldn't step up and be a real boyfriend." She locked eyes with Vickie. "You spent way too many hours worrying about what he was thinking."

Vickie knew the words were true. "So what are you saying?"

"Just that I don't want you to get hung up on another guy who clearly isn't good for you. If you really like him, I think you should lay it out there. There's no reason to waste time on someone who doesn't reciprocate your feelings."

"Has he given you any indication that he might be interested in you other than just as a research partner?" Ainsley asked gently, shooting a tone-it-down glance in Kristy's direction.

"Well, we just talk a lot. About everything." Vickie couldn't help but smile. "He always seems really interested in what I have to say. And he remembers stuff that I've told him."

Kristy bit her lip. "I haven't met him or anything, but Vick, you deserve someone who wants to be with you bad enough that he's willing to scream it from the rooftop."

Ainsley giggled. "Okay, enough drama. She doesn't want someone to cause a scene."

"Well. . .I don't want them to cause *too much* of a scene. But a little one would be okay." Vickie grinned. "How about this? I promise not to get sucked into are-we-friends-or-more land again. Once our project is over, I think I'll have my answer."

"Maybe you should continue to go on a few dates here and there in the meantime," Kristy said.

"Oh, I don't know. The last couple of guys I've gone out with weren't my type." Vickie held a hand up. "Stop. Before you say anything, I'm not being picky. But seriously—one of them took me bowling, and you'd have thought we were competing in the Olympics."

Kristy laughed. "First of all, the thought of you at a bowling alley cracks me up. Please tell me you didn't wear heels and pearls."

"Jeans and tennis shoes, thank you very much." Vickie grinned. "But I did have on diamond earrings. To class it up a bit." She laughed. "And even better, I beat him on one frame. It was so funny."

"Did he merit a nickname?" Ainsley asked.

"Gold Medal Man." Vickie smiled broadly. "But not to his face, of course. Just in my head."

Kristy shook her head. "Your nicknames crack me up. Poor guys."

"Surely there's someone else besides Gold Medal Man. Any other prospects?" Ainsley twisted her long red hair up into a bun. "Besides the professor."

"Nope. I don't have time to meet anyone right now, anyway. Between working and learning all I can about Abraham Lincoln, I stay busy."

Kristy and Ainsley exchanged a glance.

"What? I'm serious. I'm not just saying that so I can have an excuse to spend time only with Thatcher." Vickie knew that wasn't completely true. She could probably find time to date if she really wanted to.

"Well. . ." Kristy's voice trailed off. "There's sort of something we have to tell you."

"And before you get mad, just know that it was for your own good," Ainsley said.

Uh-oh. This didn't sound good. "What?" Vickie furrowed her brow and looked at Kristy. "Spill it."

"You know how upset you were about turning thirty?" Kristy asked.

Vickie nodded.

"And then you went on what you thought was a date with Thatcher."

"Yes, I remember clearly. What?"

Ainsley rose from the chair and came to sit next to Vickie on the couch. "We talked about it and decided that maybe you needed some new guys to choose from."

"So we made you an online dating profile." Kristy winced. "Please don't be mad."

"Surely I didn't hear you correctly." Vickie was stunned. She turned to Ainsley. "Are you serious? I am out there like some kind of advertisement?" Her voice was shrill.

"It's very tastefully done. And the picture is fantastic."

Vickie was horrified. "A picture? My photo is posted on an online dating site? So just any random person I pass might be looking at me and thinking, *Hey, I saw her online and she needs a date*?" She threw her head back on the couch and closed her eyes.

"At least if someone passed you and recognized you, it would only be because they were also looking for a date," Kristy said.

Vickie let out a groan and sat up. "Seriously?" She turned to Ainsley. "And you? You couldn't stop her?"

"Hey. Who says it was my idea?" Kristy feigned hurt.

Ainsley let out a laugh. "I confess. I was the one who thought you needed a little nudge." Her face grew serious. "Come on, Vick. Just give it a chance."

Vickie shook her head. "I don't think so."

"Would it make you feel better to know that you're quite popular? You've got all kinds of guys just lined up wanting to chat with you or buy you coffee." Kristy laughed. "One even proposed marriage."

"Great. Just great."

"At least promise that at some point you'll log in and look the guys over. There's one pretty cute one who seems normal. He's some kind of consultant."

"I'll think about it if you two will promise to stop pretending to be me online."

Kristy and Ainsley exchanged glances. Kristy rolled her eyes in Vickie's direction. "Fine. We will stop. But you have seriously got to get out of your rut."

Vickie leaned her head back against the couch. Were her friends right? Was it time for her to move into a new realm of dating? It sounded good in theory, but she knew her heart wouldn't be in it. She was starting to think her heart was already spoken for.

"I'll get out of my rut." *One way or the other.*

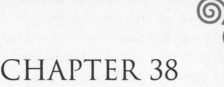

CHAPTER 38

T hatcher stood on the bottom step of the Museum of Natural History and stretched his calf muscles. Fall was finally here, and he loved the crispness of the air. He looked around. A number of people were milling about, but he was early enough that most tourists weren't out yet. He couldn't help but think of what Vickie had said about this city being a great one for students of history. He watched a family of four head into the museum, the smallest boy exclaiming about dinosaurs. Thatcher remembered going to see the dinosaurs when he was a boy, back when he'd thought he could take on the world and the good guys always won. Those were the days.

After one final stretch of his muscles, he set out at a brisk walk, crossing Madison. Once he got to the path that ran alongside the grass of the National Mall, he quickened his pace and settled into a comfortable jog. He could see the Capitol in the distance.

He wondered briefly what Vickie was doing. Getting ready for the wedding, probably. He glanced at his watch. Considering the time difference, it was probably too early for her to be doing that. Maybe she was still sleeping.

He was torn this weekend. Part of him wished she were in town so they could continue working. But on the other hand, it was good to get some distance. He had the sinking feeling they were getting too close. Last night, his fingers had itched to call her and tell her about an interesting tidbit he'd learned. And to see how her flight was. But that would've been inappropriate.

He made it to the Capitol reflecting pool and began to make a lap around the water. After his second lap, he slowed to a walk. He made his way over to the same step he'd sat on with Vickie a few weeks ago. That day, she'd really opened his eyes to the resources available in the city. He couldn't shake the thought of the sheer volume of historical spots and museums within such a small area. An idea had begun to form in the back of his mind, but he was still unsure which direction to take it. Maybe another lap or two would help. He rose and took off, this time at a faster pace, hoping it would help to clear his head.

◎◉◎

The loud rapping noise startled Thatcher. After his run, he'd gone by his office, the lure of work too great to resist. He'd been trying to make sense of a garbled freshman essay about the Revolutionary War for the past twenty minutes. "Yes?"

John poked his head inside. "You got a minute?"

"Of course." The very fact that John was on campus on a Saturday instead of at home with Megan and Avery clued him in that something was wrong.

John stepped inside, closing the door tightly behind him. "You're not going to believe this."

"Oh man. I don't think I want to know. Anything that makes you look like you just ate a lemon isn't going to be the kind of news I'm going to like."

"Clark Langston." As the name escaped from his mouth, John sank into the chair. "The man is despicable."

Thatcher sat up. "Okay, this isn't news. We've known that for a while." Thatcher had known it for the better part of twenty years, but that was beside the point. "What has he done this time?"

John shook his head. "I was playing racquetball this morning, and one of his grad assistants showed up."

"Yeah? What happened?"

John took a deep breath. "He's right outside. He wants to speak to you about something."

Thatcher raised an eyebrow. "Bring him in."

John stepped to the door and motioned at someone. A skinny guy slunk into the office, his eyes focused on the floor. "It's okay, Charley," John prodded. "Telling Dr. Torrey is the right thing to do."

Charley slowly raised his eyes to meet Thatcher's. He took a deep breath. "I'm one of Dr. Langston's graduate assistants."

"Charley Jones. I remember you," Thatcher said. "You were in one of my classes a couple of years ago." Thatcher remembered the kid as painfully shy but brilliant. "Have a seat." He motioned toward the chair John had vacated.

John stepped to the door. "I'm going to just leave you two alone. I need to get home." He nodded at Thatcher. "Call me later though." He closed the door behind him.

Thatcher directed his attention back to Charley. "So what's with all the secrecy?"

"Well, I'm taking a course this semester in ethics. We've been talking a lot lately about professional integrity." He hung his head. "I feel weird about telling you this, because I'm Dr. Langston's assistant. But I think it's my duty."

"You can tell me. And if you want whatever it is to remain between us, it will." Thatcher nodded at him encouragingly. "Go ahead."

"I'm not really friends with his other two grad assistants. They're roommates, so they, like, hang out and stuff." Charley wrinkled his nose. "Plus, they're Dr. Langston's buddies. I think he goes out with them sometimes to bars and all."

Thatcher wasn't the least bit surprised. Clark probably dumped his work on this kid and let the other two slide. He'd always played favorites.

Charley continued. "Anyway, the other day, I overheard them talking. They were laughing about Dr. Langston pulling one over on someone." He met Thatcher's eyes. "I think they didn't even realize I was in the room. The whole thing about there being some never-found Abraham Lincoln documents was just a big scam. Dr. Langston just wanted you preoccupied so he could clinch the department chair position." Charley shifted uncomfortably.

Thatcher was silent. He was such an idiot. He'd been had. "I know how hard it must have been to come and tell me this, especially since it meant you had to go behind your boss's back."

"That ethics class really made me think. What he did was wrong." Charley's face was suddenly fierce. "And if you want me to go tell the dean, I will."

Thatcher shook his head. "That won't be necessary. In fact, how about you just keep this between the two of us? I don't want life to be difficult for you because you chose to tell me the truth." He paused. "And you know, there was no real harm done. I've learned a bit more about Abraham Lincoln than I needed to, but that just makes me a better student of history. Right?"

Charley's face lit up in a smile. "I guess." He swallowed. "Thanks for being cool about it, Dr. Torrey."

"Don't give it another thought, Charley. Now go and enjoy your Saturday."

Charley quickly made his way out of the office.

Thatcher wanted to throw his computer through the window. But only for a second. Clark was a real piece of work, convincing those two grad assistants to be a part of his duplicity. Thatcher rested his head in his hands. That Clark would stoop so low surprised him, although he didn't know why. He'd been waiting for years for Clark's true colors to come out.

Once he got over the shock, he felt immense disappointment. But not because he wouldn't be revered in history. Nope. He'd never needed those kinds of accolades. Instead, he couldn't brush away the regret that he'd no longer require the services of his research partner.

CHAPTER 39

The limo would be arriving at any minute. Vickie checked her reflection in the mirror one last time. The dresses were perfect. Since it was a fall wedding, Kristy had decided on brown bridesmaids' dresses. She'd let them choose their own style. Vickie's dress was a beautiful strapless A-line gown that came just below her knees.

"That looks perfect on you," Ainsley said, stepping out into the hallway. Her dress was a full-length halter style.

"Wow." Vickie looked Ainsley up and down. "You look amazing." The dress looked perfect with her coloring. Her red hair was twisted into a simple chignon, but a few tendrils around her face softened the look.

"Can you tell I'm still carrying a little extra baby weight? Be honest."

Vickie shook her head. "No way. You look really great."

"Thanks. I've started doing yoga again but not regularly. I still feel a little like I'm in someone else's body."

A loud whistle sounded from the end of the hall. "I have the two most beautiful bridesmaids ever. No one is even going to look at me."

Vickie and Ainsley turned to see Kristy standing at the end of the hallway. Her dress was simple chiffon with an empire waist. "You look very Grecian," Vickie said, "like some kind of painting or statue."

"So gorgeous," Ainsley agreed.

Kristy's hair was curled, and it flowed around her shoulders. Instead of a veil, she wore a tiny rhinestone tiara. "What do you think?" she asked.

"Ace is going to flip out. You just look so beautiful." Vickie felt the tears well up in her eyes. If she hadn't made it to the ceremony yet and was already weepy, she hated to think of how she'd manage to listen to their vows. They'd written their own, too, which always made them more emotional.

"Better than the first time?" Kristy asked, uncertainty written all over her face.

"No comparison."

Kristy smiled broadly. "Thanks." She took a deep breath. "Okay. I think I hear the car."

Ainsley had slipped into the guest room and emerged with Faith in tow. "Let me put her in the car seat." She glanced at Kristy. "Sorry."

"Please tell me you aren't apologizing for having that angel with us today." She leaned down and kissed Faith on the cheek. "If she was a little older, she'd be my flower girl for sure."

Ainsley smiled. "Let's just be glad she isn't fussy. I don't know what we'd do."

"We'd deal with it." Kristy touched Ainsley on the arm. "She's part of you. I love her even if she is fussy. And I'm happy she's here to share this day. Someday I can tell her the story about how she got to ride in a limo with me on my wedding day."

Shades of relief colored Ainsley's face. "Thanks."

They headed out the door toward the waiting limo. The driver opened the back door, and Ainsley got in first with the car seat.

Vickie turned to Kristy. "You ready?"

"More than I ever thought I could be." They carefully climbed inside the limo, and the elderly driver closed the door behind them.

Vickie leaned her head against the leather seat. They'd stayed up so late last night, talking. She hadn't realized she was tired until she had a second to be still. She glanced over at Kristy. Her eyes were closed. Maybe she was saying a silent prayer. She looked so calm.

Ainsley leaned down and spoke to Faith in soothing tones. Vickie watched as the baby looked up at her mother with wide eyes and gave a gummy grin. She looked a lot like her dad, and Vickie couldn't fight the waves of sadness that the little girl would never get to know him.

The limo slowed to a stop. "That was fast." Vickie slid closer to the window and inhaled sharply. They were in front of Rhea Springs, Kristy's favorite spot on the park. And from the looks of things, a wedding was about to happen. "Kristy, you might want to check this out."

Kristy looked out the window. "No way," she whispered. "I wasn't paying attention to where we were going. I can't believe he did this."

Nancy opened the limo door. "How was the limo ride?" she asked, beaming.

"Mom, I can't believe this. Was this your idea?" Kristy asked.

Nancy shook her head. "Not at all. My only job was to tell you about the limo." She grinned widely. "But enough chitchat. Lots of people are waiting on you." She held out the box that was in her hands. "Here are your bouquets." She handed Vickie and Ainsley small bouquets of orange gerbera daisies tied together with brown ribbon the same color as their dresses. "Didn't these turn out nicely?" Kristy's bouquet was just like the bridesmaids' but with twice as many flowers.

"They're beautiful," Ainsley said.

Nancy leaned down. "Here comes Dorothy to take Faith."

Ainsley unbuckled Faith from the car seat. "Okay, sweet girl. Try not to fuss." Faith cooed and her pacifier fell from her mouth.

"Good thing you've got that clipped to her." Vickie laughed.

Dorothy stepped up to the open car door. "Oh girls. You look beautiful." She smiled. "I'm ready to take that precious baby for a bit." She reached into the car and took Faith from Ainsley. "Don't worry. I'll take good care of her."

Ainsley grinned. "Thanks. If she gets fussy, you might have to stand up and walk around."

"No problem," Dorothy said, as she and Faith walked off.

"Okay, it's my turn." Nancy tipped Kristy's chin upward. "You look beautiful, darling. I hope you enjoy your day."

Vickie's eyes immediately filled with tears. She should've found a way to sneak some tissue.

Ainsley grinned. "I'm guessing it's my turn next? Seems we're in unrehearsed territory. So much for me knowing how many steps it would take to get down the church aisle."

"I can't believe he did this." Kristy wore a dumbfounded expression. "Do you think he knows how much it means to me?"

"Of course. The fact that Ace set up your wedding on park grounds, knowing that was always your idea of a dream wedding, just goes to show you that he's the right man for you." Vickie grinned. "He gets a million cool points for this." She was really impressed. This was straight out of a movie ending. John Cusack couldn't have done any better.

Ainsley climbed gracefully from the limo. "See you at the front," she said, then walked around the car.

Vickie climbed from the car then turned around to help Kristy out. "No one will be able to see us as long as we're on this side of the car."

Kristy smoothed her dress. "Okay. Last chance." She twirled. "Anything out of place?"

"Nope. You're perfect." She grinned. "I'm going. Good luck." She slowly walked around the long limo. The closer she got to the altar, the louder Pachelbel's "Canon in D" sounded. *Someone must've brought a good outdoor sound system.*

Guests were seated in white wooden chairs on either side of a white runner that served as an aisle. Vickie paused until Ainsley finished walking up the runner and took her place up front. Ace stood at the end of the aisle, along with his groomsmen and the preacher. He was grinning broadly and nodded at Ainsley as she passed him.

Vickie took a breath and began walking slowly down the aisle toward the front. She smiled at Owen and Dorothy, who were so enthralled with Faith they were barely paying attention to what was going on around them. She nodded at Nancy, who was seated with Kristy's sister, Sarah, and her family. Finally, she reached Ace. The gleam in his brown eyes was enough to light a dark sky. As she took her place next to Ainsley, the first chimes of Wagner's "Wedding March" began, and the crowd rose.

Kristy stood for a moment at the end of the aisle, absorbing the scene. The shock of the location change still registered on her face. Finally, she began walking toward Ace. Her eyes never left his, even for a second.

Vickie knew it was a moment she'd remember forever. Kristy seemed to float along the white cloth runner. The late afternoon sunlight glinted off the rhinestones on her tiara.

Ace stepped forward to meet Kristy, taking her hand in his. "You're beautiful," he said softly.

Kristy handed her bouquet to Vickie with a wink then turned her attention back to Ace.

The preacher began the ceremony, welcoming the guests and thanking them on behalf of the groom for keeping the location a secret. The crowd chuckled.

"The bride and groom have chosen to write their own vows," the graying preacher said, nodding toward Kristy and Ace. "When you're ready."

Ace took a breath. "Kristy, I know you were probably surprised that I chose this location. But as soon as I realized we weren't going to make it to the beach, I knew this would be the perfect spot. I know how much you love the park—you practically grew up here. This land is equally special to me, not only because my ancestors fought here, but because it's where I found you." He paused. "I am the luckiest man in the world for finding you." He motioned to the scene around them. "I know that you've avoided this spot because of the memory it holds. But I want there to be a new memory. A memory of you, looking more beautiful than I've ever seen you look, and me, standing here with my heart in my hand, thanking God that He led me to you. I promise that I will always be by your side. I will hold your hand as we go on this journey, and I will try my best to make you happy." He reached out and brushed away a tear trickling down her face. "I love you."

Kristy was quiet for a moment. "This is the best surprise you ever could've given me. From this moment on, whenever I drive past Rhea Springs, all I will think of is you and this lovely day." She took a breath. "I never expected to find a love like the one we share. In fact, I never believed that kind of love existed. But you have been patient with me and let me trust in our love at my own pace. And today, as I walked toward you, I realized that I have no fear. I know there will be good times and bad times. I know that we will lean on each other and that together, we can face anything." She paused. "I love you with all of my heart."

Vickie brushed a tear from her face. It almost felt voyeuristic, to watch such a special moment between two people who loved one another so much. Even though she hated to think about herself, she couldn't help but wonder if she would ever find a love like that.

Ace and Kristy exchanged rings, and finally, the preacher declared them husband and wife. Ace gently pulled Kristy to him and planted a light kiss on her lips. The crowd stood and clapped as the recessional began to play. Vickie handed the bouquet back to Kristy as they began to make their way back down the aisle and to the waiting limo. It had been a perfect wedding, and as Vickie climbed into the limo, she knew she'd been part of something magical.

CHAPTER 40

Katherine felt more at home each day. Her grandparents were so thankful to have them there, it was almost as if they were trying to make up for all the lost Christmases and birthdays. But Mom wasn't getting any stronger. Katherine knew it was probably childish of her to hope that there'd soon be a marked improvement.

"How are your classes, dear?" her grandmother asked over breakfast.

"They're going pretty well." Katherine took a bite of toast.

Her grandmother peered at her. "Is your mom still sleeping?"

Katherine nodded. "I checked on her earlier. I think she had a long night."

They ate in silence for a moment.

"I wish there were something more that could be done."

Katherine jerked her head up at the defeated tone in her grandmother's voice. Was she the only one who wasn't giving up yet? "She's having some success with the alternative treatments. I really think the acupuncture is helping."

Her grandmother's eyes were sad. "I know those things are

helping to keep her comfortable." She reached across the table and patted Katherine's hand. "But honey, it isn't curing her. You know that." Her voice broke, and the older woman's eyes filled with tears.

Katherine bit back a sharp reply. This was the first time she'd seen actual emotion on her grandmother's face. "But I'm not ready to lose her." The words were out before she could stop them.

Her grandmother came around the table and pulled up a seat next to Katherine. She put her arm around her granddaughter. "Honey, neither am I." She sighed. "I've messed up so much over the years. Sometimes I think it's because out of all my children, Jane was the most like me. I wanted to teach her from my mistakes, but instead I drove her away." She brushed a strand of Katherine's hair from her face. "I know Jane has apologized and tried to take the blame for these past years, but a lot of it rests solely on me. I finally just let her go." She shrugged and met Katherine's gaze. "Can you believe that I spent a lot of years trying to pretend that she didn't exist? My own daughter. If I had it to do over, I would've stood outside her door in California, banging on it until she either let me in or had me arrested. And I wouldn't have come back home until we were on good terms." She leaned back in her chair. "But we don't get do-overs in this life. All we can do is try to make amends and move forward."

"I guess," Katherine said. She hadn't realized her grandmother felt any remorse. She'd heard her mother and grandmother talking, late at night, and she could tell they'd finally gotten their relationship mended.

"Katherine," her mother called from the sunroom. "Can you come here for a second?"

She stepped to the door. Her mom was in her usual spot on the chaise, looking out into the backyard. The large glass windows provided a great view. "Do you need something?"

Her mother patted the chaise. "Come sit with me."

Katherine pulled the door closed and went to sit next to her mother. "Is everything okay?"

"I'm tired. But I feel pretty good." Her mother sighed. "I wanted to talk to you about something."

Katherine glanced over at her mom. "What is it?" Each time she was summoned to her mother's side, she expected the worst.

"Have you thought anymore about your father?" She met Katherine's eyes. "About meeting him, I mean?"

"The thought has crossed my mind. But I'm just not sure. . . ." Her voice trailed off. "I guess I'm just having a hard time imagining what it would be like to know him. And I'm not sure what role I'd want him to play in my life."

Katherine's mom took her hand. "Honey, I know if I weren't sick, you'd probably be angrier at me about this whole thing." She shook her head. "But I hope I can be a good lesson for you. People make mistakes sometimes." Her voice was pleading. "We don't always do or say what we should, especially where the people closest to us are concerned. But I think you're going to need him."

"I've just gone all this time without him in my life. I guess I don't know where he'd fit now."

Her mother's eyes were pleading. "Promise me you'll think about it. I'd like to call him and tell him what's going on." She paused. "But I don't want to do that until you're ready."

Katherine shook her head, her eyes full of tears. "A little more time. That's all I need." She laid down next to her mom on the chaise and stared at the ceiling. Wasn't that what everyone needed? More time. Time to try and explain away the hurts and make peace. But Katherine had the sinking feeling that the hourglass was nearly empty.

CHAPTER 41

Vickie couldn't believe it. After Kristy and Ainsley had gone on and on about how Vickie always fell for men who were simply not interested, Thatcher had called her last night after the wedding. Thanks to that one gesture, she knew beyond a shadow of a doubt—or at least beyond a shadow of much doubt—that this time was different.

She'd wanted so badly to run into the room where Ainsley and Faith were sleeping and share the news. If it hadn't taken forever to get Faith to finally fall asleep, she probably would have. The episode of *Friends*, where they couldn't get the baby to stop crying after Rachel woke her up, was all that prevented Vickie from throwing caution to the wind. So she'd held it in.

Until morning.

And now that she'd spilled her news, Ainsley was giving her *the look*.

"Why are you looking at me like that?" Vickie semi snapped.

"I just don't want you to get too excited. A phone call and an offer to pick you up from the airport aren't exactly big commitments."

Vickie took a deep breath and counted to five. They'd had a wonderful time together, and she refused to ruin it by biting her friend's head off. Especially when she knew what a hard time Ainsley had been having. And especially when she knew that for Thatcher, those things did constitute a commitment. "I'll keep that in mind."

Ainsley laughed softly. "Okay, good." She deftly changed the subject, and they talked of other things until time to go to the airport.

During the flight, Vickie couldn't believe how easy it was to keep her mind off the fact that she hated flying. All she had to do was remember the shift that she'd heard in Thatcher's voice. He'd missed her. He was ready to take a step forward. She could tell.

She was glad her friends couldn't see her as she exited the plane and made her way to baggage claim. She was downright giddy.

She waited impatiently beside the luggage carousel. Thatcher was supposed to be outside at noon to pick her up. A glance at her watch sent her pulse rate soaring. *Five minutes till noon.* She took a breath. *Get a grip.* Finally, after what seemed like eons, her navy blue suitcase came out of the shoot. She snagged it from the conveyer and headed out the door, grinning when she saw the time. She'd only been waiting for five minutes. Perhaps patience was a lesson she'd never quite learn.

She spotted Thatcher's truck immediately and rolled her suitcase in his direction. Just as she got next to the truck, he looked up and grinned.

"Hey." He hopped out. "Let me get that." He grabbed her suitcase and effortlessly lifted it into the space behind the seats.

"Thanks." She climbed inside the truck. Once he was seated, she grinned. "And thanks for picking me up. I could've taken the Metro."

"I know what a pain it is to lug a suitcase on there." He glanced in her direction. "Besides, I needed to talk to you."

Vickie couldn't read his tone.

"And I have a surprise. Are you up for a little field trip, or do you need to get right home?"

She thought of the mountain of laundry waiting at home. And the cats, who'd probably been acting ugly to Dawn whenever she'd gone over to feed them. Neither of those things were enough to keep her from finding out what Thatcher's idea of a surprise might be. "A field trip sounds nice. I might need to grab something to eat though."

He nodded. "I think that can be arranged."

They sat in silence for a moment.

Thatcher merged the truck onto 395. "So, tell me about the wedding. Was it just as good as it would've been at the beach?"

"Oh, it was even better. Ace did the most amazing thing."

"Showed up?"

She shot him a glare. "Should I regret telling you about Kristy's humiliation?"

"Sorry. I couldn't resist." He grinned. "Go on."

"You know how I told you she'd always dreamed of having her wedding on park grounds?"

"Yep."

"Well, he surprised her with a ceremony there. It was awesome. We thought we were on the way to the church. He'd arranged for a limo to pick us up from Kristy's house." She glanced over at him. "But instead of taking us to the church, it took us to Rhea Springs." She sighed. "Isn't that romantic?"

Thatcher chuckled. "Are you getting all teary-eyed over there?"

"No. But I easily could. It was a very sweet gesture. I wish you could've seen it." As soon as the words left her mouth she wanted them back. "I mean, you'll have to see the video."

"Sounds like a plan."

"How about here? What's gone on since I was gone? Did you

secretly find the documents and forget to tell people I was your assistant?"

Thatcher was quiet. "We'll talk about work soon. But first. . ." He pulled into a parking space. "Check it out. I sure didn't expect to find a space so close."

"What are we doing?" Vickie looked around. They were on the National Mall.

"Come on." Thatcher hopped out of the truck.

She followed him. "Where are we going?"

"How about an afternoon at the Museum of American History?" He raised his eyebrows up and down. "Look at me being all touristy."

Vickie laughed. "I'm impressed."

Once they were through security, Thatcher grabbed a guidebook. "Okay, I know what I want to see."

"The puffy shirt?"

He grinned. "How about Abe's hat?"

They reached the escalator and stepped on. Vickie wavered for a moment between steps and toppled backward. She felt strong arms grab around her waist to steady her.

"Easy there." Thatcher's breath ruffled against her hair. "Let's try not to cause a scene at the Smithsonian."

Vickie felt the blush rise up her face, and she was glad she was in front of him so he couldn't see his effect on her. "Sorry. Escalators have never been my friend." She grabbed the rail and looked at him over her shoulder. "Once when I was a little girl, I decided it would be a good idea to sit down while I was riding."

"Did you get off unscathed?" he asked as they stepped onto solid ground.

She grinned. "I did, but my blue jeans didn't. My mother was furious."

He chuckled. "Just stick by me, and I'll protect you from the mean escalator."

"Thanks."

An hour later, they'd seen several bits of American history. "Why do I get the feeling you're buttering me up for something?" Vickie asked.

"One more exhibit, and we'll go. How about the original Star-Spangled Banner?"

"Lead the way." Vickie followed him into the exhibit. Along the right side of the wall, displays depicted the War of 1812.

Thatcher paused in front of a glass case. "Look at that."

Vickie stopped next to him and peered inside.

A charred piece of wood sat beneath the glass. "Part of the White House after the British burned Washington," Vickie read from the display board.

Thatcher let out a low whistle. "I'm beginning to think you were on to something. This place is pretty cool."

She grinned. "I don't like to say, 'I told you so,' but. . ."

They followed the corridor to the end and turned left into the next room. Vickie blinked. It was almost totally dark. She bumped against Thatcher. "Sorry," she murmured.

"That's okay." He guided her to a bench that ran along the right wall. "Let's sit."

They sat down opposite a glass wall that ran from the floor to the ceiling. Behind the wall was the gigantic flag, illuminated by special lighting.

"Wow." Vickie breathed. "It's amazing." The flag itself was huge. It seemed to fill the room.

"Incredible. I read in the guidebook that it's thirty feet high."

"Isn't this worth braving the crowds of tourists?" Vickie whispered.

Thatcher leaned close to her ear. "We're the only ones in here right now."

She grinned. "Pretend it's the middle of summer. There'd be a full house."

"I like it better this way."

Vickie turned her attention from the flag to the man sitting next to her. "Me, too," she said softly.

"I have to tell you something."

Her heart fluttered. "Anything."

And then out of nowhere, Thatcher reached over and took her hand.

CHAPTER 42

Thatcher stared down at his hand, intertwined with Vickie's. He had lost his mind. Impulsive gestures weren't common for him. So maybe this one could be chalked up to the darkness. Something about being able to hide in the shadows made him feel a little more open. "I have some bad news," he said quietly.

She stared at him in silence, her lips parted ever so slightly.

He squeezed her hand. "We've been had. Or more to the point, I've been had. You were just along for the ride."

"I'm not sure I understand."

Thatcher pulled his hand from hers. "I told you about Clark, my colleague who has it in for me."

She nodded. "Yes, but you never told me why."

He flinched. "That doesn't matter. While you were gone, I found out that Clark was never looking for the Lincoln papers. The whole thing was supposed to be a distraction for me. I guess Clark figured sending me on a wild-goose chase would keep me from concentrating on going after the chairmanship."

Vickie pulled her brows together. "I don't understand." She gave him a shaky smile. "I know I keep saying that. But why would he do that?"

Thatcher shrugged. "Revenge. Hate. Because he's a bad seed?"

"So this means. . ." Her voice trailed off, and she searched for his eyes in the semidarkness.

"It means that we can stop trying to find out new information about Abraham and Ann. It means that there probably weren't any letters to begin with."

She was silent for a moment. "That stinks."

He let out a soft chuckle. "That it does." He'd been disappointed to learn the truth about the Lincoln papers. But his was an even bigger disappointment. He lowered his voice. "It means that I should just pay you for your help and let you get back to your normal life."

Over the past few days, he'd convinced himself it was better this way. He wasn't good enough for a girl like her. It was better they part ways now, rather than spend more time together.

A family of four stepped into the flag-viewing room. A little girl pressed her face up against the glass wall. "Look at the flag, Daddy." She beckoned her father to her side.

"Come here, Macey. You're standing in front of those people," the woman said, struggling with a stroller.

"Oh, she's fine." Thatcher rose. "We've been here for a while. It's all yours." He turned to look at Vickie, who was still frozen to the bench. "Ready?"

She nodded and followed him from the exhibit.

"It seems so bright out here now," Thatcher said, blinking as they stepped from the dark room. "Is there anything else you want to see?"

Vickie shook her head.

"How about that lunch? Are you still hungry?"

"Food would be good."

A few minutes later, they were in his truck. "Do you mind if we just swing by somewhere and get you something to eat?" he asked. "I probably need to get home and let the dog out."

She glanced at him. "You know what? Don't worry about it. I just remembered I have a frozen pizza in the freezer." She gave him a tiny smile. "I think I should probably just fix that and go to bed. I'm really tired."

He nodded. "Okay."

They were silent for a moment.

"Um, listen. About the research. You never did tell me what kind of payment you wanted. I don't want you to feel like you wasted those hours." He looked at her out of the corner of his eye. She must be really tired, the way she was slumping in her seat. He'd noticed soon after they met that she almost always had perfect posture. But not today.

"Why don't we just consider you picking me up from the airport as payment? I really don't want to take any money from you." Her voice was sweet but firm.

"But think of all the time we wasted. I know we both had better things to do." He pulled the truck into a spot near her apartment.

She shook her head. "I learned a lot, actually. If it makes you feel any better, I can probably work some of the information into one of my ranger programs." She shrugged. "So it isn't like it was a complete loss."

He left the truck running and hopped out. By the time he got to the passenger side, Vickie was already lugging her suitcase from the truck. "I was going to do that." He motioned toward her suitcase.

Vickie tightened her grip on the handle. "I've got it. No problem." She pushed her carry-on bag over her shoulder. "Thanks for the ride." Vickie stood just outside the door to her apartment building, watching him.

"Take care," he said, climbing back into the truck.

As he pulled into traffic, he glanced in the rearview mirror. Vickie was still standing on the sidewalk, clutching her luggage and watching him drive away.

CHAPTER 43

Katherine had finally somewhat given in to her mother's request. She might not have called her dad, but today she was parked outside of his place. In fact, she'd been parked there nearly every day for the past week, watching.

"I am officially a stalker," she said to herself in the mirror. She glanced around the quiet street. "And his neighbors are probably getting worried about the strange girl who sits in the car every day, talking to herself."

Not only had she taken to staking out his house, she'd also learned some of the places he frequented. The little neighborhood grocery store, a bookstore around the corner, and some kind of Mexican dive. She'd come close to being seen at that one, because the lure of chips and salsa was too much. When the bubbly waitress had tried to seat her at the table next to her dad, Katherine had drawn the line. "Can you put me over there?" she'd asked, pointing to a table across the restaurant. That one had been close. Not that she thought he'd recognize her. But she might not be able to hold it in. And a crowded restaurant wasn't exactly the kind of place anyone would want their long-lost daughter finally making contact.

A man jogged past her parked car, and she felt him glance at her. Maybe he was some kind of neighborhood watchman. Right. Out with his ferocious poodle. She grinned. Muscular men and poodles seemed like an odd combination.

The faint strains of her favorite Sugarland song sounded from the depths of her purse. She dug the phone from the bag. "Hello."

"Katherine, dear, are you nearly home?" The worry was evident in her grandmother's strained voice.

She hadn't told anyone she was secretly following her father. She knew they wouldn't understand. Mom's patience was getting thin, but so far, she'd kept her promise not to contact him. "I'm on my way." She put the car in DRIVE and headed west.

The silence on the other end was deafening.

"Grandmother, is something wrong?"

"Don't be alarmed."

Her heart sank into her stomach. Ever since her mom had gotten sick, random phone calls and what they could mean were terrifying. "Is Mom okay?"

"She's been admitted to the hospital. Your grandfather is with her. They were already on their way when I got home from the salon or I'd have gone with them. But I thought if you weren't too far away, you might want to ride with me."

"No. I'm going straight there." She hung up the phone, not even bothering to say good-bye. *Please, Lord. If it's her time, please at least let her hang on until I can get there.* Her standard prayer. At least her grandfather was there. When they were in California, every time Mom had taken a turn for the worse, Katherine had been consumed by how alone she felt. Maybe having family around would lessen that feeling.

But all the family in the world couldn't make her mom well.

Katherine willed herself not to speed. She wouldn't do anyone any good if she had an accident. She took a deep breath, trying to prepare herself for what lay ahead.

"Surprise," Katherine said three days later as she burst into the hospital room and flopped onto the end of the hospital bed. "Check me out, skipping classes." She grinned.

Even in sickness, her mother could still speak volumes with just a glance. "I'm none too happy about that, young lady."

"If you feel like reprimanding me, does that mean you're feeling better?" Katherine asked hopefully.

Her mother's mouth broke into a smile. "Even though you should be in class, I'm happy to see you. And the doctor was in just before you got here. It looks like I can head home today."

Katherine leaned in for a hug. "I'm glad. I was worried." She hated to tell her mother how empty it felt at her grandparents' without her there. Having those words out in the open would only cause pain. For both of them.

"You know, Thanksgiving break is right around the corner."

Her mother nodded. "I know. I think your grandmother has a big family feast planned. Are you up for that?"

"I think the more important question is are you up for it?" Katherine met her mom's gaze.

Mom nodded. "I'm looking forward to it. Sure, it will take a lot out of me, but it's been a long time since my whole family has been in one place." She peered closer at Katherine. "What's going on?"

Katherine shook her head. "Nothing."

"I know that look on your face. It's the same one you wore when you were ten and you slammed your bike into Mrs. McClesky's car. You're hiding something."

The woman seriously had a gift. "It's nothing big." Katherine scowled.

Mom's face lit up. "I knew it." She laughed. "Look at me. In the hospital, hooked up to an IV, and I'm still not off my game."

She leveled her gaze at Katherine. "Spill it."

"Well, I've sort of been following my father."

Her mother narrowed her eyes. "What?"

"I've been following him. You know, seeing where he lives and works and how he acts."

"Okay. This I wasn't expecting. Has he noticed you?"

Katherine grinned. "No, but I'm pretty sure some of his neighbors think I'm about to stage some kind of burglary."

"Just out of curiosity, how does he look?"

"I don't know. Just normal, I guess. Kinda old."

Now it was her mother's turn to scowl. "He's my age."

Katherine grinned sweetly. "I was kidding."

"So does this mean you're getting ready to meet him?" her mother asked hopefully.

"I'm almost there. Not quite. But soon."

Her mother gave her another look.

"And you'll be the first to know, I promise."

Mom laughed her beautiful, tinkling laugh, and Katherine wished she could bottle the sound and carry it with her forever.

CHAPTER 44

D o you want to know what kind of an idiot I am?" Vickie wailed.

Dawn calmly poured steaming hot water into a teacup. "You're not an idiot." She stirred a touch of honey into the chamomile tea and set the cup in front of Vickie. "This is my best attempt at comforting you with something I've made." She paused. "Unless you're in the mood for popcorn."

Vickie managed a tiny smile. "That isn't necessary. But I appreciate the gesture."

"I'll just be honest with you." Dawn poured water over her own tea bag and came to sit across from Vickie at the table. "I've been dating for more than half of my life." She winked. "I know that's hard to believe, right? And I have to say that this guy is a mystery to me."

"Get in line," Vickie mumbled. She hadn't even bothered to call Ainsley yet to tell her she was right.

"Let's try and figure it out. So he calls you sometimes."

Vickie nodded. "Yes. He even called me while I was in Tennessee."

"And on those calls, is he all business?"

"Not entirely. Sometimes he's really chatty, telling me funny stories about his students or asking me all about my week." She shrugged. "But then sometimes he's all business and just wants to discuss Abraham Lincoln."

"Okay. What about the time you guys have spent together in person? Was it mostly business? Or pleasure?"

Vickie made a face. "That's just it. I'm not really sure. I mean, I have a great time with him. We have a lot to talk about and all. And we have fun, you know?"

Dawn shook her head. "No sense. I think he just has no sense." She grinned.

"When he told me the project was a scam, he grabbed my hand. Why would he do that?"

"It sounds like there isn't much rhyme or reason to anything he does."

"But then he turned around and told me how we'd both wasted our time and tried to pay me for helping." Vickie wrinkled her nose. "That makes it seem like it was just business. Period." She let out a heaving sigh. "I went and did it again."

"What? Now you're Britney Spears?"

Vickie grimaced. "Funny." She took a sip of hot tea. "I guess it just doesn't make sense. I know he likes spending time with me. I can tell."

"I hate to be Dawn the Downer, but maybe his liking to spend time with you isn't enough. I think you need to let him go." She held up a hand. "I know you don't want to hear it. But he drove off and left you standing on the sidewalk with a huge suitcase." Dawn gave Vickie a pointed look. "That does not bode well."

"You're right." Maybe she wouldn't bother to tell Kristy and Ainsley about this. She could just move on and pretend he didn't exist. Yeah, right.

"How about trying the online thing? You've already got a

profile," Dawn said in a singsong voice.

"It's easy for someone who just found the love of her life to give out dating advice, huh?" Vickie grinned. "I shouldn't have told you about the profile. To tell you the truth, I haven't logged on there yet." Mainly because her cheeks still flamed at the thought of her having been out on display for a few months without even knowing it. From now on, anytime someone told her she looked familiar, she knew she'd panic that they'd seen her online dating profile.

A sheepish look flashed across Dawn's face.

"What?" Vickie sat up, glad to focus the attention on someone else. "Is everything okay with Jason?"

Dawn's face turned pink. "Everything is more than okay. I hate to tell you this, especially with the way things have gone these past few days."

"Ignore me and my pity party. Tell me what's going on."

Dawn grinned. "You, of all people, are going to think this is a horribly unromantic story. But the other day, Jason and I had lunch in Georgetown. After we were through, we were just walking around, looking at all the shops. We came to a jewelry store and I was looking at some earrings that would be perfect for the upcoming holiday party season. But the next thing I knew, Jason was on one knee."

Vickie's mouth dropped open. "Right there on the street?"

"Well, the sidewalk." Dawn grinned. "I know that doesn't rank on your romance scale, but I thought it was pretty spectacular."

"So you said yes?"

Dawn nodded. "I sure did. We went right into that store and picked out a ring." She held up a ringless hand. "It's being sized today, but I'll stop in and show it to you later."

"I'm speechless." Vickie was very happy for her friend. But Dawn had always been the one person she could count on to be single, despite her many suitors. It was almost like the whole world was pairing up and leaving Vickie to fend for herself. "Congratulations."

"Thanks. I know it's sort of quick. We've only been dating for four months. But like I said earlier, I've been dating for half my life so I know what I'm looking for by now. I think I knew almost immediately that he was the one; I just had to make sure he felt the same way."

Vickie knew that technically she'd been dating for half of her life as well. Her first date had been at age fifteen. Now she was thirty. That was not a comforting thought. Especially considering she didn't seem to have gleaned the lessons from a half-lifetime of dating that Dawn had.

"I'm glad that's off my chest. It was all I could do not to tell you as soon as I walked in, but then I saw your very sad face and those awful flannel pajamas. And I knew right then that it was best that my ring was at the jeweler today."

"I'm thrilled for you." Vickie grinned. "Besides, maybe Jason has a friend."

Dawn laughed. "I've already scoped them out. I can promise you that none of them would meet up to your expectations."

"I'm not that bad."

"Too hairy, too short, doesn't use good grammar, talks while he chews, too competitive, not smart enough, too smart. . .should I go on?" Dawn regarded her with a raised eyebrow. "Because I'm pretty sure that was just the last year alone."

"I took the last several months off, though."

"Only because you were preoccupied with Thatcher. Believe me when I say that none of Jason's friends would be up to your standards."

"I don't think I'd want a fix-up right now, anyway," Vickie said. Because the last thing she needed was yet another bad date.

CHAPTER 45

Thatcher sat in his office, his head in his hands. Ever since he'd dropped Vickie off at her apartment three days ago, all he could think about was how pitiful she looked, standing there with her suitcase—like she was waiting for a train that would never come. When he closed his eyes, that's what he saw. Her standing there, watching him drive away. Why hadn't he turned around and insisted on carrying her suitcase inside the building? Because he'd been so distracted by the fact that he was leaving her. Not a good excuse. But it was all he had.

He felt like his insides were being ripped to shreds. It was quite possible that over the past two weeks, stock in Rolaids had gone sky-high, all because of him.

On the one hand, he missed her. But on the other, he was certain she'd never be able to understand all the things that had happened that led him to live his life as a loner. The truth was he was terrified of letting her get close enough to find out.

Amanda's signature knock brought him back to reality. "Come in," he called.

"Just wanted to check in to see how your presentation was

coming. Have you come up with a plan to knock their socks off at the January meeting?"

He shook his head. "Not really. I thought I might have something in mind, but I've scrapped it."

She plopped down in the chair across from his desk. "Run it by me. Maybe I can help."

"I think a large part of my plan will center on our using the local resources available to help make history come alive. Implementing things like field trips and such, even if some of them take place outside of class time. There are a lot of really interesting things to do and see right in our own backyard." He flinched. "I guess I didn't really think about it until recently."

Amanda nodded. "We're probably so used to those things, they don't have the impact they would on someone who isn't from here." She met his gaze. "Which is a good majority of our students." She chewed on her pencil for a moment. "I think you're on to something here, Thatcher. I certainly think it would make Dean White happy." She stood and stepped to the door. "Let's hope so." Thatcher turned his attention back to the essay he'd spent the last half hour trying to read. His gaze wandered to the business card Vickie had given him soon after they met. The park service logo seemed to beckon him.

Suddenly, the answer to both of his problems was solved. Excitement bubbled inside him as he set out for the National Mall.

☙◈❧

An hour later, Thatcher was en route to the Jefferson Memorial. A quick stop by Survey Lodge, and he'd found out where Vickie was stationed. The young ranger working the desk was apprehensive at first until Thatcher explained that he and Ranger Harris had been working on a research project together. That seemed to ease the young man's mind that Thatcher wasn't just a stalker on the prowl for pretty young park rangers.

Thatcher finally found an empty parking space on Ohio Drive. He was still going to have to walk quite a distance. He hopped out of the truck and pulled his tweed jacket closed. It was just about time to start wearing his heavy winter coat.

He crossed the inlet bridge where the Potomac River ran into the Tidal Basin. In the spring, this spot would give a fantastic view of the cherry blossoms in bloom. But today, it was just windy and cold. He rounded the corner and the Jefferson Memorial came in plain view. At least it didn't have as many steps as the Lincoln Memorial.

Thatcher took the steps two at a time until he was at the top. He passed between two of the large columns and into the domed memorial. He stared up at the huge bronze statue of Thomas Jefferson. It had to be nearly twenty feet tall.

"You know, the Library of Congress bought Thomas Jefferson's entire book collection after the library's books were destroyed during the War of 1812," a familiar voice said from behind him. He'd know that soft Southern drawl anywhere.

Vickie's smile seemed a little strained as he turned to face her. But at least it was a smile. More than he deserved after he'd left her on the curb with her suitcase. "You really have turned into a fan of all things touristy."

He grinned. "I blame you." He motioned toward a stone bench. "Can we sit for a second, or does that go against ranger mode?"

Vickie looked around. "There aren't too many people here right now, and I'm due for a break." She started toward the bench. "But only for a minute."

"That's fine." A minute was better than nothing.

Once they were settled onto the bench, Thatcher was unsure again. What if she felt obligated? He sighed. It was a chance he'd have to take. "I have another business proposition for you."

She wrinkled her brow. "I hope this one is going to be more legit than the last one."

"I assure you, it is." He explained the presentation he'd been assigned to put together and his idea for integrating the local area's historical resources into curriculum. "What do you think?"

"I think that's a wonderful idea," she said. "Do I get any credit for it?"

"Tons. And the truth is, I was wondering if you would lend your expertise." He met her gaze. "It would mean a few more weeks of working together." He grinned. "I know you were probably relieved to be rid of me, but my offer to pay you still stands."

Vickie was quiet for a moment. Finally she nodded. "I'll help. Just let me know when and where."

"Are you sure? You don't look too sure." He was beginning to regret his decision to ask for her help.

"I'm sure." She smiled. "Really, I am."

He wasn't convinced but decided to go along. "Okay, how about this weekend? Maybe I'll pick you up Saturday? How about 2:00? We can scope out some of the sights that I'll include in my presentation."

"Are you going to do some kind of PowerPoint?"

He grimaced. "I hate that kind of stuff."

"But you know, you could include pictures and video. . .I think it would really help highlight your ideas."

Thatcher let out a sigh. "You're right. I guess this means it's time for me to buy a digital camera, huh?"

"And a cell phone, but we'll save that for another day." She grinned and stood up. "I'd better get back to my station. See you Saturday."

"Looking forward to it," he called as he headed toward the truck. And he was. Maybe not the picture-taking, presentation-putting-together part. But the rest of it would be nice.

CHAPTER 46

W ell, is married life all it's cracked up to be?" Vickie asked, curling up on the couch. It had been one long day. Or week. Really, it had been a long month.

"It is fantastic." Kristy's glee came through the phone line. "I don't want to gush too much, and I promise I'm not going to be one of those annoying newly married girls who keeps saying 'my husband' blah, blah. But it pretty much rocks."

Vickie laughed. "Good. You know I've always hated those girls." Vickie and Kristy had spent years poking fun of their recently married friends who suddenly came down with my-husband syndrome. Every time Vickie listened to one of them replace the guy's name with his new title, she wanted to stop them. *I was at the wedding. I know he is your husband. His name is Bob. You have called him Bob for the past five years. Please just refer to him as Bob.*

"I'm only going to say this to you," Kristy said. "Not Ainsley, because I don't want to upset her." She sighed. "But knowing I get to go home to my best friend every night makes my whole life better. It's like I know there's nothing we can't face together. Does that sound way too mushy?"

"Not at all. I think I'd be a little worried if you didn't feel that way." Vickie paused. "But. . ." She trailed off. "Now, this is only a suggestion, but if you don't mention your marriage to Ainsley, she's going to know you're doing it on purpose. And I honestly think that will make her feel worse. She'll be glad to hear about your happiness." Vickie and Ainsley had gotten the chance to visit more after the wedding, and she sensed that her friend, although clearly still grieving, was starting to come out of the cloud she'd been under for the past year. The only worry with that was that some of the numbness might wear off and make the hurt more painful. Only time would tell.

"You're probably right. I think your talent is wasted as a park ranger. You should totally replace Emily Post or whoever it is that gives out advice."

"I think Emily Post is about good manners. Maybe you're thinking of Abby?" Vickie laughed. "If only I could give my own self good advice. I'm sure that's the real mark of a good advisor."

"Uh-oh. Is the professor misbehaving?"

Vickie filled Kristy in on the latest and waited for her reaction.

"Hmm. I don't know, Vick. I still say he runs hot and cold too much for my liking. It's almost like he pulls you to him and then pushes you away." She paused. "Do you think he has a split personality?"

Vickie laughed. "No. His personality is fine. I think he just doesn't know what he's doing. I don't think he's been in many relationships."

"How do you know? Have you talked about it?"

"Well, no. Why? Do you think we should?" Vickie inspected a broken pinky nail. She needed to schedule a manicure soon or else she was going to start looking completely unkempt.

"I think it's time to find out what kind of baggage he's carrying around. You know, the figurative kind. That might explain his behavior."

Vickie sighed. "But then I'll have to tell him I've never been in a serious relationship."

"True. But you are the queen of first dates." Kristy giggled.

"Thanks a lot."

"Sorry." Kristy paused for a moment. "But seriously, if you think this guy has the kind of potential you seem to think he does, then he needs to know that anyway. Honesty is the way to go. Always."

"I guess you're right."

"Um, didn't I just have my dream wedding? Let me at least consider myself an expert in happily ever after for a few days."

Vickie grinned. "Fine. He's picking me up Saturday. I promise to try and find out the dirt on him."

"I love it when you're armed with a plan. I can always count on you following through because it will be something you get to check off of your mental to-do list."

"Yep. And number one on my list for Saturday: Find out about Thatcher's past."

Saturday afternoon, Vickie threw her phone and a notepad into her bag and headed downstairs to wait for Thatcher.

"Hold it right there." Dawn's voice stopped her in her tracks.

Vickie turned, a grin on her face. "I'll bet I know what you want to show me," she said.

Without a word, Dawn held out her left hand.

Vickie let out a tiny squeal. "Oh, it's so beautiful." And it was. A simple round solitaire in a platinum setting. There was nothing better than classic jewelry. The size of the diamond wasn't too shabby, either.

"Thanks." Dawn beamed. "You know the best part? Jason

actually found this one. We went into the jewelry store and were looking at all the rings. He spotted this one and declared it was the one. And he was right." She looked Vickie up and down, as if seeing her for the first time. "Where are you headed, dressed all cutely like that? That isn't a normal Saturday errands-to-run kind of ensemble."

Vickie glanced down at her outfit. She had made an extra effort. She wore a gray sweater dress with a low-slung black belt. Black tights and slouchy black boots completed the look. "Thatcher is picking me up." She grinned and filled Dawn in on his plea for assistance.

"Is that right?" Dawn's blue eyes twinkled. "My guess is that he was already looking for an excuse to see you and it just so happened he could chalk it up to work." She waggled her eyebrows. "Have fun."

"Thanks," Vickie called as she took the final flight of stairs. She spotted his truck pulling into a space just as she exited the building.

They spent the better part of two hours traipsing around DC. They visited Ford's Theatre, the Museum of Natural History, and ended up at the National Archives.

They climbed back in the truck, exhausted. "I think I could put together an entire semester—no wait, make that an entire year—of studying just sites that are right here," Thatcher said, starting the truck.

Vickie nodded. "And that's not counting all the places in the surrounding area. There's Arlington."

"Oh yeah. That's a given."

"Mount Vernon isn't far. And then there are a number of Civil War battlefields around." She smiled. "I remember when I was in college, studying abroad for a semester. One of the things that sticks out the most was that before we traveled as a group to Rome, our professor had us draw names, places, or items out of a hat. Whatever we drew, we had to prepare a little report on and give it when we were on the spot."

"What was your assignment?"

"The Arch of Septimius Severus. It's in the Roman Forum." She laughed. "See? Your students will remember your hands-on approach to history years after they've graduated."

He looked over at her. "How many years has it been?"

Vickie made a face. "Not as many for me as for you."

"Touché." He grinned. "Hey, are you up for working at my place?"

"I've got nowhere to be today, so that sounds great." She had to admit, she was a bit curious about where he lived. Sure, she'd seen his fishing cabin. But that wouldn't be as telling as his home. "Where do you live? I don't think you've ever said."

"Columbia Heights. Just north of Dupont Circle."

Fifteen minutes later, Thatcher parked along a residential street lined with townhomes and large trees.

"This looks like a quaint neighborhood."

Thatcher grinned. "That's exactly what I thought when I first saw it. Wouldn't this be a quaint place to live?" he said in a mock British accent.

Vickie laughed and followed him up the stairs that led to a nice-sized porch. "I like your porch swing," she said.

"I wish I could take credit for it. It sort of came with the house. But I do enjoy it, especially when the weather is pleasant."

She looked up at the two-story townhome. "This is really nice."

"Thanks. I've been here for the past seven years. Before that I rented. Once I turned thirty though, I figured it was time to buy."

"And here I thought I was the only one feeling the pressure to grow up."

Thatcher opened the door and ushered her inside. Buster popped up from a red dog bed near the couch. He bounded over to Vickie, wriggling with excitement.

"Hi, Buster boy." She scratched behind his ears.

"Let me put him out back," Thatcher said. "Feel free to look around."

The open floor plan made the place seem much larger than it had appeared from the outside. The living room, dining room, and kitchen blended together, forming what seemed like one large space separated by furniture rather than walls. "This is a really great place," Vickie said, once Thatcher returned.

He grinned. "Once again, the decorations are compliments of my sisters."

"They have great taste."

Thatcher nodded. "They would love you."

She stared at him. Was he hinting that he wanted her to meet his family? Surely even Kristy and Ainsley would see that as a good sign, right? "I'm sure I would love them, too."

CHAPTER 47

Thatcher meant it. His whole family would love her. But then they'd also be waiting for him to mess things up. "Let me give you a tour," he said, changing the subject. "You can see the downstairs. Kitchen, living room, dining room. The bathroom and laundry room are down that little hallway." He pointed in the direction.

"I love the open space." Vickie looked around. "It seems so big for one person."

He nodded. "Yes. And I certainly don't entertain very often." Okay, never. "You ready to go upstairs?"

"Lead the way."

He led her up the staircase. "These are kind of narrow, so be careful." He chuckled. "Just be glad I didn't install that escalator."

"Very funny."

He gave her a quick tour of the upstairs then led the way out to the small yard. Buster came running up, wagging his tail.

"I think Buster is ready to come in." Vickie patted the dog's head. "His ears are cold."

"He's probably ready to eat, too." He looked around. Darkness was beginning to fall. "And how about you? Are you hungry?" He held the door for her to go back inside. "I make a mean pot of spaghetti." He hoped she liked spaghetti because that was the one thing he had ingredients for.

She gave him a dazzling smile. "That sounds great. Are you sure you want to cook, though? I'm okay with just grabbing takeout or something."

"I insist." He motioned toward the kitchen. "Come on." He glanced quickly around to make sure there were no dirty dishes.

Fifteen minutes later, they were standing side by side, preparing a meal.

If he'd thought it felt intimate when they were at his fishing cabin, that was nothing compared to how it felt to cook dinner with her in his kitchen. Buster was curled up at their feet, and for a second, the whole scene was so perfect he wished he could freeze it.

"You're really concentrating on chopping those tomatoes," he teased. "You know all the slices don't have to be symmetrical for the sauce to taste good."

She laughed. "Sorry. I try hard not to be such a perfectionist, but it's difficult."

"I happen to think that is a good quality. You're very conscientious. It's an admirable trait."

Vickie wrinkled her forehead. "Thanks, I think." She laughed. "Those are the words every woman wants to hear from a man. 'Baby, you're very conscientious.' "

He chuckled. "If I told you all the things I think about you, you might blush."

She whirled around to face him. "Try me."

"With that knife in your hand? I don't think so."

"Fine. I'll put it down." She let the knife clatter to the cutting board. "Better?"

"Your cheeks are turning pink, and I haven't said anything."

She met his gaze. "Maybe it's just warm in here."

"Or maybe you don't want to hear what I think about you."

She turned back to pick up the knife and resumed chopping. "Whenever you're ready."

"Okay. I think you're really smart. And kind. My dog likes you." He paused. "And I think you're the most beautiful woman I've ever known in real life." Had he really just said that out loud? Somewhere along the way, he had lost the ability to beat around the bush.

Vickie dropped the knife again and slowly turned to face him. "Really?" she whispered.

Thatcher couldn't take it any longer. He had tried, really tried to keep her at a distance. He'd told himself it was in her best interest and that there was no way she would ever want him once she knew everything about him. But standing there in his kitchen, the steady gaze from her green eyes boring into his, he could no longer deny the sparks between them. The air was practically electrified.

He tentatively reached out a hand and stroked her cheek.

She half smiled at his touch.

Thatcher hoped that meant she was going to be okay with what he was about to do. He pulled her gently to him. Their faces were inches apart. For a moment a hint of fear reflected in her eyes, but in a flash it gave way to a smile. He hesitated just before his lips touched hers, breathing in the moment. When he finally placed his lips on hers, she returned his kiss with no hesitation. Time seemed to stand still.

She pulled back, her eyes wide. "Wow," she breathed.

"I couldn't have said it better myself." He smiled.

Vickie's cell phone buzzed. She walked over to the table and picked it up. "It's my aunt Rose. I should take it."

He motioned up the stairs. "You're welcome to use one of the rooms upstairs if you want some privacy. I'll finish the food."

"Thanks."

He could hear her saying hello as she went up the stairs.

Thatcher leaned against the counter. He had crossed the line. There was no going back.

CHAPTER 48

Vickie's heart rate still wasn't back to normal. She sat down in Thatcher's office and tried to concentrate on what her aunt was saying. "I'm sorry, Aunt Rose. Can you start over?"

"Sure, hon. I might not have a good connection." Rose had been in Texas long enough that she had a distinctive twang. "I called to let you know that Mom's had a little accident."

"Mom?" Vickie was still reeling. "Gram? You mean Gram's had an accident?" She sat upright. "What happened?"

"Oh dear. I don't want to alarm you. Actually, I tried to get ahold of your mother first, but she didn't take my call." Rose delivered the last sentence with clipped words. There was no love lost between the sisters. Rose resented the fact that Vickie's mom lived in the same state as Gram and yet refused to so much as accompany her to a doctor's visit.

"I'll get in touch with her." Vickie sighed. "Just tell me what happened."

"We had a little freak ice storm. I mean, Texas hardly ever gets ice, especially in November." She paused. "Anyway, Mom was going out to get the newspaper, and she slipped. She broke her hip."

Vickie inhaled sharply. "Oh no. Is she in the hospital?"

"Just for a few days. She would've called you herself, but the medicine they gave her for pain makes her really sleepy."

"Do I need to fly out? I can be there tomorrow if I need to."

"There's no need for that. But I will go ahead and tell you that I think she's just going to stay here through New Year's. The doctor thinks it will take awhile to get her rehabbed, and I'd rather her have someone to stay with. I can take her to her appointments and all."

"Thanks for taking such good care of her, Aunt Rose. And please let me know if I need to come out to help. I'll make sure Mom knows, too, in case she wants to fly out." *As if.*

Rose's snort was unmistakable. "I've lived in Texas for twenty years, and Marilyn hasn't so much as sent me a birthday card. I'll expect her here when pigs fly."

What could she even say to that? "Thanks for letting me know. Tell Gram I love her and that I'll talk to her soon." They hung up, and Vickie said a silent prayer for Gram. And for Aunt Rose. Vickie knew all too well the destructive path her mother had cut through the family.

She turned the phone over and over in her hand. She may as well get it over with. The phone rang four times before her mother picked up. "Hello, Victory."

Vickie rolled her eyes even though she knew her mom couldn't see her. She was not going to be drawn into the same arguments tonight. "Aunt Rose tried to call you."

"She was probably calling to see what I'm getting Mother for Christmas. I don't know why she'd even care. It's not as if we shop at the same stores."

Ugh. She was in rare form. "No, Mom. She was calling to let you know that Gram had an accident." Vickie explained the situation. "It will be easier for her to stay out there with Aunt Rose until January. That way there'll be someone to take Gram to her doctors' appointments."

"My sister is such a saint, isn't she? If I hadn't been in the delivery room when you were born, going through agony I might add, I'd almost swear you belong to her instead."

Vickie knew her mother was only trying to goad her. For years, Vickie had held out hope that someday they would be close, but the older she got, the more fleeting the thought. "I'm thankful that Aunt Rose can do it. I told her I would fly out to Texas if I needed to." She paused. "And it wouldn't be a bad idea for you to do the same."

"They don't need me. Rose is a lot more capable as a nurse than I am."

"Mom, you don't have to go out there to help care for her, but you could go out just for a visit."

Her mother was silent. "Darling, I know you only want to help. But sometimes you treat me like I'm a child."

Sometimes you act like one. Vickie didn't dare say the words out loud. She knew her mother's cell reception would mysteriously cut off. As it always did when Vickie said too many things that weren't to her mother's liking. "I'm looking forward to seeing you and Daddy at Thanksgiving."

"I suppose Mother's extended stay in Texas throws a wrench in your Christmas plans, doesn't it?"

Vickie hadn't thought of that. "Oh, it will. What are y'all doing for Christmas?" Vickie spent nearly every Christmas with Gram. Her parents always preferred to travel during the holidays so they could experience Christmas among different cultures. Vickie preferred a more traditional approach.

"This year, we're doing a cruise." Finally, Mom's voice was excited. "I think it's all booked up though. Maybe you can spend the holidays with friends."

"I'll be fine."

A beep on her mother's line abruptly ended their conversation.

Clearly whoever it was rated higher than Vickie. She turned the phone over and over in her hands. Her mother got to her every time. No matter what.

She quickly bowed her head. As she'd been doing since she first began praying regularly, she asked God to help her get along with her mother. But this time, she followed up that thought with another one. *Lord, please don't let me be one of those girls who turns into her mother.*

CHAPTER 49

He might not be a master chef, but his spaghetti looked great. As did the garlic cheese toast Thatcher had thrown together at the last minute. Two plates—his only matching set—sat on the counter, ready to be filled. Buster was in his normal spot underneath the table, waiting to see if any morsels of food fell within his reach. All that was missing from the scene was Thatcher's dinner guest.

He paced the length of the kitchen. Should he go upstairs and check on her? It had been at least twenty minutes since her phone rang. Maybe she was embarrassed about the kiss they'd shared and didn't want to face him. He was a little uneasy about that himself.

Footsteps on the wooden stairs announced Vickie's impending entrance. Thatcher began stirring the spaghetti. He didn't want it to seem like he'd been waiting impatiently.

He looked up from the pot as she walked into the room and her sorrowful expression alarmed him. "What's wrong?" he asked, his hand frozen midstir.

"My gram. She's visiting my aunt Rose in Texas. Earlier today, she fell and broke her hip." Vickie's voice wavered. "She's in the hospital."

Thatcher dropped the pasta spoon, and it clattered against the side of the pot. He crossed to Vickie in one long stride and pulled her to him. "It'll be okay," he whispered, smoothing her hair.

"She's just so fragile. She never should've gone to Texas anyway." Vickie nestled her head against his chest.

Thatcher enjoyed the feeling of her against him but wished it could've been under happier circumstances. "Do you think you could've stopped her from going?"

She shook her head. "No. She's quite stubborn." Vickie pulled out of his embrace and met his gaze.

"Is that maybe a family trait?" he asked.

Her mouth twisted into a grin. "Could be."

"I'm very sorry about your grandmother." He walked back to the stove. "Do you feel like eating, or should I put a lid on this for later?"

"I'm starving." Vickie took a plate from the counter.

Thatcher removed the plate from her hand and shook his head. "Nope. You go sit down." He motioned to the table. "I'll be your waiter tonight."

She sank into the wooden chair. "I won't argue with that."

He fixed two heaping plates of spaghetti and set them on the table. "Is bottled water okay? Because if not, you're kind of out of luck. Although I might have an old bottle of Gatorade somewhere. . . ." He opened the refrigerator door and peered in.

Vickie laughed. "Water is fine."

Once they were settled, Thatcher said a prayer for the food and for Vickie's grandmother.

"Thanks for that," she said once he finished. "And if you wouldn't mind adding her to your personal prayer list, I'd appreciate it."

"Already done." He grabbed napkins from the holder and handed her one.

They ate in silence for a few minutes. "Well?" Thatcher finally asked. "Does it taste okay?" He was pleased with how the food had turned out but wanted to make sure she was suitably impressed.

Vickie paused her fork midair. "It's yummy. Who knew you were such a good cook? And here I was feeling guilty taking so long upstairs." She grinned. "You didn't need my help at all."

Thatcher shrugged. "Pasta and grilled meat. Those are my specialties." He nodded upward. "And I was wondering what was taking so long up there. I started worrying that maybe you were secretly going through my things." He winked. "Thought you might have some kind of pickpocket gene."

Vickie laughed. "I promise I don't. I didn't even look in your bathroom cabinets." She took a sip of water. "I had to call my mother and let her know about Gram."

Thatcher frowned. "I guess she was pretty upset, huh?"

"You would think. But she's far more concerned with what to pack for her upcoming Christmastime cruise." She wrinkled her brow. "Let's just say that my mom and I aren't exactly as close as we could be."

"I'm sorry."

"Don't be. I'm learning to live with it." She turned her attention back to her food.

Thatcher knew all too well what it felt like to have to learn to live with failed relationships. He also knew there was nothing he could say to take her pain away. "Do you want to talk about it?" he asked, carrying his plate to the sink.

"Maybe later." Vickie rose from the table. "Since you were so nice to fix dinner, I'll do the dishes."

He grinned and shook his head. "Nope. Don't give them another thought. I'll take care of them later."

"Well, I'm certainly not going to put up a fight." She returned his smile.

As they made their way to the living room, Thatcher noticed that Vickie's arms were crossed over her body. "Are you cold?"

She nodded. "A little. It's okay though." She grabbed her bag. "I have a jacket in here."

"That isn't necessary." He walked over to the fireplace. "This is one of the reasons I ended up buying this place. I'd always wanted a gas fireplace."

In a few moments, warmth filled the room.

Vickie sat down on the rug in front of the fireplace and leaned against the couch. "This way I'm a little closer to the heat." She grinned.

"Looks like you aren't the only one with that idea." Thatcher laughed as Buster curled up beside her on the rug.

"Smart dog." She pulled out a notepad from her bag. "Now. Let's start making a list of all the places to include in your presentation." She looked up at him, pen poised.

Thatcher shook his head and dropped down next to her. "Nope. No more work tonight." Truthfully, he'd like to pick up where they left off when her phone rang earlier but didn't know how she'd feel about that. "Tell me something."

She looked at him with puzzled eyes. "What do you want to know?"

He was close enough to her that he could see the tiny freckle underneath her eye again. Since the moment he'd first noticed it, weeks ago at the pizza place, he'd wanted to trace it with his finger. "Why are you alone? I mean, why is it that someone like you is spending her Saturday night trying to help someone like me with work? Why aren't you on a date to the theater or the ballet or an art gallery opening?"

Vickie looked away, her gaze fixed on the fireplace. She was silent for a moment. Finally she turned toward him, propping her arm on the couch. "I've never been in a serious relationship. Not that I haven't dated, because I have. My friends call me the queen of first dates."

"Well I'm the king of no dates. So I'm intrigued." *And very much attracted.* He wanted to know what made her tick.

She shrugged. "I guess I do go on a lot of first dates. But there's always a reason not to go on the second one." She sighed. "You've been around Dawn and Jason. She describes him as feeling like 'home' to her. I guess that's what I'm looking for." She glanced up at him, her green eyes serious. "Home. And I've never found it."

Thatcher frowned. "You really think you can tell if someone's going to fill that expectation from a first date?"

"Why not? If it's there, it's there."

He raked a hand through his hair. "Maybe in a movie, where someone writes the script. But not in real life. In my opinion, first dates are awkward. Neither party is really acting like themselves. The poor guy is afraid of messing up by saying or doing the wrong thing, and the girl is worried about how she looks." He shrugged. "It's hard to find out if someone is your soul mate under all that pressure."

"That's the same thing my friends say. They seem to think I'm too picky."

"Are you?"

She shook her head. "No." She grinned. "Okay, maybe sometimes I have a tendency to write people off after a few minutes. But I don't think it's picky. Just selective."

"What about me? Remember when we first met? What would you have written me off for? I mean, *if* we'd been on a date?" He knew it was a gamble for him to bring up their first disastrous dinner together but figured he may as well stay out on the limb he'd been on ever since he'd decided to kiss her.

She twisted her mouth into a smile. "Well. . .*if* it had been a date, I probably would've gone home thinking I wished you'd gotten a haircut and worn a suit." She shrugged. "But now I'm used to your longer hair and relaxed style."

"Hey." He feigned a hurt face. "For your information, I wear a tie to work most days, so in my free time I like to dress down.

And I'll have you know that last spring on my class evaluations, one of my female students said that with my hair a little longer, I could be Patrick Dempsey's brother." He laughed. "Of course, I had to use Google to find out if that was a compliment or not."

Vickie giggled. "I can totally see the Dempsey comparison." Her face grew serious. "I guess I'm just looking for something really specific. You'd be amazed how difficult it is to find a guy who is really honorable. You know? So many people, especially these days, can't be trusted when it's all said and done."

Thatcher was quiet. He wondered what would happen if he opened up to her right now. Told her the whole truth about himself, including the mistakes he'd made in the past. Would she accept him, or would that knowledge drive her away? Because the sense of home that she'd described sure fit how he felt when he was with her. And coming this close to that feeling only made him realize how much he wanted to keep it. For as long as he could. No. He couldn't tell her. Not yet. But soon.

CHAPTER 50

Vickie watched a myriad of emotions play across Thatcher's face. "How about you? Why are you alone? And more importantly, why are you the king of no dates? I mean, clearly someone who gets compared to Patrick Dempsey probably has plenty of women chasing him."

Thatcher shrugged. "To tell you the truth, I ignore any advances that come my way. And I don't do setups." He regarded her seriously. "Honestly, I've just been alone for so many years I've stopped looking for someone to spend my life with."

"Have you ever been in love?" She was proud of herself for being forward and asking such a personal question. She didn't normally delve much into other people's personal lives. But after that kiss. . .she wanted to know as much about him as she could.

"I've had crushes. Been infatuated. Been attracted. But I've never experienced the kind of love that sticks."

"Nice to know I'm not the only one who hasn't been in love." She sighed. "Most of the time I feel like a pariah."

He leaned closer to her. "Well, you're not. My inability to keep from kissing you earlier should've told you that."

Vickie laughed. "So you were unable to keep from it?"

"Guilty. But in my defense, I've waited a long time."

True. He'd also kept her in a constant state of confusion. "I thought you only saw me as a research partner. I mean, after you picked me up from the airport, I didn't hear from you for two weeks." She still didn't understand how his mind worked.

Thatcher groaned. "I know you must think I'm a total idiot. I guess it's just hard for me to let someone into my life. It's been easier for me to let you in as a research partner than a potential. . ." His voice trailed off. "A potential something else."

Something else? What did that mean? She wanted to ask him but held back. This needed to be something he could verbalize without her prodding him. Instead, she grinned. "Well, being your research partner has certainly been interesting."

Thatcher reached out and lightly ran his fingers along the curve of her jaw. She felt her heartbeat quicken at his touch. There were more questions she wanted answered, but for this second, what she wanted most was for him to kiss her again. She leaned forward and met his waiting lips. For a moment, she closed her eyes and was lost in him.

Just then, Buster wriggled between them, forcing them apart. Vickie met Thatcher's surprised gaze, and they burst out laughing.

"Looks like someone's feeling left out," Thatcher said, still laughing. He looked at his watch. "I probably do need to get you home soon though."

She nodded. Kissing him made her feel out of control. Wonderful, but out of control. "Sorry we didn't get more work done tonight."

He stood and helped her up from the floor. "Come here," he whispered. He pulled her into his arms. "We may not have gotten a lot of work done tonight, but I had fun. And I hope you did, too."

She nodded against his chest. "Thanks for dinner."

"Do you think maybe we could do this again soon?"

Was he asking her for a date? Or trying to set up time to work on his project? "Sure."

He leaned down and kissed her on the forehead. "Tomorrow then? After church? We could probably get a lot of the presentation figured out in a few hours."

"Sounds good." Guess she had her answer. Today, she was his "potential something else," but tomorrow she was back to research partner.

❧

After church the next day, Thatcher picked Vickie up for lunch. Initially, he didn't mention working. Their conversation was purely personal.

"Are you ready for the holidays?" he asked, once they were seated and waiting for their food.

"I was. But not so much anymore."

He shot her a puzzled look. "What gives?"

"Thanksgiving will be fine. I'm going to visit my dad's side of the family in Knoxville." Vickie could hardly believe they were only a couple of weeks away from Thanksgiving. "But I'm dreading Christmas. I was supposed to visit Gram, but it looks like she'll be staying in Texas."

"So will you see your parents for Christmas then?"

She shook her head. "My parents are going on a cruise over the holidays. So I'm on my own. Unless I decide to fly to Texas."

He reached across the table and grabbed her hand. "If that falls through, I'd love for you to go with me to my family's Christmas." He grinned. "If you don't mind too much food, lots of little kids running around, and board games."

"Sounds like an idyllic family." His invitation startled her. You didn't invite your research partner to meet your family for Christmas. So that must mean that he definitely saw her as more.

Vickie had the sinking feeling they could play this game forever. She knew that eventually she'd have to get up the courage to ask him how he really felt about her. But in the meantime, she'd wait to see if he'd volunteer the information. A girl could hope.

CHAPTER 51

I know. It sounds crazy." Vickie held the phone against her ear. "But we've been having the best time together."

"So now you're his research partner and more." Kristy laughed. "Sorry I was such a naysayer before. I guess he just needed a little time to figure it all out."

"I've never been happier. Things are still a little more undefined than I'd like, though."

"Oh, Vick. He's kissed you and said you're the most beautiful woman he's ever known. And invited you to have Christmas with his family. Stop overthinking it."

Vickie giggled. "You're right. I should just be content with the way things are."

"Well, either way, I'm glad it's working out. I guess that online dating profile we set up was a waste of money."

"Please don't remind me. I'm still trying to forget it exists. And yes, I think that can be canceled." She sank onto the couch. "How are things with you? Still enjoying the newly wedded bliss?"

"Yep. It's almost our one-month anniversary. And *my husband* is going to take me out to celebrate." She emphasized the words with a Southern belle voice.

They laughed together.

"Have you talked to Ainsley lately?" Vickie asked.

"Not in a couple of weeks. The holidays are going to be tough on her. I wish there was something we could do."

Jake jumped onto the couch and curled up next to Vickie. She absently patted him. "I know what you mean. But I guess all we can do is hold her to the promise she made to start grief counseling at the beginning of the year. I imagine just having someone to talk to will help her tremendously."

"You're right. I wish we lived closer to one another. She could use us about now."

"Someday we'll rule the nursing home."

Kristy laughed at their longtime pact. "Indeed, we will."

They said their good-byes, and Vickie clicked the phone off. She glanced at her watch. Thatcher would be here any minute. With less than a week until she left for Thanksgiving in Tennessee, they'd decided to spend the day out at his fishing cabin. Of course, they'd been inseparable for most of the past week. Every night after work, they'd gotten together to eat and talk and work. Usually in that order.

Twenty minutes later, she was inside the pickup truck, and they were on their way.

"Buster is so excited." Vickie laughed as the dog wriggled against her, his nose pressed against the window.

"He and I are in cahoots today." Thatcher grinned. "As long as he sits next to the door, it forces you to sit next to me."

She couldn't complain about that. Each time they went around a curve and she brushed against him, a little prickle of excitement went through her. "So he's your wingman?"

Thatcher burst out laughing. "I suppose so."

Finally they pulled up to the cabin and unloaded the truck. "How about if I start on lunch?" Vickie asked once they were inside. She held up a grocery bag. "How does vegetable beef soup sound?"

"Perfect on a cold day like this. Are you sure? I don't mind cooking."

"I'll take care of it."

Thatcher followed her into the kitchen and grabbed her around the waist. "Hold on," he whispered. "I don't think I've told you how cute you look today." He spun her around to face him.

"Cute?" She cocked her head sideways. "How so?"

"I like this sporty look you're going for today." He grinned. "I guess you've figured out that I think you're just as beautiful in jeans and a sweater as you are in a designer dress."

Vickie laughed. Earlier in the week, Thatcher had been at her apartment and she'd made the mistake of asking him to help her fix a shelf that had fallen in her closet. His reaction to seeing the vast number of dresses hanging in her closet had been priceless. She hadn't had the heart to show him the guest closet that was also full of clothes. Or the plastic totes that held her summer things.

She glanced down at her dark-washed denim jeans and soft green sweater. "I decided to choose comfort and warmth over trendy today. But I'm glad you approve."

He leaned in and lightly touched his lips to hers. "I more than approve." He motioned toward the living room. "I'm going to start working. Pretty soon, we'll be through with work and we can just relax."

"I'll call you when lunch is ready." Vickie started work on the soup. Things were going so well with Thatcher. She was falling hard for him. Just over the past week, they'd grown so much closer. She felt like she could tell him anything. She was totally herself. And she was sure he felt the same way. For the first time in her life, she'd finally found someone she trusted enough to let her heart get involved. And it felt wonderful.

CHAPTER 52

Katherine's heart raced. Was she ready to do this? She'd been sitting outside of her biological dad's place for nearly an hour. *You can do it.* She thought of all the reasons why she should go to the door.

She'd been watching him for weeks and had learned quite a bit about his life. Sure, there were some things she hadn't been able to find out, but she'd at least figured out that he seemed like a pretty decent guy.

And Mom would be so relieved. She'd promised that she wouldn't contact him until Katherine was ready. It was obvious that her mother would like to have a conversation with him. And Katherine was pretty sure she knew why.

According to her calculations, this man was the last remaining person her mother needed to apologize to. Katherine was afraid of what would happen then.

Sitting in church last Sunday with her grandparents, she'd listened to the preacher's lesson about love. He'd cited one of her favorite verses from 1 Corinthians, but this time, she'd heard something in the passage that she'd never focused on before. *Love does not insist on its own way.* Wasn't that exactly what she'd been doing? The lesson had helped her to realize how selfish she was being. If making amends was what her mother needed to do in order to be at peace, then Katherine knew she should comply.

An old basketball hoop outside of the house caught her eye. The net was missing, and Katherine couldn't help but wonder if her dad had hung the hoop or if it had been there when he'd purchased the place. At their home in California, her mother had hired someone to put a basketball hoop up so Katherine could practice. Even on days when her mother had worked late, she'd still stayed out in the driveway until dark, helping Katherine perfect her jump shot.

"I have to be your mom and your dad," her mother had always said. They'd gone on camping trips and fishing trips and had attended Lakers games because her mom didn't want her to feel like she'd missed out on anything by not having a father figure around.

But now, sitting in his driveway, she couldn't help but wonder what it might've been like. Would he have been overprotective when she was sixteen and going on her first date? Would he have been patient as he taught her how to drive? She had to face the facts. Even if she met him now and they developed some kind of relationship, she'd never know for sure what it would've been like.

Her memories of growing up were good, though. And looking back, she knew she wouldn't trade those for the world. Especially not now.

She let out the breath she hadn't realized she was holding. It was now or never. Katherine took one more look in the mirror. Her hair was in place, and her lipstick was fresh. She climbed slowly from the car, feeling like a gladiator facing an arena full of lions. But that was silly. She'd seen this man plenty of times over the past few weeks. He was harmless. Handsome, even.

Katherine marched up the front path to the door. Should she knock or ring the bell? She glanced down at the welcome mat. Would she be welcome? There was only one way to find out. She raised her fist and rapped three times on the door. Then she waited.

CHAPTER 53

T hat looks great." Thatcher looked over Vickie's shoulder at the screen. "I think we're nearly finished." He gave the computer screen one more glance. "I'll be right back."

The presentation was coming together. It was weird. For the first time in a long time, he was excited about work again. He knew the work that he and Vickie had done had helped rekindle his passion about his job. It was going to be hard to stand up in front of his colleagues and admit that he'd become complacent, but now that he had a new plan mapped out for future classes, he felt certain he'd be able to win them over. And with the project nearing completion, he'd have a few weeks to practice the presentation and work out all the kinks.

His sister had mentioned stopping by later, but he hadn't expected her so early. So when he heard the knock at the door, he threw it open, expecting to see Corinne. Instead, he was face-to-face with a young woman who seemed somehow familiar, although he couldn't place her. "Can I help you?" he asked.

"You've got to come see this," Vickie said, walking up behind him. She looked at the open door. "Oh. . .sorry."

Thatcher turned back to the girl who was still standing on the doorstep. She hadn't spoken. "Are you okay?" he asked.

She seemed rooted to the spot.

He turned and met Vickie's eyes. She'd moved to the couch, but he could see that she was concerned about the silent visitor. He shrugged at her and turned back to the mute girl. "Why don't you come inside? It's awfully cold out."

She stepped over the threshold, and he could see that she was shivering. "I'm looking for Edward Torrey."

A gasp escaped his lips. No one had called him that in years. As soon as he left high school for college, he'd taken to using his middle name. Thatcher just sounded so much more professional. Changing his name was the next best thing to becoming someone else entirely, which was what he would've liked to have done.

The young woman turned her blue eyes toward him, and he felt the room sway beneath his feet as he placed her. "You've found him," he said simply. He cast a frantic glance at Vickie, who was glued to the couch as if she were watching a scene in a movie unfold.

The girl took a deep breath. "My name is Katherine Wyatt." Her face was calm. "I'm your daughter."

Vickie let out a gasp.

Thatcher looked from Vickie, who sat wide-eyed and open-mouthed, to Katherine, who stood before him shaky and ashen. The rush of emotions was almost more than he could bear. The need to explain the situation to Vickie before it got out of hand mixed with the need to reach out to Katherine and tell her how much he'd thought of her over the years. "Katherine, I've spent many years hoping to meet you. But I gave up hope a long time ago that you'd ever want to find me."

She gave him a tiny smile. Her eyes might be her mother's, but the smile was his. "Mom didn't give me your letters and cards until a few months ago," she explained. "But don't be mad." Her words were rushed. "She felt guilty after the divorce and all." Her eyes filled with tears. "And she's really sick now and wants to make sure I have a family." The last bit came out in a whisper.

"Why don't you take your coat off and go warm up by the fire?" he asked gently. "I'll get you some hot chocolate, and then you can tell me the whole story." *She must be twenty by now.* The same age as some of his students. The same age he'd been when he'd last seen her. Feeling ancient, he ushered her toward the now-vacant couch. As soon as she was settled by the fireplace, he set off in search of Vickie.

He rounded the corner to the office where she was throwing things into her duffel bag. "Vickie," he began in a low voice so Katherine wouldn't hear. "I assure you there's an explanation for all of this. I need to speak to Katherine for a moment, and then I'll tell you what's going on."

The watery tears in her green eyes looked like they were about to spill over. "I think I can see what's going on. Am I to understand that you've been *married*?"

He nodded silently.

"And you had a *child*?"

He nodded. "But—"

"No buts. Remember when we talked about why we were still single? And you said you'd never been in love, just like me? You told me you'd never had a serious relationship." She angrily zipped her bag. "Don't you think the whole 'I'm divorced and have a daughter' was kind of an important element to that story?" The tears finally began to stream down her face. "I feel so stupid." She rushed down the hallway and to the door.

He followed her out to the porch, glancing to see Katherine, listlessly standing by the fire. "Please, Vickie. Don't do this."

She threw her bag into the cab of his pickup truck and turned to look at him. "I'm taking your truck back to the city. I'll drop it off later. I have to get out of here."

Before he could move from the porch, she'd started the truck and sped off. He raked his hands through his hair. This was a disaster.

But he couldn't think about it now. He needed to focus on Katherine, who'd clearly had a reason for coming. He walked back inside, hoping he could figure out how to be a father in the minute it would take to reach her.

CHAPTER 54

Anyone who'd ever ridden with Vickie had always said she drove like she'd stolen something. And in this instance, she guessed she had. Taking Thatcher's truck had been her only option besides setting out on foot. At least this way it would cause him a bit of an inconvenience as he tried to return to the city.

Her mind was reeling so much, for a moment she considered pulling over to catch her breath and try and slow her thoughts. Thatcher had been married. He and his wife had a child. He'd gotten divorced. And he hadn't bothered to tell her.

She thought back over the volume of time they'd spent together over the past months. Of how they'd become the kind of friends who shared personal information about their lives. Or so she'd thought. And when he'd finally gotten up the courage to kiss her, she'd believed it to be a defining moment in her life.

But now it felt cheap and empty. She'd waited her whole life to share a meaningful kiss with just the right guy and he'd turned out to be a fraud.

It wasn't the fact that he'd been married and must've been in love before and that he was a father. He was thirty-eight after all.

He'd had plenty of time to have all kinds of experiences before he met her. With an explanation, she could've accepted those things in time.

But keeping the details of his past a secret, especially when he'd had plenty of opportunities to share them, was a betrayal of her trust. It had taken so long for her to trust him in the first place. Her entire life she'd waited to find someone she cared about and who cared about her. And she'd thought she'd finally found it in him.

She thought of all the men she'd gone out with over the years. Even with those guys she'd really liked, she'd carefully guarded her heart and had always prided herself on the fact that no one had gotten close enough to hurt her. Until now.

It felt like there was an actual hole where her heart had once been. That giddy, happy feeling she'd had was gone. In its place was a hollow coldness that seemed to seep through her entire body. She was broken.

CHAPTER 55

I'm sorry I just showed up like this," Katherine said, once they were settled in front of the fireplace. "It seems like I sort of messed things up for you." She motioned toward the door where the dark-haired woman had exited.

He sighed. "Don't worry about that. She'll be okay."

"Is she your. . . ?" She paused, not sure which word to use.

"Vickie is her name. She's been working with me on a project I'm researching." He sighed. "But we're also. . ." He met her gaze. "I guess we're sort of involved," he said finally.

Katherine nodded.

He rose and began to pace in front of the fireplace. "Tell me more about what brought you here. I can't tell you how surprised I am." He stopped and faced her. "Or how happy."

"Mom is sick. Really sick. It started awhile back, and now she has liver cancer." She looked down at her hands. They'd never looked anything like her mother's tiny hands. Had she inherited those from her dad?

He sat down on the couch next to her but not too close. She was glad he was keeping his distance. She wasn't ready to hug him or anything. She wasn't even sure what to call him yet.

"What's the prognosis?" he asked softly.

She met his gaze and felt the tears stinging her eyes. "Not good," she whispered. "We sold the house in California and now we're staying with my grandparents in Maryland." She managed a tiny smile. "I've met so many family members. They've accepted me in a way I didn't expect."

"I'm glad you're getting to know them." He picked up a coaster from the coffee table and began to turn it over in his hands. "And I'm sorry to hear about Jane." He set the coaster back down and glanced over at her. "What all did she tell you about me?"

"Please don't be angry at her. She's sorry about things." Katherine took a deep breath and explained the situation to him. She could see the emotion on his face as he realized she'd spent her entire life thinking he didn't want to be her father.

He was silent for a long moment. "Jane shouldn't get all of the blame. What kind of person must you think I am, to have given up my rights?" He shook his head. "I was so unprepared for fatherhood. We were eighteen when you were born. I'd barely been around any babies at that point. I had no idea what to do with you."

"Mom said you did the best you could."

"It was nice of her to try and give me the benefit of the doubt. You know, until you were two, you used to spend time with me. I was terrified the whole time. Some nights, especially when you were just a baby, I'd stay up all night watching you sleep, just making sure you were still breathing." A haunted expression crossed his face. "When Jane took off with you to California, I bought a puppy from this breeder who lives near my parents. I thought you'd have something to play with when you came for visits, and maybe that way I could learn to take care of something so I'd be a better dad."

Her mouth turned upward in a grin. "Easton? I saw a picture in the stacks of cards and letters. He looked like a sweet dog."

He grinned. "Wait here." He walked out of the room, and she heard him open a door and whistle. A chocolate lab with big brown eyes came bounding into the room and jumped up onto the couch beside her.

"This can't be him," she exclaimed, rubbing the dog's head.

"Nope. But he's from the same breeder. This is Buster. I guess he's Easton's descendant." He grinned. "Having a chocolate lab always reminds me of you, and I've had one ever since you were born. When you were two, you and Easton loved each other so much. You'd cry and cry for your mom, but as soon as I'd bring Easton inside, you'd be all smiles and laughs." His eyes grew moist. "Those were good times."

Buster gave her one last lick and hopped down off the couch. He turned in three circles and stretched out on the rug in front of the fire.

"He's a beautiful dog."

"And you're a beautiful young woman." He stood awkwardly beside the couch. "Listen, I'm not going to pretend that I know how to do this or what to say. . ." He sat down. "I'd really like to get to know you. My family lives not too far from here." He paused. "I know it might be too soon right now, but at some point, I'd love for you to meet them. My parents, especially, have always hoped for a reunion."

She didn't know what to say. Through all of this, it hadn't occurred to her that there would be another side of the family who might want to know her. "I'd like that. At some point. And I'd like to get to know you, too." She let out a tiny laugh. "I don't even know what I should call you."

He grinned. "I go by Thatcher now. It's my middle name. My students call me Dr. Torrey. Some of my friends call me Thatch." He looked over at her. "For now, if you're most comfortable calling me Thatcher, that's fine."

She nodded. That was good. He didn't expect her to immediately call him *Dad* or anything. Not that she was opposed to it. It would just take a little while to start thinking of him that way. "Okay." She turned toward him. "I should probably be going. I need to get back to Mom. But she wants to see you. I think to apologize." Tears stung her eyes again. "It's getting harder for her to get around. Do you think maybe you could drive to my grandparents' house sometime soon?"

Thatcher nodded. "Of course. Anything." He paused. "Are you sure she wants to see me?"

She nodded. "Yes." Katherine poked around in her bag and pulled out a scrap of paper and a pen. "Here's my number," she said, scribbling her cell number on the paper. "Why don't you call me and let me know when you can come?"

He took the number. "Sure."

Katherine rose from the couch and put her coat on. "It will probably need to be soon though."

He met her eyes and nodded his understanding. "Of course. Maybe later in the week?"

"That should be fine. Just call, okay?" She leaned down where the dog was sprawled. "'Bye, Buster. Maybe I'll see you again soon." She gave him a pat and stood up.

"I'd like that." Thatcher grinned. "And so would he."

She walked to the door and paused with her hand on the knob. "So, I'll see you?"

"Later on this week. I'll call." He followed her out to the driveway to her car. "I'm so glad you came by."

"Me, too." She gave him a tiny smile and got in the car.

Thatcher stood in the driveway, watching her leave. One last glance in the rearview mirror told her he was still out there, watching and waving as she drove away.

CHAPTER 56

As soon as she parked Thatcher's old truck, Vickie called Kristy. She didn't even feel the November chill as she trudged toward her apartment.

She quickly caught her friend up to speed, through a mix of tears and bitterness. "I guess I'm just a complete idiot. Falling for a guy like him," she said, once she'd shared the story.

"Like what? Smart and handsome?" Kristy asked. "I think you're being too hard on yourself. . .and maybe him."

Vickie was silent for a moment. "Why would you even say something like that? You were the one who wanted me to proceed with caution, remember? And you were right. He let me fall for him, knowing the whole time that he wasn't telling me the truth about who he really is. I let him know all about me." Vickie couldn't remember the last time she'd been so near hysterics. "I kissed him like I'd never kissed anyone before." Her voice broke. "I was falling in love with him." Her breath came in ragged waves.

"Vick, I think maybe you need to take a step back. Think about it from his point of view. I feel certain he would've told you the truth if things had gotten any more serious between the two of you."

"Why, exactly, are you on his side all of a sudden?" Vickie asked loudly. "Take a step back? For what? To see what a fool I've been? Falling for someone I can't trust?" She paused. "I should've known from the beginning that he wasn't the guy for me. His hair is too long, and he never dresses as nicely as the occasion calls for. And all he wants to do in his spare time is fish. I don't know what I even saw in him."

"From the way you described him, I'd say you saw someone who could be your best friend and your true love. Vickie, I've known you for how many years now? Twelve? And I've never heard you talk about anyone the way you talked about him. I know it took me awhile to warm up to him, but it seemed like after you guys got past your rocky start, he started to really care about you." She took a breath. "So please don't do this."

"Do what?"

"Pick him apart. Convince yourself that his wardrobe isn't what it should be or his hobby isn't the one you'd choose. The things you always do."

"What's that supposed to mean?" She opened her apartment door and shut it firmly behind her.

Kristy let out a sigh. "It means that I've watched you for the past twelve years use superficial things as reasons to keep people at arm's length. When I think about it, I don't even know why you allow me to be your friend."

"Whoa. Where is this coming from?" Vickie was floored. "If you've spent the past twelve years thinking I was so superficial, then why would you even want to be my friend?"

"That's the thing. You aren't superficial. That's what I don't get. Are you just that scared of letting someone get close to you that you have to find reasons not to let them in your life?"

"How could you possibly understand what it's like to be me? You've just married the perfect man. Ainsley was married to the perfect man. Even Dawn, the person I thought was least likely to settle down, has now found the perfect man. And I keep finding losers." Vickie fell onto the couch, still wearing her heavy wool coat, and curled up into a ball.

"Stop. Will you just listen to yourself for a second? There is no such thing as the perfect man. Ace is not perfect. I'm quite sure that if you asked Ainsley, even though she still misses Brad something fierce, she would tell you that he wasn't perfect." Kristy paused. "And do I even need to tell you how imperfect we are?"

"No. I know how imperfect I am. There's no need for you to point that out. I'm just saying that I seem to have a special talent for finding guys who have something wrong with them."

Kristy let out a growl. "I hate to say this to you. Really, I do. But this unrealistic quest for perfection reminds me of someone."

"Who? What do you mean?" Vickie asked, sitting upright.

"For the first time, I'm starting to see your mother in you."

Vickie felt like she'd been punched in the gut. "I can't believe you'd say that. I am nothing like my mother. She has the unrealistic quest for perfection. I just have high standards."

"And there's nothing wrong with that. I want you to be choosy. I want you to find a man who will treat you right, who you can have long conversations with, and who shares your faith in God. But you need to realize that whoever that man is, he is going to have flaws. He might be a little on the short side, or a little too tall, or have a gap between his front teeth. He might not have an impeccable wardrobe, and he might be a baseball fanatic. But sometimes those things that you seem to see as 'flaws' are the things that make us individuals. Do you just want some cookie-cutter guy who oozes perfection?"

Vickie didn't know what to say. They'd been friends for a long time, and Kristy had never said anything like this before. "How long have you felt this way?"

"I'm just worried about you is all." Kristy's voice wavered. "Vick, I want you to be happy. And for some reason, you won't let yourself be. I guess I've sat back and kept my mouth shut for a long time now because I kept thinking you would snap out of it. But I know how much you care about Thatcher. And from what you've told me, I'm pretty sure he cares equally as much about you. I just don't want you to throw away something that could be such a good thing unless there's a valid reason."

"And you don't think lying to me is reason enough?"

Kristy sighed. "He didn't lie to you. He chose not to tell you about that part of his life. Yet. It sounds like he hadn't had contact with his daughter for quite some time. I seriously doubt he had any inkling there was a chance she might show up on his doorstep, or I'm sure he'd already have told you."

Vickie thought for a moment. That, at least, was true. It wasn't like he'd been seeing his ex-wife and his daughter on the weekends and just not telling Vickie where he was. But still. She didn't like feeling attacked like this. "I can't help that I feel betrayed."

"Fine. Spend a few days feeling sorry for yourself. But don't use this as a reason to run. Relationships are hard. And if you aren't willing to see them through the tough times, well then, maybe you aren't ready for one."

Vickie felt her anger boiling. "What are you trying to say? That this is the reason I've never been in a serious relationship? Because I'm not ready?"

"I don't want to argue with you. I just want you to think about what you're doing."

"Fine." Vickie couldn't take it any longer. She hit the END CALL button and threw her phone down on the couch. Twelve years, and she'd never hung up on Kristy. Or been so mad at her. Or so hurt by her. The phone began to buzz. Vickie glanced down and saw Kristy's name on the caller ID. She walked down the hallway and left the buzzing phone on the couch. She was in no mood to hear more. All she wanted was to climb into bed and hope that tomorrow was a better day.

CHAPTER 57

Vickie wondered if the hollow feeling in her heart would ever go away. Not only was she not taking calls from Thatcher, who'd become a constant in her life these past months, but now she didn't feel like she could talk to Kristy, either.

The problem was that today she'd woken up with doubts in her mind. Was Kristy right? Had she put too much stock on superficial things? It was possible. She thought back about the men she'd dated over the past decade. She'd written them off, one by one, for many reasons. Too short, too tall, too hairy, not funny enough, too funny, too fat, too skinny, and the list could go on. There'd been the one who was too religious and then the ones who weren't religious enough. The ones who were too close to their families and the ones who weren't close enough.

If it weren't so sad, it would be almost comical. Somewhere along the way, she'd turned into the Goldilocks of dating. Except that she never could find the man who was just right.

Her workday seemed to drag on forever. She considered it poetic that she was stationed at the Vietnam Memorial this week. No matter how many people were at the wall, it was always a hushed, somber place. Vickie could always count on feeling a little down after working there all day. She couldn't help but feel the reverence and see the sadness as mothers who'd lost sons came and traced their names onto notebook paper.

At least she'd been switched back to her regular shift. No more late nights. Although that also meant no more three-day weekends. But now that she was through working with Thatcher, she supposed it didn't really matter.

Quitting time finally arrived, and Vickie hotfooted it to the Metro. She didn't feel like walking home, as she often did. She wasn't even hungry. She wanted nothing more than a hot bath and to fall into bed.

A message from Thatcher waited on her machine. He'd left messages the past three days, ever since she'd run out of his cabin. She had to admit that she was a little curious as to how he'd gotten back to DC. But not curious enough to take his calls.

The hurt feeling hadn't subsided, and she knew she wasn't ready to talk to him.

A pounding on the door startled her. She peeled herself off of the couch and checked the peephole, thankful to see Dawn in the hallway.

"What gives?" Dawn asked as soon as she was inside. "You look like death warmed over."

Vickie filled her in on the situation, as well as the stream of phone messages Thatcher had left on her machine.

"Wow. That's tough." Dawn looked at Vickie with sympathy. "I don't blame you for being upset."

"Thank you." After Kristy's take on the situation, Vickie had almost been afraid to share it with someone else, lest they side with Thatcher as well. "What do you think I should do?"

Dawn shook her head. "Nope. I think this is one of those situations where you need to make the decision for yourself." She glanced over at Vickie. "I can tell you what *I* would do. But you and I are different."

Vickie managed a smile. "Okay, fine. What would you do?"

"If it were a year ago, I would've just moved on to someone else. Cut my losses." She shrugged. "But now, with Jason, I care enough about him that I would want to hear him out. It would be difficult to deal with, but I guess at this point, I love him so much that I think we could work through about anything."

Vickie was silent as she considered Dawn's words. "I think it's a different situation for you. Before you got engaged, Jason was always up front about his feelings for you, right?"

Dawn nodded. "Well, yes. All along he made sure I knew where I stood."

"Thatcher hasn't. He's become one of my best friends and he's kissed me a few times. But he's never come out and told me how he really feels about me. To tell you the truth, I've always been afraid that once his presentation was over, I might never hear from him again. After we stopped researching the Lincoln project, I didn't hear a peep from him for two weeks. Until he needed something from me." She sighed. "So I already felt uncertain about him. Not my feelings for him, but about his for me. And this. . .knowing he kept something so huge from me." She shrugged. "I think it just shows me that I wasn't as important to him as I'd hoped. Otherwise, he'd have shared it with me. He had plenty of chances."

"It sounds to me like your mind is already made up."

Vickie leaned her head back against the couch. "I guess it is."

Dawn patted her on the leg. "Do you want me to bring you anything? Chinese food? Pizza? Ice cream?"

"No." Vickie shook her head. "Thanks for offering, though. I'm just going to go to bed and watch a movie."

"How about tomorrow? When's your flight out?"

Vickie grimaced. "I'm skipping Thanksgiving. I can't face my mother right now. All she'll do is make me feel even worse.

Thankfully, I sounded bad enough on the phone yesterday that my parents assume I'm sick."

"I hate to think of you all alone on a holiday."

Vickie shrugged. "I'll pretend it's just another day. Besides, I'm looking forward to burrowing into my down comforter and watching movies all day."

Dawn frowned. "How about tonight then? I'll stay with you if you don't want to be alone."

"That's okay. I think maybe some alone time is what I need."

She locked the door behind Dawn and padded down the hallway.

CHAPTER 58

Driving to his former in-laws' home might be the most stressful thing Thatcher had done in a while. He tried to relax and enjoy the drive, but the tension crept up his shoulders and to the base of his neck until he felt like a vise was trying to crush him.

At least his presentation for work was nearly ready. Thankfully he and Vickie had gotten finished with the bulk of the work, so even though he was on his own now, he should be able to pull it together.

Vickie wouldn't take his calls. He knew she must be terribly upset to have reacted the way she had. Taking off in his pickup truck had been so uncharacteristic of her. He wanted to explain himself very soon so maybe she would understand why he'd chosen not to tell her the truth. He hoped a cooling-off period would give her more time to forgive him.

Katherine's appearance after all these years had certainly been a shocker. She was a lovely young woman. It was hard to believe that he'd been her age the last time he'd seen her. It felt like a lifetime ago. And even though she'd implored him not to be angry with Jane, it was hard not to feel a twinge of anger. But he knew he had to shoulder a lot of the blame. If he'd been a stronger man, he could've demanded to see his daughter. That's probably what most people would've done. But he'd always hated the thought of forcing someone to spend time with him if they didn't want to.

He finally arrived at his destination. His stomach churned as he climbed out of the old truck. He knew Jane's parents had never thought he was good enough for their daughter. Maybe he should've borrowed a different vehicle.

Before he could knock, the wooden door swung open.

Katherine stood before him, smiling. "Thanks for coming." She ushered him into the living room.

It hadn't changed much since the last time he was there, nearly twenty years ago. Right after he and Jane had married, her parents had moved to Maryland. Jane always said it was in case anyone in their hometown did the math and realized she'd been pregnant on their wedding day.

"Can I get you something to drink?" his daughter asked.

Thatcher shook his head. "No, I'm fine." He looked around nervously. "Are your grandparents here?"

Her mouth twisted into a smile. "Mom made them run all their Thanksgiving-dinner-related errands this morning. She said you were probably dreading coming here enough without them being around to make you more nervous."

He couldn't help but grin. "I can't say that I'm sorry about that." He met her eyes. "I guess your mom has told you the entire story by now, huh?"

Katherine nodded. "Finally. She waited long enough to tell."

"I don't think your grandparents ever forgave me." He ran his fingers through his hair. "I guess maybe I never forgave myself either."

"Mom's in the sunroom. If you're ready." She looked over her shoulder at him, her eyebrows raised.

"I am." He took a breath. What did Jane want to say to him

after all these years?

Katherine tapped on the door. "Mom?"

"Come in," Jane said, her voice weak.

Thatcher followed Katherine into the room. Jane was stretched out on a yellow chaise facing the large windows that overlooked the sprawling backyard. She looked up and smiled weakly. "Eddie. It's been so long."

Katherine grinned. "Mom, I told you he goes by his middle name now. Thatcher."

Jane's eyes were still the same blue they'd been twenty years ago. "He'll always be Eddie to me." She looked him up and down. "If the girls from Stevens High could see you now, they'd be beating your door down." She smiled.

"Hi, Jane." Thatcher felt a blush rise up his face at her words. How was it possible that she could still make him feel like an awkward teenager? In this tiny room with his ex-wife and their daughter, a lifetime of what could've been seemed to flash before his eyes.

"I'll leave you two alone." Katherine pulled the door closed.

"Well. . ." Thatcher took a seat on the couch and looked at Jane. She was frail, but her face was as beautiful as it had been twenty years ago.

"I tried calling you at work a couple of times, but didn't leave a message. And I know it was probably cruel of me to make you come all the way out here." She struggled for a moment but finally sat up. "Let's just say that once you're facing the end, you feel entitled to be demanding." She managed a smile.

"About that. I'm so sorry." He shook his head. "I can't imagine what you must be going through."

She shrugged. "I've made my peace with it. At least I know what's happening, you know? It isn't like having a sudden heart attack or car accident. This way, I'm able to get my affairs in order." Jane let out a sigh. "I thank God every night for giving me this time. Katherine and I have grown even closer over the past year. I've been making a list of things for her to remember after I'm gone." She held up a notebook. "Tips on everything from what to do with a colicky baby to things she should know about purchasing her first home."

He was impressed by her foresight. "She'll cherish that forever."

"I hope so. You know, by the time I was her age, I'd already cut ties with my own mother. There were so many times through the years that I wished I'd had someone around to give me advice and share their own experiences with me." She tapped on the notebook. "This way, it's like I'll always be around to help her."

"How is she handling everything?"

"As well as can be expected, I guess. This past year has been tough for her. She's played nursemaid to me, worked, and still managed to keep her GPA high." She paused. "But I admit I can't help but worry about how she'll do after I'm. . ." Her voice trailed off and her gaze met his eyes. "You know."

He nodded.

"That's part of the reason I wanted to meet with you. I hope the two of you can get to know one another."

"Katherine mentioned that she hadn't received any of the cards or letters I sent over the years." He didn't want to let her know how much this information had upset him. She was dealing with enough already.

Jane closed her eyes for a moment, as if to collect her strength. "I can't apologize to you enough. Once Mike adopted her and you relinquished your visitation rights, I told myself it was best if she didn't have contact with you. I selfishly thought it would be easier that way."

"But what about after you and Mike split up? Did you not consider it then?"

She nodded. "Yes. But by then, I didn't want to confuse her." She looked sheepish. "I know these are terrible excuses. Please forgive me. I'm trying really hard to make amends to everyone now."

"Of course I forgive you." He could see the pain on her face. And he knew something about what it was like to live a life full of remorse. "I'm not exactly innocent. I should've tried harder to reach out. We're both at fault." He smiled at her. "If it makes you feel any better, from what I've seen, she's wonderful. You did a fine job of raising her, and I'm sure it wasn't easy."

"She is the one thing I've done right in my life. And I did try and consider how you'd want her raised. Katherine is a good girl. She really tries to do what's right and is so considerate of others." Jane sighed. "I always felt like you would be proud." She glanced at him. "Come sit here." She patted the end of the chaise. "I need to be able to see you better for what I need to say next."

He stood and went to sit where she'd requested. "What is it?"

"I have another apology to make to you. I should have told you years ago." She sighed. "It's a difficult task to try and rectify things with so many people." She grabbed his hand. "I know I hurt you terribly all those years ago. I was young and selfish and stupid."

He swallowed hard. "You don't have to do this."

"Yes. I do." She gripped his hand even tighter. "I didn't tell Katherine this part. I guess I was embarrassed, and I didn't want her to know what a horrible person her mother had been." She inhaled sharply. "I've always felt torn about it though. I know I never should've pursued you the way I did. I was just so hurt by Clark's cheating on me that I wanted to hurt him back. And you." She looked at Thatcher. "You were always the best, the kindest guy. Always there for me when I needed a shoulder to cry on. I knew better than to lead you on."

Thatcher watched as the tears began to fall down her face. The crush he'd had on Jane all through school had been huge. But they ran in different circles. The only thing they had in common was their church youth group. So when Jane began having problems with her boyfriend, Thatcher had been only too happy when she'd confided in him. Her attention and flirting made him feel like he was finally part of the crowd. And when she invited him to be her prom date, he was ecstatic. The rest was history. He'd never forgiven himself for acting so out of character that night. "Jane, please don't." He stopped and took a breath. "You don't have to apologize."

"Please, just tell me you forgive me." She looked at him, her face taut with pain.

He nodded. "Of course."

She let go of his hand. "The one good thing that's come out of this is Katherine. And I'll be honest with you. I see so much of you in her. I'm thankful that you'll be part of her life now."

"I'm thrilled at the thought of getting to know her. I've already told her that I'd like her to meet my family when she's ready."

Jane smiled. "You can't imagine how much peace it gives me to know that there will be people to love her and look after her."

"Believe me, I'm not going anywhere. You can trust that I'll always look out for her." He may not have done the right thing by his daughter in the past, but he was ready to step up to the plate.

CHAPTER 59

I'm so sorry," Ainsley said over the phone. "Are you sure you don't at least want to hear what he has to say?"

Vickie bustled about the kitchen, getting tomorrow morning's coffee ready. "I'm sure. I mean, come on. It's been two weeks, and he's left only three lousy messages. If he doesn't care enough to come see me face-to-face to explain the situation, I think it's pretty obvious that I meant nothing to him." She sighed and leaned against the counter. "I should've listened to you and Kristy at the wedding."

There was silence from Ainsley's end of the phone. "But you're still crazy about him, right?"

"Maybe that doesn't matter. I'd be glad to hear him out if he put more effort into it than a handful of messages. He hasn't even called during times I'm normally home." She tightened her grip on the phone. "And he has my cell number, so it isn't like he couldn't reach me if he wanted to. I shouldn't have to seek him out to give him a chance to explain. Is that unreasonable?"

"I guess not. You did put yourself out there pretty well. For you, I mean." Ainsley chuckled. "I have to admit, I was impressed at the way you hung in there even though he doesn't always do or say the right thing."

"There was just something about him, you know? But I'm done. You're right that I did put myself out there. I let him in my life. He knows all about me, about the trouble I have sometimes with my mom and how I have an irrational fear of flying." She sighed. "Who knows? Maybe he's glad it all went down the way it did. I have no idea if he wanted to continue things once his presentation was over anyway. Because he never would say."

"You want a man who's able to express his feelings. That's kind of important," Ainsley agreed. "So what are you going to do now?"

"I never thought I'd say this. . .but I'm going to get right back out there. You know that guy you and Kristy sent messages to online? Which, by the way, I am still a little weirded out that I had an online dating profile for nearly two months and didn't know it. But anyway, I'm meeting him for coffee on Saturday."

"Whoa. I didn't expect to hear that." Ainsley's voice was full of uncertainty. "Are you sure you're ready for that?"

"Does it matter? I can either sit here and be sad that things didn't work out with Thatcher, or I can move on. I'm choosing to move on. Besides, I might've been able to justify spending Thanksgiving feigning sickness and curled up in bed. But Christmas and New Year's are right around the corner. I at least want to be able to ring in the new year feeling like I'm moving on."

"Just be careful, okay? I know how much you've been hurt by all of this." Ainsley cleared her throat. "Have you spoken to Kristy yet?"

"No." Vickie was suddenly even sadder. "Not since I hung up on her," she said quietly.

"She told me. She feels awful about what happened. But I think she's waiting for you to cool down some before she calls you."

"I've been thinking that I should call her. There were some

things she said that were true. And as much as I hated to, I know I needed to hear them." She flipped the kitchen light off and walked into the living room. "I don't want to be hypercritical of people anymore. I guess I don't have to tell you this, but just in case you didn't know, I might be a little bit of a control freak."

Ainsley chuckled. "You?"

"That's right." Vickie joined in her laughter as she flopped onto the couch. "I think maybe that's been part of my problem. I wanted to call all the shots in my life. And somewhere along the way, I lost sight of the fact that God should be the one in control. Not me." She sighed. "So I'm trying hard to turn over a new leaf. I'm praying a lot more than I ever have before—asking the Lord to give me patience and trying to turn things over to Him more."

"Is it helping?"

"More than I ever expected. I mean, I'm still hurt by Thatcher's secrets, but I think all the time I've spent praying has shown me something positive in this situation."

"What's that, if you don't mind me asking?"

"That I'm actually capable of letting my guard down. I think if nothing else, this has shown me how wonderful it can feel to let myself be vulnerable. Just next time I'm going to make sure it's with someone who really cares about me."

"I'm glad you've found some peace. I think that's important: to face a dark time and still be able to see the light." Vickie knew that Ainsley was referring to her own situation. It was taking a long time for Ainsley to recover from Brad's death, but she had a beautiful baby daughter to focus on.

Vickie sighed. "I'm going to call Kristy tomorrow. I hate the thought of her thinking I'm upset with her. Especially now that it's almost Christmas. You know—peace and goodwill and all that."

Ainsley laughed. " 'All that' is right. I think that's a good plan.

I know she'll be glad to hear from you."

They said their good-byes, and Vickie sat in silence. For a fleeting second, she imagined a pounding on her door and Thatcher outside with the biggest bouquet of flowers she'd ever seen. But she pushed the thought from her mind. He wasn't that kind of guy. He wasn't coming for her. And starting with Saturday's coffee date, she was going to forget him.

CHAPTER 60

Vickie still hadn't called him back. Thatcher had tried to get in touch with her a handful of times now and had even left messages. But she hadn't returned any of them. At first, he'd tried to convince himself that it was probably just because she was out of town for Thanksgiving. But he'd left a message since then and still gotten no response. He had no idea what he should do. Sure, he'd considered showing up on her doorstep. But that seemed very confrontational. She must not want to speak to him; otherwise, she'd call him back.

These past few weeks, he'd been surprised to find that Vickie was the one person he wanted to talk to the most about what was going on with Katherine and Jane. This situation was way out of his comfort zone. He needed help. But the thought of saying that out loud wasn't appealing.

So he'd decided to be sneaky. Jason Redd had left a message last week about his volleyball team. It would be a lot of the same guys who'd played softball, and Jason's message invited Thatcher to join in. They played on Thursday nights.

So after grading his last final on Thursday, Thatcher donned his athletic gear as if he were just another guy going to play a couple volleyball games. Except that in reality, he was going in the hopes that Vickie's friend Dawn would be in the audience. Maybe he could get some information from her as to what was going on inside Vickie's head.

"Hey, man," Jason called, once Thatcher arrived at the gym. The basketball court was divided into two sections so two volleyball games could be played at once. "We're on Court A." Jason pointed toward one of the courts where several guys were volleying the ball back and forth across the net. "I'm glad you could come; otherwise we'd be a little short."

"I could use some exercise." Thatcher grinned. "It's been a pretty stressful week." That might've been the understatement of the decade, but Jason didn't need to know that.

"I'll go put you on the roster." Jason jogged off toward one of the officials, who sat in the front row, holding a clipboard.

Thatcher took the opportunity to scan the crowd. He spotted Dawn sitting midway up the bleachers. She was watching him. He nodded in her direction, and she waved. According to the clock, ten minutes still remained before game time. Without another thought, he started up the bleachers. At this point, he could use any help he could get.

Her black dress and red belt were out of place in the old gymnasium. She must've come straight from work. "Hi," he said. "How are you?"

She regarded him coolly for a moment, her blue eyes narrowed. "Fancy seeing you here." She patted the seat next to her. "Have a seat."

He obliged. "I wanted to talk to you about—"

She cut him off. "You want to know how Vickie's doing." Dawn tossed her blond waves. "Let me guess. She's still not taking your calls?"

"So I guess you heard about what happened." He raked his

fingers through his hair. "There's an explanation."

She held up a manicured hand. "Save it." She flashed him a smile. "Look, Thatcher, I think you're probably a very nice man. But Vickie's my friend, and you haven't treated her very well." She narrowed her eyes at him. "She spent Thanksgiving in bed watching movies and trying to forget how much you hurt her."

He drew his face back like he'd been slapped. "But there's an explanation for why I hadn't told her everything about my past."

Dawn shook her head. "Don't you get it? It isn't just that you weren't totally up front with her. It's also that you've been lukewarm toward her from the beginning."

Thatcher was silent. "Lukewarm?"

"You gave her just enough attention to keep her hanging on. Am I right? But as soon as the two of you started to get close, you pulled back." She raised a perfect eyebrow. "Now I'm sure some of that has to do with whatever it is you've been hiding. But still, that's no way to treat a woman. Did you ever tell her how you felt?"

He was speechless. In hindsight, he probably had acted that way. But it was only because he'd felt like he wasn't good enough for Vickie. Not because he didn't care about her. And hadn't his feelings for her been obvious? "What should I do?"

Dawn let out a chuckle. "Uh-uh. This one you're going to need to figure out all by yourself. You know Vickie. In fact, she seems to think you know her pretty well. So you need to figure this out by yourself." She paused. "I shouldn't have even told you this much. The truth is, Vickie already has a date with someone else. Someone who pursues her and sends her sweet e-mails and tells her she's pretty. But I like you. So I'll give you a hint." She leaned toward him. "Think about Vickie's favorite movies. They all have something in common."

His mind raced. He did know her favorite movies. All chick flicks. He could see them now, lined up on her bookshelf. How many times had he teased her about being a hopeless romantic? "Something in common?"

"That's all you're getting." Dawn motioned toward the court. "Looks like they're ready for you."

He stood and made his way slowly down the bleachers. "Good luck," Dawn called.

Thatcher knew her words had nothing to do with the volley-ball game.

☙◉❧

Sunday afternoon, Thatcher settled onto his leather couch. Yesterday, he'd gone to the used-video store and cleaned them out of movies he knew were on Vickie's shelf. At only two dollars each, the videos proved that it paid off to apparently be one of the only remaining people in the Free World who still used a VCR.

He'd started his movie marathon last night with *Say Anything* and *Sixteen Candles*. If Vickie liked these movies enough to name her pets after the lead characters, it must mean something. But after viewing, he wasn't sure what to think. He couldn't figure out what their connection was.

When he'd found himself getting a little teary-eyed at the end of *Titanic*, he feared the ownership of a romance movie collection might've depleted his testosterone supply. The last time he could remember tearing up over something he saw on TV was during the televised funeral of Ronald Reagan. Of course, mourning the loss of his favorite American president justified tears a lot more than a chick flick. He didn't know what was wrong with him.

So after Jack had faded into the abyss of the sea and old lady Rose had thrown the big diamond in after him, Thatcher took a man break. He and Buster went for a run through the neighborhood, and when he got home, he turned the channel to ESPN for the rest of the night.

Today, it was time for round two. First up, *Fools Rush In*, followed by *An Affair to Remember*, and finally *Sabrina*. He balanced them out by wearing a faded Vanderbilt football shirt he'd had for at least ten years and eating an entire pepperoni pizza with extra cheese.

Six hours later, he paced the length of the living room, Buster at his heels. One by one, Thatcher went over each movie in his mind. Lloyd Dobler held up a boom box and played a sappy song. Jake Ryan had a red sports car and rescued Samantha from her sister's wedding reception. Jack put Rose up on that piece of board so she could stay alive. Matthew Perry went to Mexico to find Selma Hayack. Cary Grant waited at the top of the Empire State Building for Debra Kerr. And Harrison Ford as Linus Larrabee had gotten on an airplane, even though he'd never flown, and had gone all the way to Paris to find Sabrina. There must be a common denominator in there somewhere.

Thatcher stopped pacing. What did he know about Vickie? He grabbed a pen and began to make a list. She was smart. She liked pretty clothes. She had a close relationship with her gram. She loved to cook and entertain.

What else? She made him want to be a better man. A godly man. The kind of man she deserved. He thought about how she'd exclaimed over her friend's wedding in Tennessee, and how the groom had surprised the bride by giving her the wedding of her dreams.

Suddenly, it all clicked into place. He knew what he had to do. He just hoped he wasn't too late.

CHAPTER 61

Vickie hadn't slept well last night. And when she'd stumbled into the kitchen this morning, she'd been greeted with an empty coffeepot. She'd forgotten to turn the coffeepot timer on. She couldn't remember a single morning over the past five years that she hadn't woken up to a pot of coffee. She must really be losing it. *Happy Monday to me.*

She ran into Survey Lodge minutes before her shift began. Today she would be at the Korean Memorial, and she was so thankful there was a ranger station nearby where she could seek refuge. The temperature had dropped. Winter had come with a vengeance.

"You have big holiday plans this year?" Chris asked as she logged on to the computer. "I can't believe it's almost Christmas."

Vickie was silent for a moment. She'd been so focused on her plans that fell through that she hadn't even thought about what she would do for Christmas now that she wouldn't be accompanying Thatcher to his family holiday. Now it looked like she'd be spending Christmas alone. "No big plans. Just a low-key holiday. How about you?"

"We're loading up and driving to North Carolina." He grinned. "Just thinking about a road trip with two kids under age three makes me exhausted."

"I'm sure it will be fun." Vickie managed a smile. Thinking about a solo holiday made her sad. Maybe she should fly out to Texas to visit Gram and Aunt Rose. It might not be too late to get a cheap ticket.

"I'm headed out," Chris said, grabbing his hat. "Just a few more hours of work, and I'm on vacation."

"Have a merry Christmas," she called. She checked her watch. If she didn't leave now, she'd never make it to her station on time.

Vickie sat inside the ranger station nearest the Korean Memorial. So far today, only three people had stopped to speak to her: two wanting brochures and the other seeking the nearest restroom. She propped her chin on her hand and watched the people milling about outside.

The trouble with it being nearly Christmas was that there were fewer visitors to distract her. So she had plenty of time to think about Thatcher. And about her future.

She'd finally made amends with Kristy. That was such a relief. Her friend had been so apologetic, but Vickie had let her know she'd been on the right track with her accusations. She was determined to turn over a new leaf. It was time to trust that God had a plan for her and stop trying to control every little thing.

But that might be easier said than done.

Vickie watched a couple strolling hand in hand down the sidewalk in front of the ranger station. They looked so happy. Is that how she and Thatcher had looked? So enveloped in one another it was like there was no one else in the world. Had she been too hasty?

But Thatcher wasn't the man she'd thought he was. He hadn't been completely honest with her. She had to keep reminding herself of that. Not only had he kept some very important information to himself, but he'd also never come out and told her how he felt about her.

She thought about the coffee date she'd had on Saturday. The guy, Ryan, had been the most promising one on the list of potential dates from the online site. And it just so happened that he was the one Kristy and Ainsley had already communicated with. So it seemed only natural to finally take him up on the offer for coffee.

But as soon as they'd gotten settled at the local Starbucks, Vickie had been hit by the sinking feeling she wasn't ready to move on. All she could think of was Thatcher.

Ryan must not have picked up on her distractedness though, because he'd booked the second date. At least she knew where she stood. There was something to be said for that.

CHAPTER 62

"I t looks beautiful," Katherine's mother said from her normal spot in the sunroom. "Now, aren't you glad I talked you into putting a tree in here?"

Katherine grinned. "I suppose." She'd spent nearly an hour wrestling with the ancient Christmas tree her grandmother kept out in the storage shed. It had been replaced years ago with a newer, pre-lit model. But they'd never gotten around to throwing this one away.

"I'm pretty sure this is the same tree we had when I was a little girl." Her mom grinned. "It's hard to believe that was so long ago." She patted the chaise. "Come sit down for a few minutes."

Katherine stepped down from the step stool she'd been standing on so she could decorate the top branches. She crossed the room and sat down beside her mother. "Are you okay? Do I need to call someone?"

Last week, the doctor had recommended that they set up hospice care. Katherine had balked at the idea. She was afraid it meant they were totally giving up. "Let's just take it one day at a time, okay?" her mother had said.

One day at a time was fine when there were plenty of days. But Katherine knew there weren't many left. At least not many good ones.

"I feel fine. I just wanted to sit with my girl for a little while." Her mom smiled and patted her on the leg. "Honey, I think it's time we talk about what happens next."

Katherine wanted to throw a tantrum like when she was a child. She wanted to scream, *I don't want to talk about what happens next. Because I don't like it.* But she knew her mother's illness had to be faced head-on. She and her mother had gone through a lot together. They'd practically grown up together. They could face this together, too. She sighed. "What do we need to discuss?"

"How you're going to handle it." Her mom grabbed her hand. "I'm not scared. And that makes me feel so selfish. I've made my peace with those I've hurt. I've made my peace with the Lord. And I'm not scared any longer." Tears welled up in her tired eyes. "But I hate leaving you behind."

"I'm not too happy about that myself. But I don't want you to worry about me. I'll find my way. Especially now that I'll have family around to help me." Katherine held back tears. She had to be strong for her mother.

Her mom nodded. "You'll never know how much peace that gives me. Your father is a good man. He will do right by you. I hope you believe that."

Katherine nodded. "I do. The few times we've gotten together, I can tell he's sincere about wanting to be part of my life. He's not going to force me to play a traditional role or anything though." She smiled. "I appreciated him saying that. It's nice not to feel pressure to suddenly start calling him *Dad* or asking him for advice or whatever it is that daughters do with their dads when they get to be my age."

Her mom gave a tiny smile. "I'm sure you and Eddie—I mean Thatcher—will carve out your own kind of relationship that will suit both of you. You're the same age as his students, you know."

"I know. I'm considering enrolling at his school next semester."

"That's a great idea." Her mom's eyes filled with tears again. "Sorry. I know it's hard to have a conversation with someone who seems like they're always on the verge of weeping." She took a breath. "It's just that ever since you were born, I always expected I'd get to share certain milestones with you: college graduation, your first trip overseas, buying your first home, your wedding, your becoming a mother yourself." She wiped her eyes. "Only recently did I finally accept that I'm not going to be around for most of those things. Maybe none of those things."

Katherine bit her lip to keep from crying. She could see how hard this was for her mother, and she was determined not to make it any more difficult. "You don't know that."

"True. But just in case, I've been working on something for you." She reached for a red notebook on the table beside her. "I've been making lists." She met Katherine's gaze. "For you. Lists of advice and opinions. On everything from love to airlines." She handed Katherine the book.

Katherine flipped through. Nearly every page was filled. "I'll treasure it."

"There are even pages in there for your future husband." Her mother smiled. "I've had a lot of time to think about all the things I'd want to tell you over a lifetime." She patted the notebook. "At least this is a start."

Katherine leaned over and kissed her mother on the cheek. "Thank you." The tears welled up in her eyes again. This book of advice and thoughts was wonderful. Katherine knew she'd refer to it for the rest of her life. It would make lots of decisions easier. But it wouldn't lessen the grief.

CHAPTER 63

The day before Christmas Eve brought a heavy chill to the air, but the forecasters weren't calling for a white Christmas. Vickie bundled up in a red turtleneck, dark jeans, and her favorite boots. Her heavy red wool coat and the hat that made her feel like Mary Tyler Moore completed her look.

She was meeting Ryan again, this time for dinner. She wished she was more excited about it. She knew it wasn't a good sign to be so ambivalent. He sent her text messages just to check in and called to make sure she got home okay—all those little things that should make her like him.

All that time with Thatcher, she'd imagined him doing sweet things for her. Now Ryan was actually doing them—no imagination needed. And she didn't care.

She hurried down the street. They were meeting at a little pizza place not too far from her apartment. Since this was their third date, he'd tried to pressure her into letting him come pick her up. But she'd made an excuse about having some errands to run beforehand, which translated into her dropping a bill off at the nearest mailbox she passed on the way. The truth of the matter was that she wasn't ready for him to be in her space.

"Hey, gorgeous," he said as she walked up. "Red is your color."

She smiled. "Thanks."

Ryan was a handsome guy. His blue eyes and sandy blond hair made him look like the all-American boy. Each time Vickie had seen him, he'd been in clothes that she could tell were expensive. He was very well-groomed, which in her experience went along with his political career. He wasn't in office, but he worked for a consulting firm and spent the bulk of his day on Capitol Hill.

If her mother were ever to meet him, she would demand marriage on the spot.

Once they'd ordered, Ryan shimmied out of his suit jacket and loosened his tie. "Did you have a good day?"

She explained about the lack of visitors along the mall. "It was a long day. How about you?"

Ryan launched into a long tirade about his day. He'd had some kind of altercation with a senator's assistant. It might've been interesting except that his speech was peppered with expletives. Each time he used a choice word, she could feel her eyes grow wider. *Figures. Third date is when the true colors usually come out.* She began to tune him out. It wasn't worth hearing. Had she given off some kind of vibe that said "potty mouths don't bother me" or something? It wasn't like she was a prude. If he'd have spilled his drink or ran into a wall and let a colorful word slip, that would be one thing. She wouldn't like it but could at least chalk it up to being accidental. But to throw that kind of language into a regular sentence meant something else. It meant that that was ingrained in him, part of who he was.

She forced herself to make small talk until the meal was over. Once they were out front, she began to feel unsure. The last time she'd met him for dinner, he'd been going back to work, so there was no pressure to let him walk her home. But this time it was different.

"Why don't you let me walk you to your place?" he asked, grinning.

She racked her brain. Not that she thought she was in danger from him or anything, but she didn't want to have to go through the complications of him walking her to the door. "You know, I think I'm going to run by work for a minute." It was a split-second decision, but she knew it was the right one. "But thank you for dinner."

"You're welcome. Let me at least walk you to the Metro."

She nodded. "Sure. Thanks." She shoved her hands into her pockets so there'd be no danger of him trying to hold her hand.

Once they were at the escalator, she smiled. "Thanks for walking me here." She reached over and patted him on the arm. "Have a good night."

Before he could react, she'd already stepped onto the escalator. "Bye," she called.

"Good night." Confusion rang in his voice.

Poor guy. She knew he'd spend the next few weeks wondering why she wouldn't take his calls. But using foul language was a deal breaker for her. She sighed. At least Kristy wouldn't accuse her of creating an excuse this time.

ॐ

Vickie leaned back against the grooved column and looked out over the mall. Despite the chilly temperature, several people were still visiting the Lincoln Memorial. A light snow had begun to fall, and she could see the lights of the National Christmas Tree in the distance. It was magical. She sighed. It had certainly been an interesting few months.

She watched a young couple run toward each other at the reflecting pool. At least they'd had sense enough to stay out of the water for their Forrest and Jenny reenactment. Vickie couldn't help but smile.

"Come here often?"

At the sound of Thatcher's familiar voice, she turned. He stood gazing down at her and smiling.

She clambered to her feet and faced him. "What are you doing here?" she asked. She noticed his hair first. It was cut in a short, trendy style. His old, wire-rimmed glasses had been replaced with a new pair that seemed to frame his chiseled face. He wore an expensively cut suit that looked almost as if it had been made just for him.

"I've been looking all over the city for you. This was my last stop, and I was hoping you'd be here." He looked seriously at her. "There are some things I need to say."

Vickie felt numb. He was the last person she'd expected to see here, and the fact that he'd come hoping to find her was surprising. "Is everything okay?" It occurred to her that perhaps he'd been to a funeral. She remembered hearing his daughter say that her mother was sick.

He shook his head. "Everything isn't okay. It hasn't been since the day you took my truck and left." He sighed. "Can we sit down for a few minutes?"

She nodded. She still couldn't believe he was here.

Thatcher lightly grasped her arm and guided her back into her favorite spot beside the column then sat down next to her. He was silent for a moment. Finally he began to speak in a low voice. "You have every reason not to want to see me again. I betrayed your trust by not telling you the whole truth about who I am."

She met his brown eyes and was surprised to see the emotion they held. He *had* betrayed her trust. Still, she wanted to hear what he had to say.

"This is a story that goes back many, many years. It's about a boy who never felt like he was good enough."

Vickie listened quietly as he told her about the torch he'd carried for Jane.

"She was in my youth group at church. I was just the nerdy guy who was in band and read nonfiction for fun. Everyone knew I had a crush on her. But she dated Clark Langston for most of our high school years."

She drew her brows together. "Clark Langston? As in your colleague who sent us after the false documents?"

He nodded. "Yes. You know how I told you that our hard feelings went back to high school? Well, Jane was part of the reason." He sighed. "Clark and I had always rubbed each other the wrong way. We were very competitive academically. But he was the star football player at our school and Mr. Everything. It always really got him when I'd beat him at academics." Thatcher dropped his eyes. "This will sound kind of stupid to say, but he spent a lot of years bullying me." He looked over at her. "My growth spurt didn't happen until college, and before that, I was just this scrawny little nobody."

She fought the urge to grab his hand.

"Anyway, Clark cheated on Jane during the spring of our senior year. She was devastated. And for some reason, she turned to me for comfort. I was ecstatic. Jane ran in much wilder circles than I did, and she was way more socially active than I." He looked sheepish. "The night of our senior prom was the night Katherine was conceived." He shook his head. "I never forgave myself."

This time, Vickie did take his hand. "You were eighteen. That was a long time ago. It may be time to let the past go."

He shook his head. "That isn't even the worst of it." His grip on her hand grew tighter. "Jane's parents insisted that we get married. She was really scared, and I couldn't believe it. I knew she didn't love me. And honestly, I didn't love her, either. My teenage crush got out of hand. But we got married right after graduation."

Vickie nodded encouragingly. "Go on. What happened next?"

He sighed. "Jane didn't want to be my wife. I would try, you know, to do things I thought would make her fall in love with me. I'd write her poems and come home with flowers." He shook his head. "But she didn't want any of it. Right after Katherine was born, Jane started going out on me." He pushed his glasses up on his nose. "After that, it all spiraled out of control."

She listened to the rest of the story, one that spanned the past eighteen years beginning when Jane had taken Katherine to California and ending when Katherine showed up on his doorstep. "Wow. You've dealt with a lot lately."

He was quiet for a moment. "You have, too." He sighed and let go of her hand. "I'm sorry I didn't tell you the whole truth before Katherine showed up. I was afraid of what you'd think of me. I didn't want you to see me as some man who didn't care enough about his daughter to fight for her." He shook his head. "I took the easy way out."

"I don't think badly of you for your actions. You were young and scared, and it sounds like Jane didn't exactly encourage you to be part of Katherine's life." Vickie was angry, despite having heard of Jane's illness. Thatcher was a good, kind man who would be a fantastic father.

Thatcher stood up and held out his hand to her. "There's more I have to tell you, but I'm going to need you to stand up to hear it."

She grinned. "Should I be worried?" she asked, placing her hand in his.

He gently helped her to her feet. "No need to worry." He gave her a nervous smile. "Just listen." Thatcher took a breath. "Now that you know part of my history, maybe you can understand why I've behaved the way I have. For the past several years, having a relationship with someone hasn't been a goal for me. I haven't had a 'real' date in years. Only fix-ups now and then for university events. And then I met you."

CHAPTER 64

The moment was perfect. Better than any Vickie could've conjured up in her mind and wished would happen. The light of the full moon reflected in the water, the lights of the mall twinkled around them, and the light snow made a gentle swooshing sound as it swirled. They were warm and dry underneath the covering of the memorial.

Vickie looked into Thatcher's brown eyes and felt the ground sway beneath her. The fluttering in her stomach took her by surprise.

"You're the most beautiful woman I've ever known." He grabbed both of her hands. "And you're so smart. If I get offered the chairmanship, I will have you to thank." He shook his head. "But the thing that amazes me is how strong your faith is. You have faith in God and in people. Somehow, you always manage to see the best in everything. You make me want to be a better person." He smiled broadly.

She opened her mouth, but he shook his head. "Let me get this out first."

She nodded.

"I realized last week that one of the things I'm guilty of is not fighting for what I love. I didn't fight enough for Katherine, and I lost her for eighteen years." He reached out and stroked her face. "I don't want to lose you. I need you. During the past weeks, you were the one person I wanted to talk to more than anyone."

She felt the tears begin to well up in her eyes. She couldn't have imagined it better.

He continued. "I talked to Dawn last week. She wouldn't tell me what to do to win you back. But she did tell me to think about your favorite movies. I spent two very long days watching all the movies I could remember that are on your shelf."

Vickie couldn't contain herself. She burst out laughing. "You did?"

He nodded. "I am now well versed in the chick-flick genre. At first I didn't see any commonality. But then I put it together with your friend's husband surprising her with her dream wedding. I saw those tears in your eyes when you were telling me the story." He smiled. "And I figured it out."

"What's that?" Happiness had welled up inside her until she felt like she might burst.

"I know what you want, what you deserve. . .a monumental gesture. I know I might not have a boom box to hold above my head, and I might not be able to fly off to Paris to track you down. So I'll do whatever it takes." He motioned at his suit. "If you want me to start wearing expensive suits, I will. If you prefer my hair shorter, I'll wear it that way. I'll get rid of the old pickup truck and spend less time at the fishing cabin." He looked earnestly at her. "Whatever it takes to keep you in my life."

She was stunned.

"What I'm trying to say is that I love you."

Vickie took a step back. She felt a tear escape and didn't bother to brush it away. "I need to tell you something, too." She swallowed. "My whole life, I've created reasons to keep people at a distance. But with you, I almost immediately let you know the real me. I didn't censor what I said for fear that you'd judge me or disagree. I let you know about my quirkiest traits. And I was never scared of what you'd think. But it's come to my attention recently that I might demand a kind of perfection that doesn't exist.

"You look so handsome tonight in your expensive suit and your new haircut. But to tell you the truth, it's the man inside the suit and underneath the haircut who I'm in love with."

He pulled her closer to him, smiling.

"And I was sort of hoping that maybe next summer you could maybe teach me how to fish. It's about time this park ranger gained some outdoor experience, don't you think?" She returned his smile.

"Does this mean I can still count on you to come with me to my family's Christmas?" he asked.

"If you'll still have me," she whispered.

Thatcher cupped her face with his hands and leaned down, planting the sweetest kiss she'd ever imagined on her lips. For a long moment, she was lost in him, in the minty taste of his lips and the warmth of his hands on her face. He pulled away and gave her a slow grin. The love she'd been waiting for her whole life had finally arrived.

CHAPTER 65

Thatcher had heard about people whose lives were changed in an instant. But those were usually tales of lottery winners or people who'd found weird items in their food and been awarded great sums. For him, the change hadn't had anything to do with money, yet he felt somehow richer.

The past weeks had been some of the happiest of his life. The holidays had been perfect. Vickie had fit in so well with his family, and they'd had such a wonderful time. Although Katherine had spent most of the holidays with her mother, he'd gotten together with his daughter several times. It would be a slow process, but the time spent getting to know her was precious. He felt more comfortable in the fatherly role with each passing day.

And now he stood before his colleagues, surprised at his lack of nerves. But he was ready. Vickie had helped him prepare for the presentation until he practically had the entire thing memorized.

He took a deep breath and clicked to the first screen of his PowerPoint presentation. "As Abraham Lincoln once said, 'If you once forfeit the confidence of your fellow citizens, you can never regain their respect and esteem.' " He met Clark's eyes on the front row. "Friends and colleagues, I stand before you today, hoping that I still have your confidence. It's no secret that I've been resistant to changing my methods of instruction. But after much consideration, I have decided that an overhaul is needed if we want to continue to attract quality students to our esteemed program."

He paused and clicked through to the next slide. "But perhaps not in the way you might think. I still stand by my opinion that I am not here to entertain students. Instead, as a professor of American history, I am called to teach them the history of our country. One of our great presidents, Franklin Delano Roosevelt, once advised that our nation must learn from the past in order to create a better future."

Thatcher looked out over the crowd and nodded in John's direction. It was nice to have some support. "Taking that into consideration, I have come to the conclusion that one of the things I can do to increase enrollment is to make sure my students have access to the wonderful historical lessons that are provided in our great city."

He moved through the slides and took the room through some of the monuments, memorials, museums, and educational opportunities that could be found in the city or within a short drive. Many of them had clips of Vickie's ranger programs from different monuments along the National Mall. Being able to hear her voice and see her on the screen made him feel like she was right there, helping him present the information. "While it would be far too lengthy to go through each opportunity, you can consult the handout I provided. There are literally hundreds of opportunities which will enable us to offer a more hands-on approach to history."

Thatcher clicked to the final slide, this one of him and Vickie. She wore her ranger uniform, and they stood smiling in front of the Jefferson Memorial. "Thomas Jefferson, one of our founding fathers, is quoted as saying 'I cannot live without books.' And I, too, firmly believe in the importance of books and what can be learned from them. But I also believe we will better serve our students by creating partnerships with some of our local institutions, particularly the National Park Service and the Smithsonian Institute."

He concluded his presentation and took his seat. John leaned forward and clapped him on the back. "Nicely done," he whispered.

Thatcher grinned—partly because he was proud of the presentation, but mainly because he knew Vickie would be waiting when the meeting was over. He couldn't wait to share the success.

Thatcher shook Dean White's hand and made his way out the double doors of the auditorium. Vickie was standing in the lobby. He'd told her she didn't have to come, but he was glad she was there.

"Hey." He grinned.

Her eyes were wide with excitement. "Well? How did it go?"

He grabbed her hand. "Let's go for a walk, and I'll tell you." He held the door for her and ushered her out into the courtyard.

"It was a home run. They loved the idea of the partnerships and were very excited about our plan to incorporate area sites into classes."

Vickie squeezed his hand. "I knew it. What about Clark? Did he say anything ugly about it?"

"Actually, no. He wasn't exactly cheering, but he did say it was a nice job." Thatcher grew serious. "There is one thing, though."

"What?"

"They offered me the department chair."

She let out a squeal. "Oh, I'm so happy for you. I know how important this was to you."

"I turned it down."

Vickie drew her brows together. "What? I don't understand. Why would you do something like that?"

He cleared his throat. "When I set out to be named the department chair, my entire life was devoted to my job. But now I have you. And Katherine." He shook his head. "I don't want my whole life to be about work anymore." He glanced at her, trying to gauge her reaction.

"Are you sure?"

"I've been praying so much about this decision. And when Dean White told me the position was mine if I wanted it, I just knew. I'm honored to have been considered. But I don't want to add work responsibilities right now."

She grinned. "I'm glad you feel good about the decision."

"I do. But do you want to know what I feel even better about?"

"What's that?"

He pulled her close. "The thought of a future with you," he whispered.

Vickie stood on her tiptoes and planted a kiss on his grinning lips. "I feel pretty good about that myself." She stepped back. "Okay, I have to get to work. This may have been the longest lunch break ever."

Thatcher grinned. "See you after work?"

She nodded. "You know it."

CHAPTER 66

Vickie made her way up the steps of the Lincoln Memorial, hoping no one would notice she was a couple of minutes late. At least she wasn't scheduled for a ranger program. This afternoon, she'd be on hand to answer visitor questions, but that was her only duty.

She made it to the top step, and Chris waved to her from the far wall. He walked over to where she stood. "Did you have a nice lunch?" he asked.

A smile escaped her lips. "Very nice."

He raised an eyebrow. "Man, you are smitten." He laughed. "But it's nice to see. Even though I'm sad it isn't with my cousin."

Vickie laughed. "I'm sure he'll find a very nice girl who is perfect for him. But as for me, I think I've found a pretty great guy."

"Good to hear." He paused. "Uh-oh. Looks like something is going on."

She turned to face the plaza. At the bottom step a young man was holding up a sign with the letter *i* painted on it. She glanced at Chris. "Do you think it's going to be some kind of demonstration?"

"Not sure." He pulled out his radio. "Let's keep an eye out, just in case."

A young woman emerged from the mingling crowd and pulled out a sign identical to the one the man held. Her sign had a red *u* painted on it.

"This is plain weird," Vickie murmured to Chris. "They don't look like demonstrators." As she spoke, an older man stepped from the crowd holding an *l* and fell into line with the others. In a moment, people from all directions, each bearing a sign, descended upon the spot where the sign holders stood. Vickie watched, speechless, as right before her eyes the signs began to make sense and spell words: WILL YOU MARRY ME?

As soon as the final letter was in place, Thatcher stepped from behind the sign holders, grinning broadly. She'd been watching the signs form and hadn't noticed him in the crowd.

Chris gave her a little nudge, and she numbly made her way down the steps. It seemed like the entire mall had stopped. A hush had fallen over the crowd, and most people had paused to watch what was happening. Vickie finally reached Thatcher, who immediately dropped to one knee.

She gasped. Even though the letters spelled it out, it hadn't sunk in until she saw him kneel.

He took one of her hands. "I didn't even realize my life was missing anything until I met you. I was just going along, living a sort of half life. I will forever be thankful that we were sent on that wild-goose chase. But I'd like to think that even if Clark hadn't done that, we would've somehow found each other." He gripped her hand tighter. "When I thought I'd lost you, I felt like I'd lost part of me. Now when I think about the future, all I can see is you and me together and hopefully starting a family of our own." He took a breath. "Vickie Harris, will you marry me?" he asked softly.

Vickie threw her arms around him and choked back a sob. "Yes. Yes, of course I will marry you." She leaned forward and met his lips with hers as the crowd cheered around them.

EPILOGUE

Six months later

Katherine pulled in front of the fishing cabin and turned off the ignition. Any visit to the cemetery took a lot out of her, and she was looking forward to a weekend of relaxation.

Vickie met her at the door. "Hi," she said, taking the bag from Katherine's shoulder. "Lunch is almost ready if you're hungry."

"I am." She stopped in the living room and gave Buster a belly rub. These past months had been difficult. But Katherine knew how many people were on her side, and that had made a huge difference. Some days were still hard to get through, but she was learning to work through her grief.

Katherine walked into the small kitchen. "It smells great in here. Do I need to help you do anything?"

Vickie smiled as she pulled plates out of the cabinet. "Nope. Everything's almost ready." She glanced up. "Did you have a good time last night? Your dad said you had a date."

Katherine giggled. "You should've seen him. I think he's been waiting on that for the past twenty years." It was the first date she'd gone on since she'd moved from California, and since she was living at the fishing cabin for the summer, Thatcher had insisted on being there when she was picked up. "I'm pretty sure he drove all the way out here just so he could say, 'Have her home by a decent hour, son,' in a gruff voice."

Vickie joined in her laughter. "I'll bet he loved it." She made a face. "Did he wait up?"

Katherine shook her head. "No. But Darren is in Dad's class next fall, so we were back by ten." She laughed.

Vickie glanced up from the plates she was scooping enchiladas onto. "Dad?"

Katherine nodded. "Last night when I introduced him, I knew it was time. It felt right." She paused. "I think he got a little misty eyed when I said it out loud for the first time. But then, so did I."

Vickie set a steaming plate in front of Katherine, then sat down in the chair across from her. "He's still out fishing, so he'll have to eat on his own."

"That's fine. I'm starving." She grinned at Vickie.

"Would you like for me to say the blessing?"

Katherine nodded, and they bowed their heads.

Vickie thanked God for the food and for their friendship and asked Him to be with Katherine as she adjusted to all the changes in her life.

"Thanks," Katherine said. "For everything." She met Vickie's gaze. God had blessed her in ways she hadn't expected over the past months, and one of those was her relationship with Vickie. At first, she'd felt awkward spending time with her dad's fiancée. But soon, she was completely at ease. Over the months, Vickie had become a friend and mentor. After Mom died, Vickie had been the only person who'd always known just what to say. She'd seemed to sense when Katherine needed to talk or when it was best to fill her time with mindless activity. And although Katherine had known

Vickie was only trying to distract her from the pain, a simple shopping trip or movie had done wonders to help bring her out of the fog of grief. Although it would still take time—a lifetime maybe—to get used to her mom not being around, Katherine was finally starting to feel like she could breathe again.

"You're welcome." Vickie dug into her enchiladas.

Katherine couldn't help but smile as she took her first bite. She remembered the day, almost exactly a year ago, when she and her mother had left their home in California. On that day, Katherine had wondered if she'd ever feel like she had a home again. But even though she would always miss her mother, she had found a place to belong. Even better, her mother would be thrilled if she knew that by finding peace in her own life, she had helped Katherine find peace as well.

ANNALISA DAUGHETY, an Arkansas native, won first place in the Contemporary Romance category at the 2008 ACFW Genesis Awards. After graduating from Freed-Hardeman University, she worked as a park ranger for the National Park Service. She now resides in Memphis, Tennessee. Read more at www.annalisadaughety.com.

Other Books by

ANNALISA DAUGHETY

LOVE IS
A BATTLEFIELD